GRIFF DRISCOLL
AND THE
CORRUPTION OF ESSENCE

COPYRIGHT

To my amazing wife, Annette who has supported me through it all and has given me the precious gift of time to write.

To my son, Jayce, whose abundant energy, joy, and love of adventure brings me great happiness.

Acknowledgements

I'd like to first thank my parents, Jay and Teri, who always believed I would one day become a writer, even when I was still a misfit with no inkling of what I would do when I grew up. Dad, I know you would have been so proud to see what I've accomplished.

I would also like to thank two good friends of mine, Leon and David, with whom I spent way too many hours pondering over this book. Thanks for listening to my rants, offering your suggestions, and reading through my early drafts when things were still quite messy.

Thanks to Covers by Christian for an amazing book cover. Seriously. I love it.

Thanks to Sara Lawson for her keen editing eye. You kept the perfect balance between noting important changes while keeping me optimistic and encouraged.

To my family and friends who supported me in this adventure.

To the Tulsa Writers Syndicate, whose wealth of knowledge and support was immeasurable.

And lastly, to you, my reader. Thank you for trusting me to take you on a journey full of adventure, mystery, and magic. And take heart, it's not over yet!

PROLOGUE

The monster was hungry, but that was about to change.

Large, black bats squeaked and fluttered their wings at the beast, though their display did nothing but make it rumble more with anticipation. The alligator-like monster swayed its long, heavily armored tail back and forth, the three spikes at the end scraping against the stony cavern ground. It shifted its weight restlessly across all six of its legs as it stared up at the stalactite-covered ceiling and the dinner hanging from it.

A small lake of lava behind the monster cast a hellish red glow that pulsed across the stony walls. Molten bubbles popped and sizzled carelessly, but the monster ignored them, keeping its two curved horns pointed toward its desire.

As if playing with its food, it snarled and snapped its mouth open and shut, briefly revealing rows of sharp, deadly teeth.

A growing rumble shook the cave and a fiery pillar rose from the surface of the lava, distracting the monster. As soon as it turned its head toward the scene, the bats zipped across the molten lake and into one of the exit tunnels.

The monster roared and lunged for a low flyer but was unsuccessful. It huffed angrily and turned instead to watch the column of lava.

The pillar shifted slowly and methodically, changing its shape to fit the twisted magic within. One black hole emerged toward the top. Then another. The cavern continued to rumble and shake until the once-smooth column of magma molded itself into a skull.

The rumbling stopped and the skull floated in place over the lake silently, like an undead warrior on watch. Below the floating figure, the lava resumed its carefree bubbling and boiling. All was quiet and peaceful in the cavern.

Then a scream—a man's scream, one that grew in intensity and ferocity—broke the silence and filled the air.

The skull exploded. The entire cavern echoed as the blistering lava sizzled against the damp walls. The beast cocked its bulky head but held its position. A man's hand emerged from the lake and grasped the stone edge of the cavern floor. The monster bowed low.

Something big was coming.

CHAPTER I

Griff awoke with a start, heart pumping at full speed, hands trembling uncontrollably, and sweat running down his brow. He tried to rip the blankets off his uncomfortably hot skin and jump out of his cast-iron bed, however, this proved to be a more difficult task than his groggy brain could accomplish. Tangled in his sheets, Griff fell onto the hard wooden floor of his bedroom, landing on his hip with a loud *thud*.

Awesome. He thought. *I'm gonna feel that for a couple of days.*

Griff groaned and lay in the midst of the tangled mess recounting his vivid dream. Lava skulls, giant demonic creatures, a hand emerging from the lava, and what was that blood-curdling scream? His thoughts were interrupted when a small coin purse thumped against his chest.

"Really, Griffin Driscoll? You're just now getting up, you lazy bum?" his mother scolded. But then she smiled, walked over to the crumpled mess that her son was trapped in, and planted a big kiss atop his head.

"Today's your big day, miracle boy! I'd have thought you would've been up at the crack of dawn, ready for your birthday breakfast!"

Griff's head perked at the mention of his birthday breakfast.

His mother took a long look at him, and with a big smile that accentuated her energetic green eyes, exclaimed, "Happy birthday, you big goof! Your breakfast is almost ready. Oh, and don't forget to pick up your birthday present!" She pointed to the coin purse on the floor, then left Griff to wrestle unsuccessfully with his sheets.

Almost as soon as she had left, Griff's dad walked to the door in his blacksmith uniform, stained from the years of demanding work in the blacksmithing forge next to the barn.

"C'mere boy!" His dad bent down, and with much effort, picked a tangled Griff off the floor and tossed him onto his old bed, which groaned in complaint.

Slightly winded, his dad said, "You may be sixteen, miracle boy, but I can still take you. Show me what'cha got!"

Having been loosed from his sheets, Griff snatched his old, worn-out pillow and heaved it at his dad. While the pillow was still in mid-air, he launched himself off his bed and tackled his dad to the floor. He smiled down victoriously at his dad, who himself wore a smile of victory.

"Why are *you* smiling? I won!"

"Did you?"

Griff looked around, but his dad's arms were still pinned to the dirty wooden floor. Just then, in a moment of intense effort, his dad swung his legs and rolled to the side, pushing Griff off. Before he had a chance to recover, Griff felt his dad's weight pressed against his arms and chest.

"You may be strong, but I'm *still* stronger." His face was red, and sweat had beaded on his forehead, but Griff knew that he was right.

"All right, all right, I yield!" Griff said through pained laughs.

His dad let up and helped him from the ground before they both sat on the bed breathing heavily.

"Happy birthday, miracle boy," he said, resting his bulky arm across Griff's shoulders. "You're becoming a young man today. As with every sixteen-year-old boy, you're gaining new freedoms, but that also means new responsibilities." He picked up the coin purse from the floor and held it out to Griff. "Like earning your keep for one—"

"And joining the Cordelian guard too, right?"

"Right ..." his dad said. "More on that later. But right now, we're just gonna celebrate your journey into manhood."

The old bed creaked as his dad stood. He turned to face Griff, a goofy grin on his face, and said, "But before we do that, please, for all that is good and holy, put some pants on!"

He slapped the top of Griff's doorframe on his way out and could be heard chuckling all the way down the hallway.

Griff entered the kitchen, having adhered to his dad's request. Across the room, bacon hissed in an iron pan atop the wood burning stove while his mom finished placing the buttery pancakes on a plate. Today was going to be a good day.

He sat at the kitchen table with his dad who was carefully drawing on a large sheet of parchment. He barely noticed Griff observing as he continued to sketch. It was the most beautiful sword Griff had ever seen. It was a slim build, made for quick combat. The handle itself was simple, yet as it neared the hilt the metal curved outward and formed beautiful-yet-fierce-looking wings.

"Dragon wings," Griff observed. "Those are dragon wings, aren't they?"

Snatched from his thoughts, his dad looked up, smiled, and said, "Oh, my boy, these aren't just any dragon wings. These wings belong to the fiercest of all dragon species: the Nightflame dragon."

He set his pencil down and continued. "It's said that the flames of a Nightflame dragon are blacker than a moonless, starless night. They say, Griff, that hidden inside those flames is death itself."

"C'mon, dad. You and I both know that's just a myth."

Griff pulled a chair up next to his dad. "That story doesn't work on me anymore. I'm too old for you to use it to scare me into doing my chores. Plus, everyone knows that there's no actual proof those creatures exist."

"No chores this time, miracle boy," Griff's dad replied, "but with a creature as deadly as *that* beast, who's to say they would leave any proof?

"You've got one thing right, though—Thank you, Leena," he said as Griff's mom set a plate of breakfast in front of him. "Nobody's ever actually seen a Nightflame, not that I've heard of anyways. Though ... there are whispers of people who claim to have seen their bright, fiery-red eyes in the night sky just beyond the Dracorian Sea ready to mangle any little boys who cross their paren—"

"All right, Gale, that's enough of that," Leena elbowed her husband before placing a steaming hot plate in front of Griff. "Son, enjoy your birthday breakfast, and then I want you to get ready to join your dad in the forge."

Griff, who had already buried his face into his breakfast, looked up with excitement, "Rwearry!" he exclaimed, as bits of pancake shot from his overstuffed mouth. His parents stared at Griff with confused looks on their faces. Griff swallowed and exclaimed, "You mean it? I'm finally allowed in the forge?"

"That's what the coin purse was for," his mom said. "And some extra birthday money too."

Gale rustled Griff's jet-black bangs. "It'll be nice to finally have an assistant in there, instead of spending my time trying to keep a troublesome little boy from getting in an' messin' stuff up!"

"No way!" Griff said playfully, "I would never do anything like that!"

Leena chuckled. "You poor boy, you're so old now that your memory is starting to go. Well, in either case, now it'll be easier for me to take care of this house *and* the goats *and* the chickens, instead of trying to keep you from sneaking in there!"

"And even though you're our little miracle boy," his dad added, "we're *not* taking our chances with you, Griff Driscoll. You may have escaped death once, but your mom and I are gonna make sure you don't have another reason to escape it again!"

Griff sighed. "Oh boy. Is it story time?"

"Yep!" Gale said. "It's that time of year, ain't it?"

"Wouldn't be a birthday without it," Griff mumbled.

"You better believe it," Gale said, crunching on a piece of bacon.

"Besides, stories like this help us keep an attitude of gratefulness," his mom added. "Makes you appreciate life a little more when you remember where you came from."

"As you know, you were really sick when you were born. Your mother and I didn't think you were gonna make it. We did our best, but you just weren't gettin' any better. Cryin' nonstop. Coughin' up blood. Constantly runnin' a fever. It was horrible."

"We didn't know what was happening to our little boy," Leena said, placing a gentle hand on Griff's arm. "You'd had a clean birth—Sylva's mom made sure of that."

"Yep. Nessa took real good care of you and your mom that day. Definitely wasn't anything she did," Gale added. "We wondered if maybe something didn't develop correctly. We'd had a hard time having kids, and as hard as that was for your mom and I, seeing you so sick was worse. So much worse. And we didn't know what was happening. We were at a complete loss."

"We kept taking you back to see Nessa, but every time she examined you, she was baffled. And no sickness or injury's ever gotten past that woman," Leena mentioned.

"Son, you were gonna die," Gale leaned in, eyes serious as a storm, "and there was nothing we could do about it."

Silence hung thick in the air like the final note of a somber song, when at last Leena's chipper voice cut through, "But then, one morning ..."

"Ah, yes, sorry …" Griff's dad coughed, rubbed his eyes, and smiled, "then one morning, you were all better!"

"No clue how it happened, but I woke up in the chair next to your crib, and you looked at me and smiled! You hadn't smiled at me since you were born!" Griff's mom said.

"What can I say, I'm just full of surprises." Griff smiled.

"Yeah, well, no more surprises like that, you hear?" Leena said.

"Deal. No more surprises like that, Mom." Griff hugged her tight. "Now, story time's over, I'm full, and I wanna go hang out with Dad in the forge. Is that okay, or do we need to relive the next ten years of my life?"

"Nah, the first couple of months is fine. But just know that the story's comin' around next year too! And the year after that, and after that, and after that!" Gale got up to drop his dishes in the sink, then returned to finish the final details of his drawing.

"Your dad's excited for you to come with him. So, you leave your dishes to me, go get cleaned up, and meet him in the back."

Gale looked up from his work, "Hey, Griff, maybe we oughta shave your head first, to make sure the fire doesn't burn off that long, crazy hair of yours!"

"Crazy? Hey, I got this hair from you, thanks!" Griff said, filling up a spoon with a small portion of egg.

"True, true. It may be thick and black like mine, but at least I keep it short. For obvious safety reasons, that is."

When Griff saw an opening, he launched the egg toward his dad. It flew across the table, headed straight for Gale's face, but his dad, with the lightning-fast reflexes of a well-trained soldier, swatted it out of the air just before it hit its target.

"Ha! Nice try, miracle boy, you're gonna have to be faster than that if you want to …" His dad's voice trailed off once he realized where the egg had landed: Leena's face.

Both Griff and his dad paused, eyes opened wide, ready for the worst. Slowly, she set her fork down, wiped her forehead with her napkin, and narrowed her eyes at them. Seconds seemed to tick down into eternity, when finally, she began to laugh hysterically.

All the air that Griff had been holding in came out with a whoosh, and he and his dad joined in the moment, hooting and snorting with laughter until they had no more air in their lungs. When things finally settled down, all three were holding their sides and chuckling. Griff turned toward his dad and asked, "So, weapons training, then the forge, right?"

"Well, you clearly need more target practice," his dad said, eyeing Leena as she pulled a clean rag from the sink and wiped her face. Then, he reached over to the old parchment paper and slid it toward Griff with a twinkle of excitement in his eyes. "No weapons training today, miracle boy. We're gonna work on your birthday gift."

CHAPTER 2

The familiar smell of metal, coal, and dust welcomed Griff to the forge. It was strange to stand in the large stone building without having to look over his shoulder for one of his parents. There was something about this place that had always captivated Griff. He was unsure whether it was the dangerous weapons he was never allowed to play with, the blazing hot fire that could melt metal, or his father's ferocity and focus as he worked.

Although all of those appealed to Griff, he believed it was the exciting and endless possibilities that came from the forge. Given the right tools and time, his dad could make almost anything. And every day in the forge was different. Some days he crafted everyday household tools like shovels or cooking utensils; other days he forged something decorative, like intricate curtain rods, door knockers, or wall art. Most often, though, he crafted weapons.

As Gale heated up the forge, Griff wandered from table to table, marveling at the intricate designs and shapes that were carefully placed on leather pads in front of the shop.

"Those, m'boy, are ready for sale," Gale called over his shoulder.

Griff nodded and continued his tour deeper in the shop, looking around to see many unfinished projects strewn about on different tables, chairs, and even a few unfinished pieces that had made it to the dirt floor.

"And ... those are not," the blacksmith laughed.

Gale's shop reminded Griff of his own bedroom, which was in a constant state of organized clutter. Clothes on the floor, toys in one corner, books in another. To the outside eye, his room was a cluttered mess. To Griff, it was home. He and his dad were more alike than he'd realized.

Griff noticed a table against the wall, far from the other projects. He went to it and picked up a small silver dagger from among the finished pieces carefully positioned on a leather mat. The dagger was extremely light, yet, as he tightly gripped the handle, it felt strong and firm. This dagger would be an excellent backup should a warrior find himself without his primary weapon. He lifted the weapon and stared down the blade: It was straight and true; no warping or chipping of any kind. This was the mark of a master.

Staring at Griff from the base of the short blade was a wolf's face surrounded by a circular frame of twisted branches and leaves—the king's mark.

"Ah, so you found my special collection." The proud blacksmith stood next to Griff and carefully took the dagger from him. He affectionately rubbed his thumb over the king's mark as he spoke. "This set has been my most recent labor of love."

"Why is the mark of the king on all these weapons?" Griff asked.

"Why do you think?"

Griff thought it over for a moment before bursting out, "You're selling to the king! You're selling to the king aren'tcha? Seriously, Dad? The king?"

"Well, okay, maybe I should have asked that a little differently." Gale sat down next to the table, eyes on the dagger, but his mind clearly in another world. A world where dreams spark and come alive.

"I *want* to sell to the king. I've been putting together this collection in the hope of makin' my way into his employment. Could you imagine that, Griff?" He laughed. "Your old man working for the king? Our family wouldn't want for anything if that happened!"

"True, but our family doesn't want for anything now, don'tcha think?"

"Yes, but imagine the good we could bring to Cordelia if I worked for the king. I mean, we could expand our town, breathe new life into it. Bring more families in. We could build bigger, better walls. And more people means less nights I'd have to stand guard at the gates!"

Although Griff loved the idea of his dad smithing for the king, the mention of more guards was even more exciting. Ever since he could remember, his dad would leave the house every Tuesday evening just as the sun was setting, and then he would wearily return, dragging his gear behind him, as the sun rose the next day. Griff was never allowed to be outside after dark. Nobody was, except the Cordelian guard.

The shadows of night housed nightstalkers, dark and mystical creatures that lurked in the forests just past town. Never did they come close to the town or disturb its inhabitants, but woe to the ignorant or foolish traveler caught outside the walls past sunset. Never were they seen in the day, but at night, their footsteps could be heard skulking just out of light's reach.

These creatures thrived in the darkness, feeding on whatever was dumb enough to wander into their paths. They came in a variety of shapes and sizes—half-animal, half-demon. One boy, Sylva Karlsen, who was three years younger than Griff and lived just around the corner from him, swore that he saw one beast that resembled an average household cat although it was covered in dense armored plates. Its legs were twice as long; tall and skinny, yet this creature was extremely agile.

"Black as a No Moon Night," Sylva explained, eyes full of fear. "I saw it hidin' in the giant oak tree just outside my window. I swear it was starin' right at me, bright white demon eyes and all! Then, it was gone."

Sylva's mother, Nessa, later investigated, but came up emptyhanded and assumed he was having night terrors again. Though there were all different types of nightstalkers, the one thing these beasts of the night all had in common was that they had an insatiable bloodlust and not a soul who crossed their paths alone ever survived.

"Well, I don't like the idea of more people in our town, but I love the idea of spreading out the guard. I've come to hate Tuesday nights because of that," Griff admitted.

"Hear, hear," Gale said. "If we could expand this town, I wouldn't have to stand guard every Tuesday night. King's sake, I could even retire and let some younger men take on the task! Now I just need to find a way to pitch these projects to the king."

"Just walk into his castle with all those weapons. I'm sure it wouldn't be a problem!" Griff laughed.

"Son, I'd have a better chance surviving the woods at night with a sharpened stick! Now, before you go and give me more terrible advice, how about we start on your birthday present?"

He walked over to the now red-hot forge, "Normally, we would start with the blade, but this is a special sword. And to be honest, I'm really excited about this handle. It's not a great first project for a blacksmith-in-training, but as the son of a master blacksmith," he poked his chest out comically, "I think you'll pick it up pretty quickly."

Griff and his dad worked all day on his birthday present. They heated up the steel and hammered it into an awkward "U" shape. From there, Griff was taught how to grind the metal to make a smooth curve, which his dad would eventually use as the wings of the Nightflame dragon. It was intense work.

Although Griff enjoyed every moment, he quickly tired to the point of exhaustion. The hammer grew heavier in his arms with the rhythmic up and down motion. Each downward swing of the hammer took all of Griff's energy and focus as he wanted to make sure that each strike hit true to its aim. From time to time, Griff's dad would take charge and give Griff a break, which he gladly accepted.

By the time they had sanded the wood for the handle, wrapped it in fine black leather, and begun etching in the final touches, Griff's mom called from the entrance of the forge, "Hey boys! Time to get cleaned up! We're having an early dinner, and I'll not have you fillin' up the kitchen with your stank!"

Nothing had ever felt so good to Griff as being clean after a hard first day as an apprentice blacksmith. To top it off, his mother had made the most delicious, tender, and juicy stagmoose steaks for dinner. Life couldn't get any better than this.

"Hey, we haven't been to our hunting spot in ages. Where did these steaks come from?" Gale asked.

"Nessa Karlsen," Leena answered. "She says 'Happy birthday, Griff' and 'Be careful tonight, Gale.'"

"Aww, man, that's tonight?" Griff asked before diving into another bite of the enormous steak in front of him. With the rush of birthday excitement, he had completely forgotten what day it was.

"Aye," his dad answered, scooping a large spoonful of corn into his mouth. "Tonide's da nide!"

"Well, like Nessa said, you be careful out there tonight, Gale. You know I don't sleep well during No Moon Night."

"Thanks, dear. But seriously, you guys don't have to worry about me. I know tonight's No Moon Night, but for as long as I can remember, the nightstalkers have never come close to the edge of the forest. I mean, sure, they get more active when the moon's not out, but we just gotta keep them torches burnin' bright. Plus, with these muscles, those demons don't stand a chance!"

Gale stood and flexed in awkward poses until both Griff and his mother were rolling with laughter.

"Yeah, you keep thinking it's your muscles, Dad, but we all know with a face like that, they're more scared of you than you are of them!" Griff exclaimed. "That's the real reason they don't come near town! The torches are just so they can see you!"

"You've got a good point there, miracle boy," his dad frowned, playfully scratching his chin. "Well, if that's the case, then we need to put you on the front lines and scare them back from whence they came! They'll never come near us again!"

Griff and his dad roared with laughter, while his mother shook her head and chuckled. "You boys are too much."

Now that their bellies were full of food and their hearts full of laughter, Griff and his family worked together to clean their dinner mess, momentarily forgetting the dark undertones of No Moon Night.

With less than two remaining hours of daylight, Griff's mother went to help Nessa ready her family for the night. Without Sylva's dad around anymore, the whole town pitched in to help his mom raise Sylva and his younger sister, Lilly, when they could. As the only one with medical training or knowledge in herbal medicines, the Cordelians did their best to free her up, should her medical abilities be necessary.

Though Griff wouldn't start his watch with the Cordelian guard tonight, Gale had still invited Griff to Talley's Tavern, the most social place in town. If you ever needed to find anyone in Cordelia, you could probably find them at Talley's. Griff snatched his cloak and joined his dad outside. It was starting to get cooler. A warm summer had just ended, and fall was settling in. It wouldn't be long until snow covered the small town of Cordelia in a beautiful blanket of white.

Griff was never a fan of the early snow. He preferred tromping through the Cordelian forest unhindered by coats and jackets. He had heard of places farther south that boasted of nearly year-round summers. Unfortunately for Griff, he had grown up surviving the unforgiving winters of Cordelia.

As they walked down the cobblestone street with hands in their pockets, Griff looked up at the fall sky. It was like a sea of orange and purple paint, swirling together in a marvelous dance. The sun was beginning to set, and Griff wondered how such beauty could preclude such darkness.

The street was empty save for the few people scurrying past to get home for the evening. Those who weren't already at Talley's were locking themselves inside for the night. Most who walked by Griff and his dad were tense, barely acknowledging their existence, as they were eager to get home and light every lantern in and around their house. Although Cordelia was surrounded by tall, stone walls that were patched over with scrap metal, and there had never been a nightstalker attack since the Cordelian guard was implemented, the residents took every possible precaution, especially during No Moon Night.

They passed by empty wooden benches where older people would sit to watch the sunrise, and an old, rusted swing set with empty seats that swayed in the cool breeze, sending an eerie creaking sound down the street. Griff stared at the rows of tall, wooden beams standing on either side of the main walkway through town. They were like mysterious guardians that towered over the townspeople. Nobody knew what they were or why they were there. They were just another strange part of reality that everyone had accepted, much like the monsters that came out at night.

Griff snapped back to the present when his dad opened the double doors of Talley's Tavern. Several groups of men and their boys were scattered throughout the tavern—enjoying a meal or a hearty snack before the sun set. Off in a corner, red-faced men roared with laughter, many leaning back in their wooden chairs with their feet on the table.

Behind the bar, a scarred older gentleman with thick mutton-chops was drying a clean mug with a dirty towel. He stared unwaveringly at the rowdy bunch before turning to Griff and Gale with a big smile. "Well, lookey who it is! The Driscoll boys made it to me place!"

Talley set the mug underneath the bar and slammed his large fist on the countertop.

"What'll it be tonight, Gale? The usual?"

"Aye, the usual. One Dragon's Beard for me."

"Aye, same." Griff added.

Talley nodded and grabbed two mugs of undetermined cleanness and began his dance around the bar, grabbing spices and other necessities for their order.

"Well, tonight's the big'n!" Talley exclaimed, grabbing a giant wooden spoon, and stirring the final ingredients into the large black cauldron. "No Moon Night. Ye all set, Gale?" Talley asked, nervously glancing toward the rowdy corner.

"Ready as I'll ever be, Talley. This Dragon's Beard's gonna warm me up nice and keep me goin' through the night, though!"

The once-fierce warrior handed Griff his mug of Dragon's Beard. Although everyone knew of Talley's previous career in the king's army, they knew almost nothing about what he did. It was ironic to think that the man behind the bar who could talk to an empty chair for hours could be tight-lipped about anything, let alone his accolades on behalf of the king. Griff leaned over the steaming hot tea and watched the froth on top dance as it continued to boil. He closed his eyes and relished the strong, sweet cinnamon aroma that flirted with hints of citrus and apple.

Talley was more than a barkeeper, he was an artist, and Dragon's Beard was his greatest accomplishment. Griff was only one of many who enjoyed Talley's creations. Watching Talley's still-muscular frame move with ease and agility as he crafted and created behind that bar, Griff could only imagine that he must have been quite the artist on the battlefield too.

"Well, you know as well as I do that those creatures tend to stay put," Talley said, handing Gale his own mug with one hand, and stroking one side of his mutton chops with the other. "Long's we got the torches ablaze, you'll be just fine. Griff, you be tailin' yer dad tonight?"

"I wish!" Griff exclaimed, looking over at his dad to see if he had changed his mind.

"But—" his dad started, taking a swig from his mug.

"But tonight's not the best night for my first experience with the guard. Ya know, No Moon Night and all." Griff recited his dad's earlier response.

"Aye, yer not wrong lad! I know yer strong, but trust me, even the fiercest of warriors can lose their bladders on nights like these!" Talley cackled long and hard as he walked away to check on the noisy bunch in the corner.

"Sorry tonight's got to be the way it is, son," Gale said as he placed a large hand on Griff's shoulder. "There's a time to be brave, but bravery must always be tempered with wisdom. The difference between a good man and a great man is that a great man always pursues wisdom." He took a long swig from his mug for effect before adding, "Aye, and sometimes the difference between a dead man and a living one is the same!

"She's a slippery one, wisdom, but if you can catch her, you'll be on the path that leads toward greatness. A day's coming soon, Griff, when you'll be makin' decisions for yourself, and when that time comes, I know you'll have her on your side."

"Ready there, Gaelic?"

A tall, skinny man with a shaved head and a thick amber beard approached them at the bar: Janson Horter. He wore brand-new black leather armor that had clearly never been used. In one hand he casually held a stout longbow, cleverly crafted and clearly a work of art. His other arm was wrapped around one of Griff's least favorite people in the world: Kaden Horter.

The Horters were one of the richest families in Cordelia. They had an exceptionally successful leatherworking shop that supplied many towns in the land of Oriel with leather armor, clothing, saddles, satchels, and just about darn near everything else. He wasn't jealous of the Horters for their success; he just hated their arrogant "we own this place" attitude. Sadly, because of their wealth and impeccable ability to run competition out of town, they did own nearly all of Cordelia.

Though Mr. Horter was a pompous and arrogant man, he was largely outclassed by his son, whose ability to bring the coarsest words to even the saintliest of tongues was well-known. A large boy with thick curly blond hair, Kaden stood at least a head taller than Griff, though supposedly they were the same age. Griff often joked that this couldn't be true because Kaden was also well-known for his ability to act like a child in need of a diaper change. Sylva and Griff often pondered whether perhaps he still wore diapers. Why would a boy who had someone to answer his every beck and call be bothered by such things as going to the bathroom on his own?

"Yes, thanks for asking," Mr. Horter said with a smile, snapping Griff from his thoughts, "This *is* my brand-new longbow. I made it myself from the rare Pacific Yew wood. You know, I brought the wood back with me from one of my many travels to the south. You should go there sometime if you get the chance, Gaelic, it's marvelous."

"Right, well, I didn't ask, but thanks for telling me about ... that," Gale said. "As you know, some of us don't have the luxury of travel like you do, Janson. We have to rely on you to tell us how marvelous those other places are."

"Ahoy there, Griffina! Comin' with yer dad tonight, are ya?" Kaden inquired.

Griff rolled his eyes, "Not tonight, Kaden. No Moon Night. Bad night for us to be out." Griff did his best to ignore the constant girl names and other poorly executed jokes from Kaden. It was the best way to get back at him. Kaden thrived under attention, even if it was negative, and Griff wasn't going to give him any.

"So says you!" Kaden exclaimed. "Dad's got me a brand-new sword, and I'm tryin' it out tonight. Those nightstalkers don't stand a chance against the Horter family!" He stuck out his chest and laid a chubby hand on the hilt of his shiny new weapon.

"Good luck with that, boy," Griff's dad smiled compassionately, "No monster has ever stepped foot past the forest. Not with all the bright torches out there. We just guard the gates as a precaution."

"Well, I'm looking for action, Driscoll, and I *always* get what I want." Kaden said, locking eyes with Gale.

"Aye, so I hear. Just be warned that what we want, and what's best are often two very different things. Trust me son, you don't want action tonight." Gale stood and smiled at Talley as he placed several silver pieces on the bar. "C'mon Griff, darkness is approaching. Time for you to go home."

Griff finished the final drops from his Dragon's Beard, stood up, and clapped a hand on Kaden's back. "Don't go gettin' yourself killed, Kaden, all right?" And with that, he followed his dad out into the night.

CHAPTER 3

Griff awoke in a panic, arms and legs flailing in bedsheets that were yet again stuck to his thoroughly-soaked body. His hands were shaking, his heart pounding, and his mind racing. Something felt wrong. Very wrong. Griff ran his trembling hands through his matted black hair and tried to calm down, but he couldn't shake this uneasy feeling. He was radiating so much heat, he felt it coming out of his nightshirt in waves. He needed air.

At once, he rolled out of bed and ripped off his shirt. He threw on a pair of dirty shorts, slipped on some shoes, and silently crept outside into the cool night. Once the door was closed, he allowed himself a heavy sigh of relief. The night air soothed his broiling body, though it did nothing to ease his persistent, anxious feelings. Griff looked toward the sky, trying to find the moon and determine the time. Then he remembered it was No Moon Night.

He stood in the cool night air recollecting his thoughts after yet a second nightmare. As he did every time he had a troubled mind, he climbed the giant oak tree in his front yard. As he climbed, images from his dream flashed through his mind.

He had been surrounded by darkness. Pervasive, unending darkness. But it wasn't the fact that he was totally enveloped in darkness that disturbed him. It was the sense of pure evil seeping from his mysterious surroundings that sent chills crawling over his skin. He remembered running in the dark. Seeing an orange light that grew with every pounding step forward. Turning a corner and bursting into the light. And then, what he would probably never forget, the smile that greeted him. It was as empty and hollow as the two eyes above it. There it was again: the fiery skull formed from lava. Griff remembered the panic and fear that surged through his veins when he realized he was back in the cave. Back with the lava and the crocodile-like creature.

The lava skull floated mid-air, facing his direction as if expecting his arrival. The mouth opened wide, and the skull spoke. "Who are you, *boy*?" It spat that last word in a deep growling voice and stared at him, its empty, malevolent, soul-searching eyes pinning him to the cavern floor in pure terror. Then, without warning, the massive skull roared in a fit of rage and exploded in a brilliant orange light. While most of the details from the dream were fading, he still couldn't shake the lingering discomfort.

Griff had arrived at his spot. Twenty feet up, he could catch a breeze, as well as see Cordelia's perimeter. The towering stone and metal walls had been carefully crafted to surround the entire town, although that wasn't saying a whole lot as Cordelia was a small settlement. Griff estimated maybe a couple hundred citizens lived within the perimeter.

From this vantage point, he could easily see all three entrances into Cordelia. There was the main gate to the northeast, which Griff's dad was guarding, then two smaller gates, one to the northwest by the shops, and one to the southwest. Griff and Sylva jokingly called the southwest entrance, "Horter's Hole," since Janson Horter himself couldn't be bothered to cross the entire town for his business travels. And considering his family owned pretty much all of Cordelia, they did as they pleased, making Horter's Hole a reality.

Each gate could be easily seen at night from this tree, thanks to the large torches meant to discourage nightstalkers from making an appearance. However, there was something off about the northeast gate: He couldn't see it. Which meant the torches weren't lit. Griff felt more uneasy.

He quickly began climbing down. Just as he reached the bottom branches, he heard a loud, familiar voice bellow out in pain from the direction of the northeast gate.

"Dad!" Griff screamed into the night.

He let go of the branch, and with feline agility and skill, landed on his feet. He broke into an all-out sprint, hopped the short fence in his front yard, and ran down the cobblestone street without so much as a second thought.

Though the night was blacker than normal, Griff made it to the gate without any issues. The tall metal doors stood slightly open, revealing nothing. No guards, no torches, no Gale Driscoll. Fear seeped deeper and deeper into Griff with every bounding step as he raced through the gate and out into the open. Now that he was on the other side, Griff was able to see things he had not been able to see from the tree or the gate. A jacket had been slashed open on the backside, and based upon a quick observation, Griff determined that it was Kaden's. It was also covered with blood. Just a few feet from the jacket, several arrows protruded from the ground, near a pair of gloves and a bloody patch of grass.

As he leaned closer, he noticed several peculiar tracks. While clearly from the feline family, this print was significantly larger and the claw marks penetrated deep into the ground. Whereas most felines had four or five toes, this print had seven. The two back toes resembled long opposable thumbs. Griff had only ever seen tracks like these deep in the forest. And only on the days following No Moon Night.

As his eyes adjusted to the eerie scene around him, he noticed more blood on the ground and decided to follow it. It led him to a large black shape twitching on the ground. He stopped for just a moment, not sure what the seizing figure was. A few moments seemed to last an eternity before Griff gathered the courage to cautiously step forward and get a better look. Whatever was writhing on the ground was also moving toward the forest, making a strange sound as it seized, rolled, and flexed its way forward.

Fear wanted to keep Griff's feet planted firmly on the ground, but curiosity and a sense of duty to his father pushed him forward. One step turned into two, and two turned into three. With each passing step, Griff's heartbeat grew louder, and his hands shook harder as he closed the gap between himself and the mysterious figure. When he was within ten feet of the writhing shadow, he realized that it was a piece of the creature that had made the tracks, a dismembered leg covered in deep black scales, its seven deadly claws twisting in excruciating pain. Griff had seen snakes do this whenever he or his dad chopped off their heads with their swords. He was used to seeing their tails flail around wildly after death, but this was so unusual, so creepy, that Griff could no longer stand to look at it. With a shudder that shook his very core, he hurried past the mangled mess to search for his dad.

Almost as if on cue, Griff heard yet another bellow, but this time, it was closer. His heart jumped to his throat. That sound came from the forest. He braced himself; he had no choice but to press on into the jungle of almost certain death. *No matter what*, Griff thought. He ran back to the gate, grabbed a torch, and lit it. *I'm coming for you, Dad.*

Griff knew the forest like the back of his hand. And he was thankful for that. It was pitch black, save for the light of his torch. The treetops were so dense, they blocked out the starlight. And the torch's light seemed to be immediately swallowed by the darkness, so it didn't reveal much, other than what was right in front of him. Swatting bugs and tree branches away, he dashed through the brush almost on instinct alone. He passed the familiar rusty, overgrown chain-link fence and the tall tower of intersecting metal beams that were covered in vines, then took a hard right. To a visitor, these objects might seem random, but to Griff, they were just a few of the signs and markers that told him exactly where he was.

Should he yell out for his dad? Should he make some sort of noise to let him know that he was here, searching? He didn't want to attract any nightstalkers. Even though light was one of the best defenses against a nightstalker, the rising panic in his chest told him to keep his mouth shut. With trembling hands and his forehead wet with nervous sweat, Griff pushed forward in the direction he'd last heard his dad.

It wasn't long before he looked down and noticed a trail in the dirt. There were more of the same tracks he had seen back at the gate, but these looked as though they had been dragging something. Griff clenched his teeth in anger and picked up his pace, following the trail. Branches slapped at his face, arms, and bare chest but he barely noticed. He was running out of time, and nothing was going to slow him down. He broke through the branches into a clearing and came to a complete stop.

About thirty paces away stood a tall cat-like creature. It was about waist high with deep black scales and three legs—one was missing. This nightstalker was all muscle, with powerful legs, a strong neck, and large, bony spikes that trailed down its back. Enormous and deadly fangs protruded from its snarling mouth. Griff was immediately drawn toward its eyes which were as white as fresh snow and seemed to glow in the night.

Suddenly, four identical creatures stepped out from the shadows. They began to encircle a dark figure huddled on the ground. Griff's eyes widened, and he clenched his teeth. It was his dad. Was he still alive? A million questions flooded through Griff's mind, but he stood frozen in fear, his heart pounding as if it were trying to escape his chest. His mind screamed at him to run forward to save his dad, but Griff's body stood motionless. If only he'd been smart enough to grab a sword from the forge before running blindly into the forest, then maybe, just maybe, his hours of training would have paid off.

The nightstalker with the missing leg reared its head back and let out a shriek of victory as it hobbled closer. Goosebumps erupted all over Griff, but that horrific sound was enough to break through the icy fear that froze him. He stabbed the torch into the ground, grabbed a thick branch, and ran at full speed toward the monsters. He hated these nightstalkers with a hatred he hadn't known he was capable of. Anger surged through him, powering his legs as they brought him closer to the enemy. With a roar, Griff wound back with the branch and swung with all his might, connecting with the first nightstalker's midsection and sending it flying into the shadows. That blow was enough to snap the branch in half, but Griff didn't care. It was still long enough to be dangerous.

The other four nightstalkers were stunned by the sudden turn of events, but it didn't take long for them to recover and focus their attention on Griff. One lunged forward, snapping its jaws dangerously close to Griff's face and knocking him to the ground. Griff shoved what was left of the branch in front of him as he fell, causing the nightstalker to chomp on it instead; its powerful jaws sunk its teeth into the wood. The beast took a step backward and frantically bucked like a wild bull, shaking its head to loosen the branch.

Griff seized the opportunity to jump up from the ground and swing his fist upward as hard as he could. He made perfect contact, bashing the monster under its jaw and sending it to the ground. But then his world exploded in pain, and he found himself back on the forest floor, disoriented. Another nightstalker had tackled him and now stood inches away, ready to devour him.

Anger flooded through him. He was not about to lose to these beasts. With a grunt of frustration and rage, Griff rolled to the side, just in time to miss a deadly swipe. He stumbled to his feet and tried to put some distance between them. But the beast was faster and shredded his back with one swipe of its deadly claws. He cried out in agony as he fell and rolled across the ground, grass and leaves sticking to his bloody torso. Using all his might to push himself back up, Griff made it to his knees only to find all five nightstalkers surrounding him.

Defeat. He had lost. A wave of emotions hit Griff all at once: anger and hatred toward these creatures, fear as his imminent death was near, and most of all, frustration at himself for being unable to save his dad. He clenched his fists and gritted his teeth. The emotions continued to build and swell within him, causing his adrenaline to pump even more. *This can't happen*, Griff thought. *This can't be the end.* His muscles were tense, and his mind was a swirling mess.

Light. White light erupted into the darkness. Griff looked down, surprised to see it coming from his bare chest. A large, strange glowing symbol had appeared over his heart—almost like a tattoo of light being drawn onto his skin by an invisible hand. The gleaming symbol was pulsing and slowly began to grow until his very veins radiated. The light slowly snaked across his skin, like neon tendrils wrapping themselves around his body.

Power. He felt it coursing through his veins, as though his whole body would explode from it. For an adrenaline-fueled second, Griff roared and somehow forced all that energy into his fists, slamming them into the ground. The place of impact erupted with a thundering noise, and bright white light shot out from the ground in every direction, forcing grass, flowers, and bushes to be ripped from the ground and thrown into the forest.

Silence. It was quiet now, the snarling sounds of the nightstalkers eerily absent. Griff slowly straightened up, completely drained. As the bright white tendrils started to retract and fade along with the glowing symbol on his chest, he looked around to discover the bodies of the nightstalkers lying a stone's throw from him. They weren't moving. The clearing dimmed as the strange light faded. Griff succumbed to weakness and fell to the forest floor. Just before his eyes rolled to the back of his head, he noticed a dark shadow approaching his limp body.

CHAPTER 4

Griff could hear muffled conversation but decided to keep his eyes closed. He was exhausted and his whole body ached.

"How's Gaelic?" Griff heard his mother whisper.

"He's resting now," answered a gentle, yet unfamiliar voice. "Your husband is a resilient man. To have been attacked by a nightstalker and then to carry your son out of the forest is remarkable."

"Couldn't believe me eyes, meself, Your Majesty!" Talley's voice whispered in wonder. "His will is as strong as the steel he smiths. Carryin' Griff on his shoulders with his leg mangled! Nightstalker's fury!"

At the mention of his dad, Griff's eyes popped open. He strained to sit up and asked, "Is Dad okay? Where is he?"

Griff was back in his bedroom. It was still dark outside. His mother and Talley sat in kitchen chairs that had been placed next to his bed. He was still shirtless, but someone had wrapped his torso in bandages. Griff realized that his back, which the nightstalker had used for a scratching post, was no longer in excruciating pain. Now it just throbbed uncomfortably.

Across the room, a man whom he had never met, yet immediately knew, stood at his bedroom door. He was tall and well-built, and his long white beard and short hair contrasted with his clear strength and energy. Wisdom that shone through bright blue eyes displayed kindness and concern. This man's stature would be enough to intimidate many people, but it was the wolf head crest carefully embroidered on his leather vest that made Griff's heart race. The crest of the Aldamund family. The king of Oriel was standing in his bedroom.

"Uhhh, hi … Your Majesty." The words fumbled out of his mouth. Awkwardly, he bent as low as the bandages around his torso would allow, before he glanced toward his mother and asked, "I-Is dad okay? What happened?"

"Yer dad is an 'ero!" Talley slapped Griff's shoulder, causing him to wince in pain.

"Sorry …" Talley muttered, leaning back in his chair. "Gone and got all excited, I did."

"It's true," King Aldamund responded. "Griff, your dad saved your life."

"I went to bring yer dad the last of me Dragon's Beard after I had cleaned me place up for closing, when I noticed the torches weren't lit as they usually be. That's when I saw yer dad, his leg all bloodied and disgusting. And Griff, ye should've seen the way it—"

"Talley …" Leena raised her eyebrows at him.

"Right, er, anywho, yer dad was a bit injured and yet he carried ya outta that forest. Once you both were outta there and yer dad saw me, he laid you on the grass and then passed out. I pulled ya both inside the gate and ran to get help. Lost me precious cup of Dragon's Beard in all the hubbub, mind you …" King Aldamund raised an eyebrow. "But, uh, hey, that's all right! It was an honor to serve the Driscoll family, and I'm glad ye both be safe!"

"Yes, thank you, Talley, for helping my boys. That was very brave and kind of you," Leena said.

"Shucks, Leena, I'd do 'bout near anythin' for your family. But what's a nightstalker doin' so close to the gates anyways? Those torches are s'posed to keep 'em away!"

"That's what we'd like to know as well." The king sighed. "Talley, thank you for helping Gaelic and Griffin and sharing your side of the story. Might I ask you to be excused while I talk with Leena and Griffin in private?"

"As ya wish, Majesty." Talley stood up and bowed low. As he straightened, he smiled at the king and said, "I'll be at me tavern when you're ready for a round of me Dragon's Beard. I know you got your own business to 'tend to, but I know my king'll never say no to a hot mug!"

With that, Talley grabbed the cloak from the back of his chair and left. King Aldamund walked across the room, took Talley's place, and sat in silence until he heard the front door open and close.

"Griff, how are you feeling right now?" King Aldamund asked kindly.

"Um, I'm fine." Griff said as he twisted uncomfortably in his bed. He wasn't sure if his discomfort was because his back had been raked by a nightstalker or because he was having a one-on-one conversation with the king of Oriel in his bedroom after he had sneaked out and entered the forest on No Moon Night. Surely he wasn't here to give Griff a lecture on staying out of the forest at night. He knew better than to believe the king made personal house calls for such reasons. Maybe the king had come to see the Horters. After all, business was doing well, and they often met with important people in Oriel, a point that they managed to sneak into every conversation they could. No matter the reason, given the choice, Griff would have rather faced another group of nightstalkers than talk to the king about what had happened.

"What do you remember from earlier?"

"Well, I woke up from a bad dream and decided to get some fresh air, so I stepped outside." It was probably just a silly nightmare, so Griff decided to keep the dream to himself. But before he could continue, King Aldamund held up a hand.

"Tell me more about this dream."

Griff heaved a heavy sigh, closed his eyes, and described the dream in as much detail as he could remember. King Aldamund only pulled at his long beard when Griff was finished, then politely asked him to continue his story. He recounted the rest of the night's events, from the scene at the front gates, to the amputated leg of the nightstalker, to the attack in the forest clearing.

He paused for a moment, wondering whether he should continue or not. He didn't know how his mother or the king would respond to the rest of the events. His mom looked as though she was already about to have a heart attack. The next part of the story would definitely not ease her stress.

Griff allowed the silence to hang in the air for too long. The king stopped stroking his beard, looked Griff right in the eyes, and asked, "And how did you survive the nightstalkers, Griffin?"

It was best not to lie to the king. And so, Griff described in full detail the confusing moment where his body lit up in white light and the impact his fists made in the ground. His mother's eyes grew wide as he told his story, but King Aldamund's face revealed nothing. Griff finished his report of the night's events, then he leaned back against his headboard, physically and mentally exhausted.

He had so many questions running through his mind. Was his dad okay? How bad were his injuries? And what in the nightstalker's fury had happened to his body back in the forest? His dad had told him that as he got older his body would go through some changes, but Griff was pretty sure this wasn't what he meant. No other boy he knew had ever mentioned his whole body lighting up with weird symbols.

King Aldamund opened his mouth to speak after a few moments of silence, but before he could say anything, there was a rustling in the living room followed by a loud grunt of pain.

"That didn't take long." Leena rolled her eyes and walked out of the room. Griff clenched his teeth, doing his best to ignore his injuries, and followed his mom to the living room. His dad had been placed on the couch, his right leg heavily bandaged. Now he was sitting up and trying to take his bandages off.

"This thing itches," he said with gritted teeth.

"Healing magic," King Aldamund whispered quietly from behind Griff. "It works wonders, but it can be quite annoying at times." Griff turned around, and the king winked.

"Gale, leave it alone! The magic's working, just let it be." Leena fussed at her husband, slapping his hand away from the bandages.

"Well, it better work faster, 'cause I'm on the verge of killing that Horter kid, just as soon as I make sure Griff's okay."

"Umm, hi, Dad," Griff answered with a smile.

His dad's attention shifted from his bandaged leg. He looked up at Griff, surprised, and exclaimed, "Son! You're okay! Boy, I was worried 'bout you!" He patted the worn couch cushion next to him. Griff slowly walked over and happily sat next to his dad, knowing he was going to be all right.

"Nightstalker's fury, son! What were you doing in the forest during No Moon Night?" Gale asked.

"I know, I know. I'm sorry, Dad. I heard you yell, and I panicked and ran to find you. But ... I *did* save your life." Griff finished with a sheepish grin.

"Aye, you saved my life, and in return I saved yours. I'd say we're even." His dad gave him a wink. "But you may not be so lucky next time. I've always vowed to protect you and your mother with my life. Next time, let me honor that vow. Don't make protecting you harder than it already is. Deal?"

"Deal," Griff replied, readily accepting a shoulder squeeze from his dad.

"Why do you want to kill the Horter kid?" Leena asked.

"Well," Gale looked at her, "maybe not kill, just ... mangle slightly. Okay, more than slightly. It's because of him that the nightstalkers attacked."

"What do you mean?" she asked.

"That boy was bound and determined to kill a nightstalker. We could hear 'em prowling nearby in the bushes. We even saw their creepy glowing eyes just inside the forest perimeter. But we were safe as long as those torches stayed lit.

"But then, Kaden '*accidentally*' stumbled, breaking two of the torches. I went just inside the gate to grab replacements, and when I came back, he was knocking the rest of 'em over. 'Course, Janson just stood to the side watching his son hollerin' for the nightstalkers to 'come and get a piece of him.' Well, that's exactly what they did. They ran right over Janson, knocking him on his back"—Gale paused before muttering—"which I would have enjoyed more if that's all that had happened …"

Leena cleared her throat, her eyes locking on Gale's as if to say, *Move on, Gale Driscoll.*

Gale coughed and continued, "Anyway, they tackled Kaden to the ground and pinned him belly down and were about to tear into the boy."

"And how did Mr. Horter respond to *that*?" Griff asked.

"Well, when they went after his boy, he was shootin' his fancy arrows and yellin' for them to get off his son. Turns out, he's actually a really good shot. 'Course, the arrows just bounced right off the beasts—they barely even noticed. He might as well've just been blowing kisses at 'em.

"Anyway, that's when I came in and chopped off one of the nightstalker's legs, which he didn't appreciate. He lashed out with his spikey tail and stabbed me right through the leg. Then they left Kaden alone and dragged me through the woods, and that's when I blacked out. Must've hit a tree or something on my way in."

Gale rubbed the back of his head, and squinted his eyes as he tried to remember.

"I woke up to a bright white light and noticed the whole ground was shaking like an earthquake. I looked over and saw Griff lying on the ground. Kinda looked like you were glowin' a little too."

He looked over at Griff, "Son, what happened? What were you doin' out there?"

"I think I can best answer that, Gaelic." King Aldamund confidently stepped forward to address Griff's dad. Gale straightened up on the couch in immediate recognition.

"Your Majesty! Uh … I'm so sorry. I didn't see you standing there. Please, please, come take a seat." He tried to move his leg off the couch to make room for the king, but Leena was too quick, and grabbed his heel, forcing it to stay on the couch.

"You will *not*!" she said with authority, ignoring the initial cry of pain from her husband.

"No need to get up, Gaelic. Please, rest your leg. It will take some time to heal, even with my restorative magic at work."

With a great deal of effort, Griff's dad settled back onto the couch before his wife released her vicelike grip on his ankle. When Gale had gotten comfortable, he muttered, "I was wonderin' where the healing magic came from."

"Gaelic, Leena, your son has a remarkable gift. Griff has the ability to manipulate the very essence of life—magic, as you call it. From what Talley tells me, you all don't see very many magical folk here in Cordelia, is that true?"

The Driscolls all nodded in unison, eyes glued to their king.

"I see. That's a shame. You know, I think I will have a seat. Don't mind me, Leena, I'll fetch one myself." He snapped his fingers and one of the kitchen chairs from Griff's bedroom shot into the living room with blazing speed and halted just behind the king, who sat down and faced Griff. All the Driscolls' eyes grew wide, though the king didn't seem to notice.

"Now, the ability to manipulate essence is a special gift that requires significant training, or it can have devastating results."

Leena's eyes grew big. "What do you mean?"

"What happened to Griff tonight was undoubtedly the result of his abilities at work. You've heard of the fight or flight response, correct?" The king looked around and noticed Griff's questioning eyes.

"When faced with conflict, we tend to have one of two tendencies: to fight or to run. Our bodies respond to impending conflict by helping us with either the fight or the flight. However, for those of us who have the ability to manipulate essence, our bodies respond with magic.

"It is not until about this stage in life, around the age of fifteen or sixteen, that these abilities manifest themselves. For most young people, the first sign of magical ability appears through sibling rivalry or the simple act of playing a game. Usually, the first signs of magic are harmless: a levitating toy, a door slamming shut, or even a watermelon exploding during a heated family dinner discussion. However, if left untrained, they can become increasingly volatile and dangerous.

"In Griff's case, the strong emotions he faced in the rescue of his father must have enabled him to use his powers to fight the nightstalkers. Griff, I must say, taking out five nightstalkers with one powerful blast like that takes serious magical power. Your gift is strong. Much stronger than most youth your age."

"How is this possible?" Leena asked. "How is it possible that he has these powers?"

"It is indeed curious, Leena, that Griff should have these powers. As a rule of thumb, essence manipulation is genetic, and as such, magical abilities are normally passed down through the family line. However, no one in your family has ever had such a skill, am I correct?"

Gale, speechless for once in his life, nodded.

"Well, then, it is indeed a mystery. But nonetheless, Griff, you are a mage and quite an extraordinary one at that. Might I make a suggestion to you and your family?" The king turned to face the new mage, a hint of excitement in his eyes.

"There is an academy in a castle far away from here for those who can manipulate essence. It is a place for those, like you, who have discovered these abilities and are in need of instruction. At Bergots Academy, young mages study for three years under the finest professors, mages who have dedicated their lives to training them in all areas of essence manipulation. I would like you to attend Bergots, Griff, so that you can learn the extent of your power as well as how to control it."

Kind Aldamund paused to let the weight of his words sink in. In less than a day, life had completely changed for the Driscoll family. Griff was a mage, able to manipulate the very essence of life. And the king himself was offering Griff a spot at a prestigious academy where he would learn how to control his abilities. Griff had one question left unanswered.

"Your Majesty, thank you for explaining all of this to me and my family. But"—Griff gulped a little before asking his next question—"why are *you* telling us this? I mean, you're, well, you're the *king*, in charge of all of Oriel, and surely you have more important matters to attend to than telling a sixteen-year-old boy that he's a mage."

The king chuckled softly before responding. "Indeed, young Griff, I am the king." His genuine smile remained as he held out his right hand and beautiful, multicolored sparks ignited in a dazzling display of magic. The sparks zipped around the room before they assembled in a spherical shape above his hand.

Griff's eyes grew wide in wonder as he watched the ball turn in place above the king's hand. One snap of the king's fingers and the orb of greens, blues, yellows, purples, and pinks whizzed around the living room and collided with the king's mark on his chest and disappeared into nothingness.

"There are three reasons I am here in your house telling you about your abilities," he continued, ignoring the stares from the Driscoll family. "Firstly, I just happened to be in this area while you and your dad were out saving each other. Secondly, to those extremely gifted, magic can leave ... footprints. Difficult though it may be, those footprints can be discovered and tracked by experienced mages. So, when you fought off those nightstalkers, I was immediately aware that there was strong magic near this town. And thirdly"—the king's smile widened—"I'm the king! I can do whatever I want!"

Griff laughed along with the rest of his family, although Gale clutched his leg to keep it from bouncing with every intake of breath.

"Now Griffin, Gaelic, Leena"—the king stood from his chair—"I know that this is a lot of information to process. But know that what I am telling you is as true as time. I shall allow you all to rest for what remains of the night. I will be back tomorrow for your answer. And Gaelic, no need to worry about the northeast gate. I have my mages watching it closely. Take care of yourself and get some sleep."

The king of Oriel turned to leave the room, but paused and looked back at Griff. "Oh, and one last thing. Classes start next week." The king smiled, and with a wave of his hand, he disappeared completely from sight. The Driscolls stared wide-eyed at each other in disbelief.

"Where'd he go?" Leena asked.

CHAPTER 5

Griff woke from a deep and dreamless sleep, for which he was thankful. What an intense night it had been! The decision before him weighed heavy on his heart, but he couldn't give an answer last night as his eyelids were even heavier. Should he choose to go to Bergots, it would mean leaving his family, his blacksmith apprenticeship, and everything he'd ever known to journey to an unknown world.

Should he choose to stay, he wouldn't learn to control his abilities, which could be dangerous. Plus, he would miss out on learning spells that could be beneficial. In either scenario, there were a lot of unknowns. Growing up in a small, predictable town meant that Griff was not used to the unknown, and that's how he liked it.

His parents, believing this to be a "defining moment for him as a man," left the decision up to him. They promised to offer wisdom when he asked for it, but otherwise wanted him to chart his own path forward. After a lengthy breakfast conversation, Griff had made up his mind: He would leave Cordelia and all that was safe and predictable to go to Bergots.

Sylva came over after breakfast to hear the story from a reliable source. He was also quite excited to share his own tale from the evening, so Griff leaned back against the tree in his front yard as Sylva talked.

The Horters had come knocking on Sylva's door, telling his mom a version of the tale where they'd been the victims and looking for minor patch-ups. Kaden, who had only trivial scratches, seemed to soak up all the attention he was getting from his parents. Griff, still mentally, emotionally, and physically exhausted, barely had the energy to explain what had really happened.

"Wow! So you're like ... you're like, magical! You can do magic stuff, huh? That's so cool!" Sylva exclaimed.

"Guess so," Griff answered. "Dunno what it all means yet, or why or how I have these abilities, but I guess it's best to learn how to use 'em."

Then Sylva did something that Griff never expected: He wrapped his arms around the new mage as tightly as he could.

"Things are gonna be different around here, y'know? I'm gonna miss you."

The king arrived before he could respond. Giving Sylva a squeeze on the shoulder and a nod, he hurried back inside to finish getting ready. The king told Griff that he funded the academy and provided everything, so students only needed to bring the bare necessities. The king would provide everything else, for which Griff was grateful.

"Having citizens rightly trained in the art of essence manipulation is essential for this kingdom. Plus, I'm always on the lookout for especially gifted mages who can join my special forces," he admitted.

Griff withdrew to his room to remove the unnecessary items from his overflowing trunk before dragging it into the living room, where his parents and the king waited patiently. His dad, whose leg had miraculously healed overnight, stood from the couch with a sad smile and gave Griff a giant hug.

"I'm so proud of you, miracle boy," he whispered. "You've made the right decision. We'll miss you here, but we know you're off on a grand adventure. Now, go learn how to kick some nightstalker butt for me, will ya?"

His dad released him from his bear hug and stepped out of the way so Griff's mom could say goodbye.

"We love you, Griff. Come home to us soon. And don't be reckless like you were last night!" she said with a final squeeze.

"One last thing, son." Griff's dad held a hastily wrapped brown package. He gently extended it toward Griff, who carefully unwrapped the brown paper to find the sword handle he and his dad had crafted just the day before. It felt like a century had passed since he had stepped into the forge with his dad and made the very piece he now held.

"I'm sorry we didn't get to finish your sword, but I hope one day we will. I want you to hold onto it and remember that your family loves you every time you see it."

With a tear forming in his eye and his lip starting to tremble, Griff was barely able to say, "I will, Dad."

The king coughed. "I hate to interrupt this beautiful moment, but it appears that our transportation has arrived. Griff, how do you feel about wargs?"

By the time they broke through the thick cloud cover, Griff's stomach had finally adjusted to traveling on the back of the majestic beast. He had heard of such creatures, but never thought he would actually see one in real life. This large winged wolf stood taller than Griff's shoulders, its thick white mane whipping violently to and fro as it flew at top speed. The long wings gracefully beat the air, pushing them higher above the clouds.

The double saddle that sat atop the winged wolf was big enough for Griff and the king to ride together comfortably. Once they had reached the optimum altitude, the warg slowed to a steady, sustainable pace, gliding almost effortlessly. Griff sat back and looked around at the vast, cloudy terrain below. He enjoyed the deafening roar of the wind rushing past, and the adrenaline coursing through his body. Griff was on top of the world.

Off in the distance, he could barely make out the forms of others riding wargs of different colors. "Your personal guards, sir?" Griff yelled over the noise, pointing in their direction.

"Indeed!" the king replied. "They normally keep their distance, maintaining security on all sides, but should they ever get any closer, then trouble is nigh!

"Now, your trunk will be waiting for us in the town of Solastran, which is several hours north of here," King Aldamund said. "Solastran is located at the base of the mountain where Bergots resides. It's the closest place to find all the supplies you will need for the academy. It was also the very first place in Oriel where magical and non-magical folk came to live together in harmony. Professor Coen from the school has kindly offered to show you around and help you get your provisions."

"How's my trunk getting to Solastran, Your Majesty?" Griff asked.

The king turned with the ease of an experienced rider and pointed to one of the guards behind them. Floating carelessly behind the bulky man was his trunk. It was not strapped down like most of their other supplies, instead it hovered off to the side, following the guard like a loyal hound, dipping and swaying with the motion of the warg underneath.

"King's crown!" Griff whispered, "Sir, how is he doing that?"

"Welcome to the world of magic, Griff! You'll learn for yourself soon enough!" And with that, the king pushed his warg to fly faster, the wind making it impossible to continue the conversation.

Dreaming about the magical supplies awaiting him in Solastran filled Griff with excitement. Outside of the king's healing magic, he had never experienced the magical world. Occasionally, he would hear rumors passed back and forth by bored townsfolk. Some were jealous of the mages' abilities. They would complain that mages didn't have to worry about things like lighting a fire by hand—that at the drop of a hat, they could have a roaring fire without all the work of dealing with kindling, flint, and steel. Others told stories of their heroic deeds, rescuing a boy in trouble or a pretty lady in need of help.

Having never left the safe confines of the Cordelian walls except to hunt by daylight, Griff certainly had no experience in these matters. Travelers were scarce in his town, and only occasionally stayed the night as they were passing through. What had once seemed like innocent and insignificant tales from worlds away was now knocking at Griff's door, changing his future in unforeseen ways. He would have much to learn in a short amount of time.

After a few hours of riding in silence, the clouds disappeared to reveal beautiful countryside and rolling hills. Overshadowing the vibrant green grass and the smooth, endless slopes were charred craters in the earth, like large droplets of ink on clean parchment—if the ink were alive and trying to escape, that is. From this height, it looked like black tendrils were trying to flee the craters, ever grasping, ever reaching further.

Upon closer examination, it looked as though the grass was dying, and the black tendrils were moving, as if the rot of death was crawling out from its pit. Areas that were once untouched grassy portraits of perfection now lay scorched and bare, like a growing, black scar on the face of beauty.

Off in the distance, Griff could see a lush pine forest brimming with life: birds flying in and out of the thick canopy like fish in the sea. However, just at the edge of the woods stood another scar upon the earth: several black trees perfectly preserved in death, collapsed in a large semi-circle with bushes nearby to match. And yet again, the black tendrils of death snaked out from its center. Never before had Griff seen such beauty overtaken by such a blemish.

"Your Majesty?" Griff almost yelled, trying to sound polite but still be heard over the whipping wind. "What happened here? What are those large black holes in the ground? And why do they almost look … alive?"

The king grabbed the reins of his mount and gently pulled, decreasing their speed so he could respond. His guards immediately did the same.

"I'm afraid that what you see is merely the dot of an 'i' in a rather long and depressing essay on the horrors of our world."

King Aldamund's almost permanent joyful temperament had disappeared as he heaved a heavy sigh.

"So … there's … there's more? There are other places that look just like this?"

"Indeed. Many more." King Aldamund looked over the beautiful blight and scratched his long white beard as if deep in thought.

"Unfortunately, Griff, now is not the time or place, nor am I the person to teach you all that this scene reveals about our world. But I will say this," he turned toward Griff and stared at him, his bright blue eyes piercing him with the intensity of a warrior.

"Remember this moment. Remember all that you see before you. It is important that you do. Professor Erebus will teach you much about what you see here. You would do well to pay attention to him.

"There is still great mystery in our land, and while for most of my lifetime it has eluded my grasp, I believe I am now closer to unearthing much of that mystery."

The king's demeanor lightened as he gently smiled before turning back around and snapping the reins of his warg.

"And who knows? You might find yourself on the same journey and make grand discoveries as well! Only time will tell what mysteries you will unravel, what adventures you will take, and what friends and foes you will encounter along the way! That is why Bergots will be so important for you, Griff. It will prepare you for what is to come!"

The king shouted each sentence louder as his mount picked up speed and the wind grew back into a roar. With only a few more flaps of the warg's enormous wings, they would soon reach top speed, again unable to continue their conversation. Griff shouted his word of thanks to the king as they sought to make up for the lost time.

Griff's head was spinning. He had encountered so many new things in just one day, and his safe and predictable paradigm of the world was beginning to crack around him. It was difficult to steel himself against thoughts of inadequacy. Every other young mage at Bergots would be much more prepared than him. Since magic was passed down genetically, they had likely grown up around magic, watching their family members use it. King's crown, they would probably have practiced before coming to the academy. And here he was, a nobody from a tiny town far away from any semblance of magic.

Lost inside his own wandering mind, Griff didn't notice that they were approaching an enormous mountain whose base stretched from one end of the land to the other. The sun was making its way toward the western horizon, causing the towering mountain to cast a long shadow over the landscape. Night was coming quickly. Between the setting sun and the northern fall air, the temperature had dropped drastically, causing Griff to clench his teeth against the cold. The warg slowly made its descent toward a cluster of brilliant lights at the base of the mountain, for which Griff was grateful. His rumbling stomach reminded him of their long, foodless journey. He hoped a meal was in his near future.

As they flew closer to Solastran, Griff found himself mesmerized by their destination. This town was much larger than Cordelia. There were a few tall stone buildings in the town square, wide cobblestone roads, and many shops and houses. Curiously, there were no walls surrounding the town. Griff made a mental note to ask King Aldamund about that. The king and his entourage touched down just outside of Solastran, where a middle-aged man with dark brown hair and a brown and gray speckled beard awaited them.

"Errick! So good to see you again!" The king dismounted with an agility and energy Griff did not expect.

"Your Majesty, it's an honor to see you as well." Professor Coen firmly grasped the king's forearm and smiled as though they were old friends.

"Griff, I would like to introduce you to Errick Coen. Professor Coen to you. He is one of your new teachers at Bergots."

"Professor of essence crafting." Professor Coen smiled graciously, extending a hand to help Griff off the warg. "Pleasure to meet ya, Griff."

"Thanks," Griff said, trying to pat his wild black hair back into place. "It's good to meet you too."

Professor Coen stroked the head of the beast, which rumbled with gratitude. "I love wargs. Beautiful beasts they are." He turned toward the king. "When will you let me get one?"

King Aldamund laughed. "Whenever you're ready to rejoin my forces, Errick. You know these are just for my mages."

"With all due respect, Your Majesty, the day that nightstalkers cease to exist will be the day you can find me at your doorstep, ready to reenlist. Until that day, I shall find myself molding young minds within the walls of Bergots," he responded with an overexaggerated bow.

Seeing Griff's confused look, the king said, "You see, Griff, Erri—I mean, Professor Coen—used to be the commander of my battlemages."

"Best of the best, I was!" Professor Coen interjected.

"Indeed, you were," the king responded with a smile, "but your professor here decided it was time to retire from the force and invest in the next generation of mages, which is most admirable."

"Thank you, Your Majesty," Professor Coen responded. "And in the interest of 'investing in the next generation,' Griff, we had better get you to Solastran Inn before too long. You must be hungry! If I know my king, I would venture a guess that he didn't feed you, did he?"

"No, I did not," King Aldamund answered. "How unkind of me, Griff. Forgive me, but we needed to get you here before nightfall. Please, enjoy a meal on me." And then, for the second time in two days, Griff found himself holding another money bag, this one much heavier than the last. "This should cover your meal and the rest of your supplies," the king added.

"Sir"—Griff's eyes widened—"thank you for your generosity, but, well, I came with my own money. I'm sure I can make do."

He extended the money bag back toward the king, but the man merely placed his hand on Griff's and responded, "Tut, tut. This is yours, Griff. As your king, I command you to take it. I fund the academy because it is important work, seeing that young mages like you learn to control their abilities." The king released Griff's hand to stroke his long white beard. "But I also fund it for another reason. Would you like to know what that is?"

Griff nodded, not sure how else to respond.

"I fund Bergots because I want mages to learn how to use their abilities to do *good*! You see, Griff, those who possess the ability to manipulate essence have an enormous power, but they also have an enormous responsibility to use that power to make the world a better place. To protect those who cannot protect themselves. To be strong for the weak. To execute justice on those whose actions call for it, and to overcome the evil in the world with good. That is why I fund Bergots, because as your king, I demand that those who have power wield it for good."

"I can't argue with that, Your Majesty," Griff responded with an awkward smile.

"Aye, the king has a way with words, Griff. You'll do well to listen to what he says!" Professor Coen gave Griff a wink before turning back to the king. "King Aldamund, I bid you farewell, and may it not be long before we see each other again."

The king climbed onto his warg and, with a final wave, disappeared quickly into the sunset.

"Our king certainly knows how to make an exit," Professor Coen said, shielding his eyes from the setting sun. "All right, Griff. Let's get you some food, how does that sound?"

"Great!" Griff responded, putting a hand to his stomach to ease the rumbling.

Professor Coen turned and walked to the entrance of the town, held up his hands, and with a big smile said, "Welcome to Solastran!"

CHAPTER 6

As they strolled through the wide, ever-darkening cobblestone streets of Solastran, Griff's nervousness transformed into curiosity. Griff was amazed to see evidence of magic everywhere. They passed by numerous colorful shops with random assorted magical items and equipment: Magical Merchandise and More, the Weapons Warehouse, Bert's Beastly Bargains, and Vander's Enchanted Library. Every store had their doors propped open for the last of their customers to freely come and go, and every store exhibited its own unique treasures. Strange magical items were displayed in the front windows; some whirred and whizzed, others bubbled and boiled, still others steamed and sizzled, and some exhibited dim, glowing lights.

As if to signal the end of the business day, each merchant began packing up the wares they had carefully positioned outside their doors to draw customers in. Once the shopkeepers had their storefronts clean and free of all merchandise, Griff watched them point their fingers at the lanterns hanging by their front doors. There was a burst of light, and they began to glow. The sights, sounds, and smells made Griff eager to dash to the front window of each store and explore their wares, but his grumbling stomach wouldn't allow it.

They ventured farther into town, where Griff passed a large white stone building with a statue of three men raising their hats victoriously in the air. Underneath, a marble sign read, "Solastran: where real magic is found not in our humanity, but our human-unity." Next to the white building was a park as large as ten of Talley's Taverns put together. Parents and guardians gathered their children from the plastic slides and shiny metal swings. Couples sat on blankets in a grassy area. Some of the older couples even had balls of colorful lights slowly dancing around them. Non-magical children were begging their friend's parents to show them more magical spells before they parted ways.

As they walked toward the middle of town, Griff couldn't help noticing unique buildings and diverse people. He did his best not to gawk, however, his eyes were about as hungry to take in the sights as his stomach was for food.

"Ah, here we are, Solastran Inn," Professor Coen announced, stopping in front of a large building. Set in the center of the city, the elegant stone and wooden structure was almost as tall as it was wide, able to host many guests at once if needed. Since Solastran sat at the base of what was probably the only magical school in all of Oriel, the inn's magnitude seemed necessary. Between numerous lanterns hanging from the building and luminous windows reflecting the life inside, Solastran Inn was a beacon of light against the dark background of night.

The tall wooden double doors opened to reveal a large and busy room, full of people eating at small round tables. Many guests had sought refuge from the crisp fall air next to the great stone fireplace along the far wall. The professor and the new mage spotted an empty table near the fire, and slowly worked their way toward it. Almost immediately, they were greeted by an energetic blonde woman named Nyall.

"Fancy a stagmoose trencher or hawk's egg soup?" Nyall asked politely.

In response to Griff's confused look, Professor Coen leaned over to him and explained, "A trencher is a large sandwich. You're in a different part of Oriel now, lad." Professor Coen gave Griff a wink, and returned his attention to Nyall, "Hawk's egg soup for me, good lass!"

"And I guess I'll have the stagmoose trencher," Griff said.

Griff and Professor Coen sat in awkward silence for a moment while they waited for their meals. Griff thought back on the day's experiences: the pack of wargs and their riders, the beautiful landscape of Oriel tarnished by death, and Solastran's unique sights, shops, and people.

"Professor," Griff said, remembering his question from earlier, "why does Solastran not have any protection from the nightstalkers?"

Professor Coen smiled. "What makes you say there's no protection?"

"Well, I don't see any walls, and there's no guard at the entrance. There's just ... nothing."

"Ah," Professor Coen leaned forward, "Lesson number one. When it comes to magic, just because you can't see it, don't assume it's not there. Do you wonder what would happen if a nightstalker *did* try to run into Solastran?"

Griff nodded his head in response.

"It would disintegrate on the spot! The reason? The founders of Solastran were very powerful mages. When they first established this town for magical folk, they decided to erect an invisible shield around the town that protects its citizens from the nightstalkers. Not to mention, in a town full of mages, those creatures of corruption don't stand a chance. So, to answer your question, Griff, there *are* protections in place here at Solastran."

"Creatures of corruption?" Griff asked. It felt like he was in a foreign country trying to pick up their language and common sayings.

"Boy, the king told me that he was bringing someone from a small town, but by the wings of a warg, you really have been kept in the dark, haven't you?"

Professor Coen ran a hand through his wavy brown hair before continuing. "All of life is made up of essence. It's the building block of everything around you. Magic, as I'm sure the king has told you, is the manipulation of essence. Now, for some reason, and we don't quite know why, there is a disease, a plague, that has been infecting our world for quite some time. We call it the Corruption. Something has been corrupting the very essence of life and bringing about these creatures of the dark. But the nightstalkers are merely a symptom of a much larger problem."

"The Corruption," Griff repeated.

"Correct. So the king has made it his number one priority to cure the world of this corruption and bring about a new era of peace—where there are no creatures of corruption. Heck, where there's no corruption at all."

Griff sat in silence and pondered Professor Coen's words. He couldn't believe that nightstalkers were not the main problem. Living in the small town of Cordelia, he never knew of any threats apart from these beasts, but it was becoming clear why the Corruption was a top priority for the king.

Griff's thoughts were abruptly interrupted by Nyall. She had somehow navigated through the dense crowd with a large tray of steaming hot food hovering just over her hands—a sight that nobody else seemed to notice or appreciate. After two stagmoose trenchers and a cup of hot tea, Griff's burning questions disappeared along with his hunger, allowing his exhaustion to surface in full force.

Professor Coen introduced Griff to the owner of Solastran Inn, Mr. Colm, and then excused himself. After climbing many stairs and winding through several corridors, Mr. Colm and Griff finally reached a room at the far end of the hallway.

"The king wanted to welcome you properly to Solastran, so he arranged for you to have the Enchanted Guest Suite."

Surprised, Griff responded, "What makes it enchanted, Mr. Colm?"

"Oh, nothing. It's just fancy wordplay. But it's much bigger than the other rooms and far away from the noise, which"—he looked around before continuing—"at this time of year, can be quite enchanting."

He opened the door to the room and allowed Griff to enter first. Griff stepped inside. He marveled at the tall ceilings, a large four poster bed with his trunk at its foot, and a soaking tub next to a window that overlooked the lake whose calm, mirror-like surface revealed a thin crescent moon. A stagmoose head with a rather exquisite array of antlers on top had been mounted high on the wall along with the heads of other animals.

"Enjoy your rest, Mr. Driscoll." And with a slight bow, Mr. Colm exited the room, leaving an exhausted Griff to relish in the comfort of his suite. He dragged his feet to what appeared to be the most comfortable bed he had ever seen and fell face first into its warm and welcoming embrace.

The next couple of days proved to be both exhilarating and exhausting. Every day offered new and exciting experiences for Griff. He begged Professor Coen to show him the park, the town hall with the founders' statue, the greenhouses, and the shops. He tried new food and tasted new drinks, though nothing compared to Talley's Dragon's Beard. As much as possible, Griff wanted to drink in the town, its history, and its experiences. One day, Griff tromped through store after store, spending more gold than he could have gained from a lifetime of allowances. He bought a leather satchel and a larger trunk at Magical Merchandise and More, and a unique sword holster with a style that Griff had never seen before from Weapons Warehouse. When he asked his new teacher what he would use that last item for, the man merely smiled and said, "You'll see."

Professor Coen helped him find his required texts at Vander's Enchanted Library, titles such as *The Magic of Essence Manipulation*; *Magical, Historical Happenings*; and *A Beginner's Guide to Essence Crafting*.

Griff had just followed Professor Coen out of Vander's Enchanted Library with a towering stack of textbooks, notebooks, pencils, parchment, and other supplies when the professor stopped unexpectedly. Several of Griff's new possessions toppled to the ground when he tried to avoid a collision.

"Griff, you don't have clothes made from enchanted fabric, do you?" Professor Coen asked.

Griff mumbled a frustrated "no" from the ground where he was retrieving his fallen books.

"You'll want those," Professor Coen said. "You don't just learn essence manipulation through textbooks. You'll also spend a lot of time practicing. And, boy, can that do a number on your clothes!"

"What do you mean?" Griff asked, once again holding his heavy stack of new purchases.

"Enchanted clothes are much more resistant to wear. As you practice your spells and abilities alongside your other classmates, you're going to need clothes that can take that sort of beating!"

While Griff didn't like the sound of "that sort of beating," he was excited by the thought of actually getting to practice essence manipulation. Remembering the destructive power of his magic several nights earlier, he could understand the benefits of having his clothing laced with protective magic.

After the professor received a nod from Griff, he loudly announced, "Off to Wizards' Wear!"

The young man that stared back at Griff in the mirror may have looked the same as the boy who left Cordelia—the same wild black hair and blue eyes like his father's—but he felt older, having experienced so much since then. The beige, long-sleeved tunic fit his athletic frame perfectly, and the dark brown pants, thick and protective as they felt, moved with ease when Griff walked around. Having found suitable clothing, he stepped out from behind the changing curtain, where Professor Coen waited patiently.

"Now, Griff, let me show you what I mean by 'enchanted clothes!'" And with one swift motion, Professor Coen spread his feet and twirled his pointer finger, shooting a small flaming orb that zipped across the room and collided with Griff's chest, sending him flying backward into the curtain.

"Sorry! Sorry!" Professor Coen said. "I got a little too excited!" He ran over and offered a hand to his frazzled student who was fighting through the tangles of the curtain.

Griff jumped up as soon as he was free, and frantically felt his chest, searching for burn marks or melted flesh. Surprisingly, neither of those fears had come true. His shirt was still intact as though the incident was merely imagined, though the tender spot on his rump said otherwise.

"See?" Professor Coen said, dusting off Griff's shoulders, "These clothes were meant to withstand basic magic. Now, you get into a more serious magical fight, and you'll want some better armor, but for the purposes of the academy, these'll do just fine."

With wide eyes, Griff looked at Professor Coen and asked, "Can you teach me to do that?"

"All in good time, my boy. All in good time. Professor Hatlen will be your essence manipulation teacher, and he's an excellent teacher. He'll have you shooting fireballs and freezing water before you know it!"

The lady at the counter, not too happy about Professor Coen's stunt, readily accepted payment before shooing them both out of her store. Griff enjoyed the company of Professor Coen; he was a likeable man with many accomplishments and had traveled the world in service to the king. The only frustrating aspect of their relationship was that it was only through Griff's constant prodding that he shared stories of his adventures as captain of the king's battlemages.

"Why did you leave the king's service to come to Bergots, anyway?" Griff inquired one afternoon as they were sitting on the curb outside Magical Merchandise and More telling stories and watching the sky transform from bright blue to dark amber.

"Well, as the king mentioned, it was to 'mold the minds of young mages,'" Professor Coen said, giving his best imitation of King Aldamund.

"Aww, c'mon Professor. I know there's gotta be more to the story than that. I mean, why leave a successful career where you got to travel the world, beat up bad guys, and get paid handsomely while doing it?"

"Well," Professor Coen paused for a moment, as if contemplating his answer. "You're right, Griff. I did do all those things. And more. I've trained the best mages at the castle. I've led squads into strange and exciting adventures. I've battled against some of the toughest magical monsters out there. And on top of that, I've traveled the world seeing things that most people would never dream of. But while I have lots of exciting stories, not all of them *are* exciting, and not all of them are adventures I want to relive."

Professor Coen heaved a heavy sigh and looked up into orange and purple swirls of the ever-darkening skies, brows furrowed, as though lost in his own thoughts.

"As exciting as the magical world is—and trust me, Griff, it is exciting—magic is a lot like fire." Professor Coen held out his hand, a ball of flame hovering gently above his palm. The warmth the orb generated was a welcome friend against the ever-cooling fall air.

"Let me ask you, Griff, is fire bad?"

Griff's mind traveled a thousand miles away to his dad's forge, where fire was used regularly to help shape and create objects that would later be sold. Fire was one of the main ingredients that kept his family in the blacksmithing business. And not only that, but fire was used in the kitchen in the wood burning stove to make some of his favorite meals.

"I—I don't think so?" Griff answered, unsure of what else to say.

"So would you say fire's good, then?"

"Most of the time, yeah, I think it is."

The ball of fire expanded; its heat increased but was not unpleasant. Professor Coen, whose gaze was lost to the warm glow of the fire, swirled his hand around. The flame followed in a mesmerizing dance.

"Fire is neither inherently good nor bad. Fire just ... exists. When fire is used to heat a couple of friends sitting outside on an evening like this, it can be a good thing. But when fire ravages a forest or burns down a house, it can be a bad thing. Fire isn't inherently good or evil, it is the circumstances in which it finds itself that makes fire good or evil. The same is true of magic.

"Magic, you'll find, can be extremely helpful. You'll come to appreciate that benefit soon. But magic in the wrong circumstances ... well, it can be even more destructive than fire. I've seen what magic in the wrong hands can do, Griff. I've seen magic at the wrong place and the wrong time. And it's those memories I don't wish to revisit, and it's certainly memories like those I don't wish to recreate."

Before standing to his feet, the professor smashed his hands together, the ball of fire disappearing upon impact. He held out a hand to help his student up from the ground. While Griff feared he might grasp scorching skin, he still allowed himself to be assisted, surprised when his hands were met with only a slight warmth.

"But those are the experiences that have shaped me and led me to where I am today. And I'm afraid that's all you're gonna get outta this old man." Professor Coen stood up, stretched, and seemed to return to his lighthearted self.

"Now"—he looked at Griff with a twinkle in his eyes—"it's time for you to pack up and organize your things. Tomorrow, we are heading to Bergots."

CHAPTER 7

Sleep eluded Griff that night. The excitement and anticipation of finally stepping onto the grounds of Bergots kept him tossing and turning in his sheets. Whether asleep or awake, his mind drifted toward fantasies of what the castle would look like, how the other students would receive him, and—what excited him most—learning to manipulate essence.

What kind of abilities would he learn? How hard would it be to learn magic? Would he be able to keep up with the rest of the students who had grown up knowing about essence manipulation? What would his classmates be like? Would he be able to make friends?

At the first sign of the rising sun, Griff jumped out of bed, put on some warm clothes, and gathered his things before taking one last look at what had been his home for nearly a week. It had been a very comfortable room, and Griff was coming to the realization that his living situation at Bergots might not be quite so cozy. He reached for the door. *This is it*, he thought. *No turning back now.*

Griff propped his door open and fumbled with the heavy trunk. He was strong, but the new trunk containing all of his new magical supplies was awfully heavy. The two handles on either side made it possible for Griff to grab it, but the enormous weight made it difficult for him to carry very far. He didn't know how he was going to get his trunk all the way down to the first floor, but he was determined.

With a grunt, he mustered all his energy, hoisted his trunk up, and shuffled down the hallway like a confused crab. It wasn't long before

Griff's sweaty hand slipped and with a loud thud, the contents of his trunk spilled out onto the wooden floor.

"Oy! You need some help, mate?"

A skinny blond boy, no older than Griff, came over and helped clean up the muddled pile of books, bedding, and other random items. The boy's own trunk followed closely behind him, but he didn't seem to notice or care.

"Marth's the name. Marth Hayes," the blond boy said, dusting off his hands before offering one in welcome.

"Griff. Griff Driscoll," he said, grasping Marth's hand. "Thanks for the help."

"Naw, not a problem. Hey! *The Magic of Essence Manipulation*? Looks like we're both first years, eh?"

"Guess so," Griff responded. "This whole essence manipulation stuff's all new to me."

"New?" Marth responded. "How can it be new? Parents refuse to do any magic around you or somethin'?"

"Nope. I'm the only one in my family who can, actually."

Marth crossed his arms and frowned, "That's weird. I've never met any magical folk who didn't have family who could manipulate essence. Well, no worries." He smiled. "You're in luck my friend! I come from a long line of magical folk and my whole family's already been through the academy. You stick with me, and you'll be just fine. Here, check this out."

The young blond boy stepped back, pressed his eyes tightly shut, and stretched out his hand with the palm facing toward the re-packed trunk. For a few silent seconds, Griff stared at the bulging vein protruding from his forehead, thinking that perhaps Marth might pass out from exertion, or at least that his eyes would pop out of their sockets. Just as Griff was about to point out Marth's purpling face, his trunk started to twitch and slowly rose into the air until it was hovering next to Griff's waist. What was once nearly impossible to carry was now floating around Griff like a child's bath toy.

Marth lowered his hand with a proud smile and said, "There ya go! Now this thing'll follow you wherever you go!"

"How'd you do that?" Griff waved his hand under the trunk, feeling nothing.

"Magic! Duh! Isn't that what you're going to Bergots for? To learn magic?"

"Well, yeah, but aren't you a first year? How did you know how to do that already?"

"Started workin' on that one as soon as I finally surfaced. My sisters have been tryin' to teach me as much as possible, but I knew I was definitely gonna need that trick before comin' here."

"Surfaced?"

"Yeah! Surfaced. You know, like, demonstrated that you can finally manipulate essence? I finally surfaced back in the spring. Sisters kept teasing me, saying it was never gonna happen."

"Gotcha. Well, I'm glad you did. Otherwise, I'd be stuck trying to carry all this stuff on my own. Can't wait to learn that trick for myself. Thanks!"

Griff's nervousness was starting to disappear. He had someone to go downstairs with, someone who seemed to know his way around. And who knows? Maybe Marth would help him catch up on all the magical things that he'd missed out on.

"Well, then, let's get goin'! We gotta get breakfast in before they send us to Bergots."

It was strange watching his trunk follow him around, but he enjoyed no longer needing to carry it.

They walked downstairs and joined in the hustle and bustle of activity. Students of various ages sat around tables with their families and friends. Many had trunks similar to Griff's hovering next to them while they maneuvered through the thick crowd, looking for a place to eat their breakfast.

Nyall scrambled from table to table amid the chaos, taking orders, refilling beverages, and bringing food to tables. Griff and Marth stepped aside to let her through, right as she mumbled something about "getting crazier every year." The only available spots were next to a giant of a boy who sat alone at a table munching on a plate of sausages. His height and warrior-like build were intimidating. His dark skin reflected the candlelight in front of him, accentuating his large muscles with every bite.

Griff and Marth exchanged looks before Griff shrugged and led them over to the table.

"Umm, hey there," Griff said awkwardly. "Mind if we grab a seat with you? We've got no place to sit."

The giant paused mid-chew and wiped his mouth on his sleeve. It was hard to see from the other side of the room, but now that they were closer, Griff noticed the short dark stubble across his face. "I would enjoy the company." He spoke with a deep voice. After swallowing the rest of his bite, he wiped his dark hands on his pants and reached out in welcome. "Vincent."

"Vincent. Good to meet you. I'm Griff, and this is Marth." Griff said, grasping Vincent's large hand. Griff half expected the giant to crush every bone in his hand, but surprisingly, that was not the case.

"Vincent! May I call you Vince, good sir?" Marth asked as he sat in a chair next to Griff.

Vincent shrugged his shoulders, "Whatever." Then he continued his breakfast.

"So ... Vincent, are you going to Bergots as well?" Griff asked after ordering his meal.

"I am. First year."

"First year!" Marth responded in shock, "You look old enough to be graduating out of the program."

"Got a late start on this magic thing … I'm nineteen." The giant looked up from his plate with a smile. "I *should* be graduating out of the program."

"I'll say!" Marth answered. "Well, sorry for the late start stuff, but hey, I'm happy to make your acquaintance nonetheless. By the way, are you an actual giant?"

Vincent chuckled and shook his head. "I don't think they exist."

Marth looked over to see Griff eyeing his trunk floating next to him, "Well, don't just stare at it. Tell it to go to the floor."

"What do you mean, 'Tell it to go to the floor'?" Griff asked. "How in the world do I do that?"

"You mean, you don't feel that connection you've had with that thing ever since I tethered it to you?" Marth answered, pointing to Griff's awkwardly floating luggage.

It was then that Griff realized it. Yes, the feeling had been there all along, at the edge of his consciousness, a mental bond to his trunk.

"Weird, right?" Marth said. "It's kinda like taking a bath. You jump in, you notice the water immediately, but after a while, your mind accepts it as a part of your reality, and then you don't really think about it much after that. Except in your case, you didn't realize you had jumped into the bathtub."

"Wow, Marth, that was actually pretty profound," Griff said.

"Hey! Don't act all surprised now. Remember, I'm smarter than you when it comes to this magic stuff."

"For now," Griff smiled. Sure enough, he grasped the faint connection and concentrated hard to tell it to float down to the floor, but with no luck. He closed his eyes and fixated on that connection, picturing the trunk on the floor, but still nothing.

"Get on the floor, you stupid trunk," Griff whispered.

"Really now, Griff?" Marth said as he accepted a plate of eggs and sausages from a flustered Nyall. "Talking to it ain't gonna do nothin'. I'll spot ya this time, but we'll work on it later. I'm starvin'!"

Marth closed his eyes and held out his hand. After a few seconds, Griff felt his mental connection slowly disappear and the trunk slammed to the floor with a loud *thud*, causing several tables around them to turn toward the sound.

"Whoops," Marth said, embarrassed. "Guess I still have a few things to work on."

As the three of them ate, they talked about their families, their childhood, and their surfacing stories. Marth, coming from a long line of magical folk, expected his abilities. After all, since magic was passed down genetically, it made sense he would one day display the gift for essence manipulation. So, he practiced and practiced, until earlier that year, he made a vase levitate for just a second, before losing control and breaking it against the wall.

"My mom was mad, but my dad was way worse, let me tell you!" Marth said, "He had to go buy my mom another one after that, and those things are *not* cheap!"

Vincent, on the other hand, was adopted.

"Don't remember much, just what my adopted parents told me. Guess they saw a bright light in the woods at night and heard a baby's cry. Dad went to check it out, and they found me and my parents. I was the only one to make it through the night."

"Man, Vincent. Sorry ..." Griff said, not really sure how to finish.

He shrugged his shoulders, "I mean ... I wish I could've gotten to know my real parents, but I'm thankful for my adopted ones. They saved my life. I owe 'em a lot."

"Then cheers to your parents, Vince. All four of 'em," Marth said, raising his glass of milk. Griff and Vincent followed suit.

"So, what did you mean, 'late start,' Vince?" Marth asked. Griff had quickly realized that Marth never seemed to mind saying things that others wondered but wouldn't dare to ask.

"Dunno," Vincent said. "I just never showed signs of having any magical abilities. My adoptive parents knew very little about that stuff. They didn't know what that light was the night they found me. Could've been one of my parents. Could've been me. Not sure." He leaned back in his chair, placing his large hands behind his head, revealing exceptionally bulky biceps. "Plus, Ma thinks I'm not one to get easily stressed, which I've heard is how most people surface."

Good thing, Griff thought, eyeing his new comrade's build. Though it might take a lot to upset Vincent, Griff decided never to test those limits. Thankfully, though, it looked like Griff might have more in common with him than he thought. He wouldn't be the only one trying to play catch up at Bergots.

As they were finishing their meal, the crowd's attention was drawn to a loud voice by the tavern entryway.

"Thank you!" Professor Coen shouted. "Students and families, it is a pleasure to see you here this morning. In five minutes, we will depart for Bergots. If you would, please, say your goodbyes, and then we will take our leave."

Griff thought the room couldn't have been any busier, but as soon as Professor Coen turned toward the lobby, the tavern became a madhouse. People shouted at each other to be heard over the chorus of chairs scraping across the floor, trunks were thrown open and closed as last-minute items were hastily thrown inside, and several mothers sobbed as they said goodbye.

Watching the chaos made Griff appreciate the simplicity and space his smaller town had offered him. Never had he needed to maneuver through such a tightly packed crowd, but he was determined not to get stuck in the back. Marth quickly helped both Griff and Vincent with their trunks, and the three of them weaved through the crowd.

Marth and Vincent, while less enthusiastic about pushing their way to the front, reluctantly followed Griff. Having waded through the dense swarm of people, trunks, and crying mothers, Griff exited on the other side.

"Hello there, Griff!" Professor Coen smiled, "Glad you've got a front row spot. Get ready for a real treat."

Turning once more to the crowd, Professor Coen bellowed, "All right everyone, let's move 'em out!"

Shoulder to shoulder, the mass followed Professor Coen as they walked past the inn's main lobby and through another large hallway before coming to a plain wooden door that was held open by a smiling Mr. Colm. Griff peered through the opening and guessed that it led to the basement.

Professor Coen exclaimed, "Let's not dawdle, everyone! Bergots awaits!" And with that, he slapped the edges of the doorframe before heading down the stairs.

Griff moved to follow his lead but froze as he watched the opening morph before his eyes. The upper door frame came alive, stretching, shifting, and swirling until it formed a large double arch. The opening slowly grew wider and taller, as though the door itself was in the middle of a powerful yawn. Two large columns, one on each side, emerged from the wall, as though they had been there all along, hiding out of view.

What had once been a plain door, so ordinary that one might pass by without noticing it, was now an ornate work of art, crafted by a master, able to fit the horde of students and all their trunks. And just beside this new entryway was an equally ornate sign that read: BERGOTS AWAITS.

It was easy to tell who was new; older students shuffled through the materialized masterpiece without a second glance, and the younger students gawked alongside Griff and his new friends.

"My sisters told me all about this," Marth said as he eyed every exquisite detail of the transfigured entryway, "But I've never seen it myself until now."

Griff's shoulder suddenly jolted forward, as a girl with dark auburn hair and a determined look pushed past.

"Watch it!" she said, smugly.

"Sorry," he mumbled in response, though judging by the distance she had already made through the crowd, she didn't hear it.

"Nightstalker's fury!" Griff said to Marth who still stood beside him, "I hope the rest of Bergots isn't like this!"

"Nah, probably not," he responded. "Just don't get in that girl's way again, I guess."

"Noted," Griff said.

As they joined the rest of the group going down the stairs and into the large, mostly-empty basement, Griff was careful not to make any more enemies or bump into any floating trunks. He wondered how this basement would lead them to Bergots. Would there be some sort of tunnel? Was this just a place to have some sort of initial welcome before they turned around to trudge up the mountain? Would they have to prove their magical abilities? Surely he wouldn't be required to manipulate essence right this moment? There'd been no time to practice, no one to teach him. His heart beat faster, and sweat formed on his brow as the different possibilities raced across his mind.

Thankfully, he didn't have to wonder long. He noticed a door beside Professor Coen. No, not a door. A doorframe. One that was just as elegant and large as the one he had just walked through, although there was no opening. There was just cold gray stone.

"Ladies and gentlemen, boys and girls!" Professor Coen announced once everyone had crammed into the large basement. "The time has come for another year of Bergots Academy. Please remember that you are here by the king's good wishes to study the art of essence manipulation. This is both a lovely and deadly magical art, and while you all have the capacity to perform, this does not justify stupidity or danger. So please, be careful, and don't do anything stupid. I don't want to send you back to your parents in a body bag, or even worse, in pieces, because of something foolish you have done. Have a wonderful and safe year. I shall see some of you in my own classes soon enough. Now, if you don't mind, we'll need just a moment. Mr. Colm, if you please."

The owner of the inn stepped to the opposing side of the door frame, before giving the professor a nod. They placed their hands on the stone wall and closed their eyes. A small humming sound could be faintly heard over the hushed whispers of the crowd; however, the longer the two men concentrated, the louder the hum grew. Griff found it more and more satisfying, as if an entire orchestra were holding out one long beautiful note.

Slowly the stones inside the frame started to move. No longer rigid, it was as if they had turned to liquid and began a gentle rhythmic dance like a slow rippling of water. The ripples of stone, rather than swelling and shrinking away from the center, were moving toward the center of the frame where Griff saw a dull blue light start to form. As the light grew, it also became more brilliant and harder to look at. The stones changed their dance and started to swirl into the center, disappearing as the radiant blue light grew stronger.

Time ticked slowly, having lost all meaning for Griff as he stood mesmerized at the beautiful display. After what felt like an eternity, a beautiful blue vortex appeared on the cold stone wall of the basement. Swirling and dancing enticingly to the orchestra's tune, it invited the crowd before it into a new adventure of magic and wonder.

"It's time!" Professor Coen shouted above the symphony. "Please step forward and walk through the portal without stopping. I'll be waiting for you on the other side." And with that, Professor Coen disappeared into the light.

CHAPTER 8

Griff's nerves were on edge as the crowd slowly diminished, and more students stepped into the swirling blue portal. He hoped walking through the vortex wouldn't hurt. But why would they create a portal that was painful? Perhaps it would be nothing more than a strange sensation. Still, with each step, he found his mind coming up with more unpleasant possibilities. Griff steeled his mind against the thought of running away.

No, he thought, *I've made my decision. Just go already!* He glanced over at Vincent, who was standing to his right, and found the friendly giant staring fearlessly at the entryway. He glanced at Marth on his left and found him staring right back, his eyes sparking with excitement. With a nod to his new comrade, Griff inhaled sharply and stepped through the blue veil.

The moment his torso touched the swirling mass, Griff's feet left the ground as though an invisible rope had yanked him forcefully forward. He didn't have time to yell or even process what had happened before his feet stumbled onto solid ground again. His eyes didn't immediately focus; it felt like he had walked from the sunny outdoors into a dark room. Dark colors rained from the ceiling and a loud, upbeat symphony greeted him.

When his eyes finally adjusted, he realized the colored rain was actually confetti. It excitedly zipped and zoomed around the room, bouncing and darting to the sounds of the music. The crowd behind him spilled out from a decorated doorway similar to the one they had all just walked through and pushed him forward. He took one last look at the ornate door, wondering if it normally looked like an inconspicuous broom closet in this impressive foyer, then marched toward his new future. As he walked, he eagerly took in the sights, sounds, and smells of his new home. He walked past the orchestra, only to find a single conductor directing an array of floating instruments with no musicians in sight. Two sticks rhythmically slammed against a tall, upright drum. Three trumpets blasted loudly and victoriously. A floating piped instrument with an attached red and black bag danced and squealed with glee.

Suddenly, a loud voice boomed across the room, "Welcome, new and returning students, to Bergots Academy! Please continue to move forward in an orderly fashion. New students, set your personal items by Professor Hatlen, then follow Professor Coen to your orientation. Returning students, please make your way directly to the dormitories and get settled before lunch."

Griff looked around and found the source of the voice: a tall, attractive, blonde woman who had now turned to walk alongside Professor Coen as he waded through the dense crowd of excited students. A plump, older gentleman with a long bushy mustache and a brown bowler hat stood among a large pile of trunks and bags that grew with each passing student.

"You must be Professor Hatlen!" Marth hollered over the musician-less band.

"Indeed, lad! Professor Padraig Hatlen." He gave a slight bow, tipping his hat. "Professor of essence manipulation at your service. And you are?"

"I'm Marth, Marth Hayes. Also at your service!" he said with a slight bow and a grin.

"Aye, I like you, Marth Hayes!" Professor Hatlen roared.

Marth and Vincent were soon swallowed by the crowd of new students and floating trunks, while Griff stared awkwardly at his luggage. He closed his eyes and tried to focus his thoughts on his trunk, hoping to quickly make it drop to the floor before somebody noticed his inability.

"Need some help?"

Griff turned to find a beautiful girl with tan skin, dark brown hair, and bright green eyes standing with a hand on one hip, an eyebrow raised, and a smile forming on her lips. Griff looked past her to see several other first years with their floating entourage impatiently waiting for him so they could drop off their trunks and scurry past to their next destination.

"Hi, um, yeah," Griff awkwardly laughed. "Yeah, I don't quite have this down just yet. Still workin' on it." He ran a hand through his black hair.

"You'll get it soon enough. I take it your parents didn't teach you?" the girl asked.

"Er, yeah, no. They didn't teach me," he said, not really knowing how to answer. He didn't feel like having someone else look at him strangely for being the only one in his family with magical abilities.

"Well, here, let me help you." She closed her eyes, and Griff felt his connection to the trunk slowly melt away as he watched it carelessly float to the stone ground.

"Thanks a bunch," Griff said, trying to hide his embarrassment. "By the way, I'm Griff, Griff Driscoll," he called after her as she hurried toward their orientation.

She turned and smiled briefly at him before calling back, "Nice to meet you, Griff Driscoll." And with that, she disappeared into the crowd.

"I didn't even get your name," he muttered under his breath.

Finally untethered from his baggage, Griff found his two friends, and together they followed the crowds to a beautiful stone staircase that split into two opposite directions halfway up.

"This way, Griff!" Professor Coen yelled from the left side of the staircase. "Off to orientation!"

"Hey guys, over here!" Griff called to his comrades.

The three shuffled along with the rest of the new students, walking down long hallways with tall arched ceilings and passing by towering-yet-elegant stained-glass windows that sparkled brilliantly as the mid-morning sun passed through them.

Griff, Marth, and Vincent joined in the "oohs" and "ahhs" with each passing corridor, window, or painting of a past king or queen. Even Vincent's stoic face wavered at the beauty of the castle.

The group paused before a large double door, where Professor Coen waited patiently. The group quieted rather quickly, eager to see what would greet them on the other side.

"I'm sure you are all excited to be here, and rightfully so!" Professor Coen announced to the crowd. "Though there are still lots of sights to be seen, I ask you all to remain especially focused during this next bit. You are about to meet Headmaster Aldamund, who will answer many of your questions, as well as explain our expectations of you. Headmaster Aldamund is a good man and deserving of your respect. So, take care to pay extra attention to whatever he says."

"*Headmaster* Aldamund?" Griff whispered excitedly to Marth.

"Yeah? What about him?"

"Is he somehow related to the king?"

"Duh, Griff! He's the king's son!"

The doors opened wide, cutting Griff off from the millions of questions now flooding his head. The crowd hustled forward into a large stone room with tables and desks meticulously stacked against the walls. Neatly placed in the middle of the room, facing a large window that overlooked the castle grounds, were just enough chairs for the assembly of new students—eight carefully arranged sections of five rows each, with each row containing exactly five chairs.

New recruits were grabbing seats quickly, so Griff looked over at his friends and asked, "Front row, anybody?"

"You betcha!" Marth said. "Vince, how 'bout you, friend?"

"I think I'll sit in the back." He grumbled, "Most folks don't like it when I sit in front of 'em."

"Ah, I see," Marth answered. "Well, Griff, whatd'ya say?"

"Easy. Vincent, us guys gotta stick together. We'll sit with you," he said, reaching up and slapping Vincent on the shoulder.

They followed the giant to the back row where a familiar red-headed girl was already sitting—the one who had run into him back at the inn. She was slouching low in her chair, crossing her arms, and wearing a familiar scowl that seemed to be permanently glued in place. Griff quickly averted his eyes and decided to leave a chair between him and the girl, to avoid another confrontation.

The sea of students hushed each other into silence as a tall man with long flowing robes approached the ornate podium in front of the crowd. The man's long brown hair and well-kept beard only revealed a few grays. Griff estimated he was in his mid-forties. Elegant as his robes were, they couldn't hide his muscular frame. His stunning blue eyes communicated kindness, yet irrefutable authority, just like his father's. Headmaster Aldamund commanded the attention of the entire room, students and faculty alike, even before uttering a single word.

The son of the king of Oriel scanned the entire room as if personally welcoming each student. Perhaps Griff imagined it, but it seemed as though the headmaster paused a bit longer when his gaze landed on him in the back row. Seconds seemed to tick into eternity before Headmaster Aldamund broke into a warm and welcoming smile.

"Greetings, students! Welcome to Bergots Academy, a place of learning and growing. A place where each day holds new and exciting adventures for each of you. Bergots exists to train new mages in essence manipulation in all its forms. And not only do we exist to train you in essence manipulation, but to instill wisdom and decency in the way you practice. It is my hope that by the end of your time here—"

"Excuse me! Sorry! So sorry!"

Hushed, panicked whispers snapped Griff's attention away from the front. Lost in the headmaster's welcome speech, Vincent had apparently not noticed the girl standing next to him, hoping he would let her past into the very last seat available. The giant stood, quietly offering his apologies, as she sneaked by. With an exasperated sigh, the girl who had helped Griff with his trunk plopped down in the open seat next to him, looking completely embarrassed.

"Welcome to orientation!" Griff quietly chuckled.

"I stopped by the library to talk to Mrs. Finnegan about something important, okay!" she hissed.

"Whoa, kidding! I was just kidding. Nightstalker's fury, you are on edge."

"Sorry, I just ... I hate being late. I thought I had more time."

"Hey, I get it, today's a big day." Griff wasn't really sure what else to say. "Well ... um ... enjoy orientation. Seriously, this time."

He sat back in his chair and sighed in defeat. Other than Marth and Vincent, he hadn't had any luck getting acquainted with the other students. If this was any indication of how interactions with the others were going to be, it would be a hard year. Thankfully, Headmaster Aldamund was still speaking; his voice pulled Griff out of his depressing spiral.

"Remember, you are here to train on the king's goodwill. It is a privilege for you to be here, not a right. As a student of Bergots, you represent the king and me, so be sure that while you are here, you make wise decisions and follow the rules.

"You are not allowed to leave the campus unless otherwise specified. Especially for—and I can't believe this even needs to be said—nightstalker hunting." Several gruff-looking boys in the crowd groaned at the headmaster's statement, which made the headmaster smile. "No animals, alive or dead"—he glanced toward the boys—"are allowed on the premises at all. Come your second year, you will get plenty of experience with magical creatures in your Mythical Animology classes. Weekend visits to Solastran are permitted, provided that you use the portal located in the lower library, operated by Professors Coen and Strickland.

"Although you may be eager to learn and practice essence manipulation, you may only do so under the supervision of your professors. Dueling and hazing are especially prohibited. You will not use your spells against each other unless a teacher is nearby and has given consent. And yes, that does mean no levitating others without their permission. We are all mages united under King Aldamund. As such, we will demonstrate unity, temperance, and respect.

"Now," he continued, his eyes almost aglow with excitement, "one of the ways you will be tested later this year and in the coming years is through Altar Storm. This is a battle to the death, with only one mage left standing victorious!"

Whispers and gasps echoed through the crowd, mimicking Griff's own inward reaction. Even the scowling ginger seemed to sit up a little straighter. A battle to the death? Seriously? What had he just signed up for?

The son of the king gazed about the crowd before he chuckled. "I am, of course, kidding."

"Every year." Marth whispered to Griff, shaking his head. "Every year, it's the same joke. He thinks it's hilarious, or so my sisters say."

"Altar Storm is a sport we have devised here at Bergots for young mages. It is a sport of skill, wit, determination, creativity, and, yes, teamwork. In the Altar Storm arena, your battlegroup consisting of you and four other mages must work together, facing difficult challenges and other battlegroups to achieve a goal. These challenges will require you to utilize all the skills you have gained and knowledge you have learned here at Bergots. You will need to pay attention in your classes, as the very lessons you learn will help as you encounter trials of many kinds in the arena.

"You will be judged both individually and as a team. Some of you will excel in areas of combat or spell casting. Others will excel in areas of wit and creative problem solving. Still others might find their skills useful in survival or even reconnaissance. Whatever obstacles you may face in the arena, the goal remains constant: Place your storm orb on the opposing battlegroup's altar before they do the same."

Griff felt a slap on his leg. "Get ready, mate," Marth whispered excitedly. "You're gonna love it. My sisters won't stop talking about the Altar Storm battles whenever they come home. Some games last hours, others last seconds. It's wild!"

Headmaster Aldamund carefully rolled up the sleeves on his robe as he continued to talk, "Make no mistake: While this may be considered a sport, it is also how we test your training. Those with top marks during their years at Bergots will be prioritized for elite positions in the king's employ. You may be the next battlemages, healers, botanists, or magical archaeologists.

"Should the king choose you, and should you agree to join him, you will personally report to the king, which will place you in a position of importance, influence, and prosperity for your family.

"Many seek the wealth that comes from such an appointment, but a worthy mage serving the king seeks the prosperity of Oriel's people over their own wellbeing. Show yourself worthy in the arena, humble before others, and intelligent in the face of adversity, and you may find yourself sitting at the king's table."

Marth elbowed Griff and whispered proudly, "If he's looking for humility, he needs to look no farther than right here. You'll never meet a mage more humble than me!"

Griff rolled his eyes and tried to stifle a laugh, lest he upset anyone else today.

Once he had finished rolling up his sleeves, Headmaster Aldamund waved his hand, and the podium in front of him slid gracefully to the side. He stepped toward the crowd of excited first years, who had been hanging on his every word.

"Do not fret. Your first semester will focus strictly on learning and controlling your abilities and getting to know your battlegroup." He smiled. "You won't be out in the arena anytime soon, I can promise you that! Now, I believe it is time for you to meet your groups."

He waved his hands again, and this time golden sparks ignited from the ground in front of him and zipped down the aisles, splitting off at each row. The sparks raced behind each chair, and once the golden trail reached the end of a row, it exploded in a fountain of vibrant sparks, each row displaying a different color that continued to hover over the students, like a brilliant galaxy.

Griff sat amazed as he watched row after row burst into color before the golden sparks finally whizzed behind him and exploded into a galaxy of purple, swirling over their heads. The violet sparks seemed to dance joyously over the new mages and their freshly formed battlegroup.

"Well, king's crown, lookie there. Welcome to the battlegroup!" Marth shook Griff's hand vigorously. "It's gonna be a fun semester, mates!" He reached up and slapped Vincent on the shoulder.

"The four other mages in your group will be your comrades during your first semester here at Bergots," the headmaster said, gazing at the swirling galaxies along with everyone else in the room.

"You will attend classes together, and you will train together. This semester, you will get to know yourself and your peers better. Each one of you has unique gifts and talents that can be used in the Altar Storm arena, and each group will have their own unique strengths. If you identify the strengths within your team and use them to your advantage in every match, you will do well. Your ability to come together as one unit and play to your strengths will be more useful than raw talent alone.

And as you discover more about your own abilities, pay attention to the skillsets of your other battlegroup members. While I believe that the most successful teams find the strengths they already have and utilize them, we understand that sometimes a change is necessary. Therefore, at the end of this semester, changes can be made to the team roster at the request of the battlegroup. Beginning next semester, you and your team will be tested through Altar Storm, so be prepared."

Professor Coen rushed past Griff and quickly marched to the front, his complexion changing color to match the hovering sparks of each row he passed. As cheery as the scene was before him—excited students under the brilliant glow of their battlegroup banner dreaming of their coming years at Bergots—Professor Coen didn't seem to share their sentiments. The spark for life Griff had grown accustomed to in the last several days seemed to have been drenched.

He reached Headmaster Aldamund, who had paused. Professor Coen leaned over and whispered furiously to the headmaster, who listened intently. His kind smile disappeared for a moment as he nodded to the professor. Then his smile returned, and he addressed the confused crowd before him."

"Now, lest I keep dragging on, we have a lunch feast prepared, so Professor Coen will lead you to the dining hall where the rest of Bergots is waiting to welcome you!"

CHAPTER 9

"Okay, folks, here's the deal: We're about to enter the dining hall, where everyone is eagerly awaiting your arrival. Mostly because they're starving. You're going to come in, jump in the food line, and then sit at any of the empty tables in the middle with your battlegroup."

Professor Coen displayed his usually cheery self as he led the first years to their next destination. Griff's head was still reeling from orientation. He had one semester to learn essence manipulation before he stepped into the Altar Storm arena. And not only would he face difficult trials on the battlefield, whatever those might be, he would also have to go up against other mages. While they might be first years like him, they knew much more about the magical world than he did. At the very least, these mages had at least seen their family members use essence manipulation, and they knew what possibilities such skills could offer in the arena. Each demonstration of magic was a reminder of how little Griff actually knew about the magical world.

Griff walked next to Vincent on the way to the dining hall, as Marth introduced himself to the girl who had helped Griff with his trunk. Her name was Mira. The scowling ginger made it clear to the battlegroup that she wanted to be left alone. Even Marth seemed to get the message. For Griff, small talk was almost always preferable to awkward silence, but as they walked through the maze of hallways, letting Marth do all the talking was a welcome relief. It had allowed him the mental space to process the last few hours.

"Welcome to your first feast at Bergots!" the professor called, though he was barely audible over the heavy wooden doors creaking open and the raucous cheering from the older students.

Three long wooden tables stretched from one side of the enormous room to the other; the outer tables were filled with second and third years, while the center tables were left open for the firsts. Sounds of shouting and table pounding reverberated off the tall arched ceilings and beautifully tiled floor, making it impossible to hear anything with clarity. Candles hung majestically from stagmoose chandeliers, though the large windows overlooking Solastran made them unnecessary during the day.

The crowd was comprised of mages from all over Oriel smiling and laughing with their battlegroups, without a care in the world. Their camaraderie made Griff feel hopeful—maybe things would be all right. Maybe he too could form friendships like this. Maybe he could find his place in this new magical world. On the other hand, these mages had nothing to worry about. They had expected to come here, to learn magic. They had experienced magic firsthand from family and friends. It was natural for them to feel at ease in a world they had known their whole lives. But that reason also left Griff feeling unsettled. He would have to fight to catch up and find his place at Bergots.

He silently followed Marth, Vincent, and the sea of excited first years into the food line, gladly accepting every spoonful of meat, fruit, and veggies onto his plate. The savory aroma welcomed him warmly and eased his troubled mind slightly. Intentionally seating himself between Marth and Vincent, Griff began silently stuffing his face, listening as Marth once again tried and failed to make conversation with the red-haired girl.

"Mmm ..." Marth's eyes rolled to the top of his head as he savored his first bite of rotisserie lamb. "They don't make 'em like this in Whisperspell."

"You're from Whisperspell?" Mira asked.

"Mmhmm," Marth said, shoveling another bite in.

"Where's Whisperspell?" Griff asked.

"'Bout haff a day's wide." At least he covered his mouth. Mira raised an eyebrow but didn't say a word. Vincent was too busy with his own pile of food to notice.

"Half a day's ride, huh?' Griff said. "Must be nice. It took the king and me literally all day on his warg to get here."

That got the group's attention. Vincent set his fork down and tuned into the conversation. Even the red-headed girl turned her scowl at him.

"The *king?*" Marth asked, almost spitting his food at the ginger—which earned him another glare. "Mate, you didn't tell me the *king* brought you here! What makes you so special?"

"Uh ... I dunno. I don't ... I don't think I'm special." Griff ran a hand through his black hair as everyone continued to stare at him like he was a nightstalker. "He said he was just near my town when I, you know, surfaced or whatever. He offered to escort me to Solastran."

Thankfully, Marth came to Griff's rescue "Well, it's a good thing, Griff. You being the only one in your family who can do magic—king's crown!—I bet you'da died just tryin' to get to Bergots if you'd had to make it on your own!"

"Wait, you're the only one in your family who can do magic?" Mira asked.

"Well ... yeah. But Vincent's the same way. He's the only one in his family too."

The friendly giant smiled, his bright teeth contrasting his dark complexion, "Yeah. But I'm adopted. My birth parents must've been mages. Your birth parents are not. You are different than me." Vincent smiled at Griff and dove back into his half-empty plate.

"So how is it that you can do magic, but your parents can't?" Mira asked. "After all, the ability to manipulate essence comes from your family tree."

"That's the mystery, Mira," Marth exclaimed excitedly. "He doesn't know *how* he got the gift. He just has it."

"So, *no one* in your family—grandparents, brothers or sisters, aunts or uncles—can manipulate essence?" Mira asked.

"Nope. Nobody. My grandparents didn't have these abilities, both my parents were only children, and nobody that I know has ever shown signs of magic. Nobody."

"Ah, well, who knows. You probably had a great, great, great, great aunt Betsy who could do it, and she just kept it all a secret." Marth leaned back in his chair and placed his arms behind his head.

"Now it makes sense why you sat there and stared at your trunk for so long," Mira said, leaning in. "I'm sorry I gave you such a hard time. I tend to get really impatient when it comes to incompetence. But ... well ... I guess I should make an exception for your situation." She smiled.

"Gee, thanks," Griff laughed. "Thanks for bearing with my ... incompetence, did you say?"

"Don't worry, mate. We've got your back. We're part of your battle-group now—well, at least this semester. We're all just one big, happy family. Right, Vince?"

"Right."

Marth turned to Mira. "This guy will talk your ears off if you're not careful. Don't ask too many questions or you'll never hear the end of it. Right, Vince?"

Vincent shrugged, then grabbed his empty plate and left for what Griff assumed was a second round of food.

"Stop it, big guy! You're just too talkative," Marth called after him.

"So, where did you come from if it took you and the king all day to get here?" Mira asked.

"Cordelia, right, Griff? Cordelia: so far north, only the crazies live there. Did I get it right?" Marth interjected.

Griff rolled his eyes. "Sure, Marth. Sure." He snatched the extra roll Marth stole from the food line and waved it in front of him. "Cordelia's my home, and I'm crazy. You nailed it on both fronts." He plunged the roll into his mouth while his friend watched. It was so satisfying to see Marth's reaction that when Griff had swallowed it, he licked the tips of his fingers to rub it in.

"Where are you from, Mira?" Griff asked, ignoring Marth's stink-eye. "What's your story?"

She straightened up, as though a professor had asked her a question. "My name is Mira. Mira Dunn. I'm sixteen. I'm from Duskhaven. I surfaced last year, but I couldn't get away from working on my family's farm until now. But I've been practicing ever since I could do magic. I've been able to borrow a few books here and there, and when I'm not watching my sister—which is rare—I would try to read them and practice some."

"Wow. But why wouldn't your parents teach you?" Griff asked. If his parents could have taught him essence manipulation, they absolutely would have. Here he had been jealous of all the students who grew up around magic. He assumed their families taught them prior to their arrival. It didn't make sense why Mira's family wouldn't have done the same.

"It's called work, Griff. My parents have to work all the time. It's not easy for everyone just because they can do magic. You still have to work. You still have to put food on the table every night. My parents work themselves ragged to make that happen for our family. Just because we mages have magical abilities doesn't mean we can conjure gold, okay?"

Her words were a punch to the gut. He hadn't considered that life might still be difficult for those who could manipulate essence.

"That's why my number one focus is to learn as much as I can and try to get into the king's service. I don't want my family to have to live like that anymore, and I've got this one shot to make life better for them. So, as long as you all don't get in my way, we won't have any problems."

"Nightstalker's fury!—yeah, we won't go messin' with you, that's for sure!" Marth said.

"That's for sure," Griff mumbled.

"Hey!" Marth turned to the red head. "I know we've had a rocky start ..." He held out his hands defensively as though she were pointing a bow and arrow at his throat. "'Cause ... 'cause I can sometimes be annoying, I get it. But can we at least know your name?"

The girl looked at her battlegroup and scowled. She turned her back toward them. "No."

Marth slumped back in his chair.

Calmly and carefully, Vincent reached across the table toward her—a risky move—and gently placed his large hand on her arm.

"What's your name?" he asked softly, his hazel eyes never leaving hers.

Her eyes widened as if no one had ever had the courage to make skin-to-skin contact unless it was in a fight. Her posture relaxed for a moment as the giant removed his hand.

"Sadie. My name's Sadie."

Mira smiled. "Nice to meet you, Sadie. We're glad you're here."

After another trip through the food line, and after Griff couldn't fit any more food in his stomach, Professor Coen called for all the boys to follow him to their dormitories, while Professor Strickland, the attractive blonde woman from the foyer, led the girls to theirs. While the trip through the long extravagant hallways and picturesque staircases would normally be a delight to Griff, trudging down corridor after corridor and up flight after flight was much more difficult due to the extra baggage he carried in his belly.

A tall boy with spiky brown hair introduced himself as Milo Ofner, a second year. Griff was happy to finally meet another friendly student. Milo was an excitable boy with a battlegroup that ranked first in Altar Storm the previous semester. He recapped some of his favorite moments for Griff, who was eager to hear every detail about Altar Storm. Milo, a gifted mage whose skillset focused mainly on spell casting, told heroic stories of fending off multiple mages from other battlegroups, as well as protecting his own group from the ever-changing dangers of the battlefield. Griff quickly learned that, should he ever need any help, he should talk to this guy.

Just as Milo was starting to talk about the classes Griff would be taking this year, they paused before a set of large wooden double doors with a sign overhead: FIRST YEAR BOYS' DORMITORIES. Milo bid his new friend farewell and joined the rest of the older boys as they trekked down the hallway to their own quarters. Even though the entrance was wide, Griff wondered how the academy would house a hundred boys on the other side. He half expected to step into cramped living quarters, with tiny bunks and hardly any space to walk. He was pleasantly surprised to find that was not the case.

Inside the open two-story common room, ornate stagmoose chandeliers with candles bathed the room in a warm glow. Several plush leather couches and chairs centered around a large fireplace where the happy popping and crackling sounds from within reverberated off the tall, vaulted ceilings. The warmth of the fire and the ever-present smell of mahogany warmly welcomed Griff to his new home. All the first year boys fit comfortably into the large common room and stood to face Professor Coen.

"First years," Professor Coen began, "welcome to your new home." He wasn't using his announcement voice anymore. It sounded more as if he were talking to a few friends around a campfire. "Your belongings can be found at the foot of your beds in one of the ten bedrooms here. There are five bedrooms upstairs, and five on this level. Please, unpack your things, make yourselves at home, and dinner will be ready in a couple of hours. Tomorrow you will start your classes. Schedules have been placed on the outside of your trunks."

The professor exited the common room, giving Griff a gentle slap on the back before disappearing into the giant castle.

Some of Griff's peers settled on the couches and began chatting. Others marched past the sitting area and searched for their trunks in one of the downstairs bedrooms. Some gathered at the corners of the large room, where several small tavern-like tables, each accompanied with four chairs, formed an intimate seating area for study or small group conversations. And others climbed one of the two arched stairways on either side of the stone fireplace. Griff watched them disappear for a moment, then reappear, leaning against the railings that overlooked the common room. He wondered if there were more couches and tables scattered around the second story to accommodate the vast number of first years. But before he could see for himself, he needed to find his room.

After discovering his trunk next to a bunk on the first floor, Griff made his bed and placed his new clothes into the provided wardrobe. He stared at the ten other bunks in the room and wondered who would eventually fill them. Would he make friends with any of his other roommates? Would anyone snore too loud? Would they be messy or obnoxious and keep him awake at night? Being an only child had its perks. One was not having to share a room.

Marth and Vincent grabbed their trunks from the other rooms and brought them to the bunks next to his. When all three had finally arranged their new sleeping quarters to their liking, they sat at one of the tavern-like tables near their bedroom door and began digesting all that they had seen and heard that day.

Just then, a boy with close-cropped brown hair and a rigid stride stepped out from another downstairs bedroom door and bumped into a mousy boy. Griff recognized the boy as another first year from the dining hall. Finn, if Griff had heard correctly. Amid Finn's stuttering apologies, the uptight boy shouted, "Watch where you're going!"

"Leave 'im alone, Ty," Marth called, looking annoyed and not a bit intimidated by the mage's glare.

"Stay in your place, Hayes." Ty pointed before marching across the common room and out the dormitory door.

"I take it you two know each other?" Griff asked.

"Yeah," Marth said. "Tyrell Falkenburg. Grew up in the same town. I know him all too well."

"Is he always this angry?" Vincent asked.

"No." Marth sighed. "We actually used to be friends. Till his dad abandoned the king's battlemages, that is."

"Wait, his dad was a battlemage? Like, one of the king's personal battlemages?" Griff asked.

"That's right. Worked right under our very own Professor Coen too."

"So, what happened? Why did he desert the battlemages?" Griff asked.

"Nobody knows. He just left one day. Never came back. We were ten when that happened. Ty never really figured out how to deal with it. I don't blame him for being angry. I would be too. You don't desert the battlemages and keep any sense of honor. His family used to be the pride of our town. Now ... well ... now, they're the shame of it."

"I feel bad for him," Vincent said.

"Don't," Marth answered. "His family's story is tragic, but he doesn't need to take that out on everyone else. Which he does, if you couldn't tell."

Since they had a couple of hours before dinner, the group decided to explore the castle. They grabbed their schedules—all identical—and toured as much of the monstrous labyrinth as they could. Now that the uncomfortable, food induced haze had subsided, Griff was able to enjoy the overwhelming splendor of Bergots. Each hallway, staircase, classroom, and even bathroom had a unique and elaborate design. From the stagmoose chandeliers that hung from tall domed ceilings, to the lofty marble columns that seemed to turn the spacious hallways into a grid, all the way down to the crown molding in every room which was engraved with dragons and wargs. He passed by large classrooms where great chandeliers remained unlit, while the numerous crystal-clear windows illuminated them with the afternoon autumn sun.

The new mages drifted from the classrooms, past the dining hall, to the grand courtyard, where the sounds of laughter and excited conversations filled the air as students were reconnecting after their summer break. Griff watched in amazement as some older mages were playing a game of pass, but rather than use a ball, he saw them tossing another student. Swirling their hands through the air, they passed the hovering student back and forth between each of them, all laughing as though this was a regular, everyday game. Even some of the first years were lining up to have their turn. The only shadow to this otherwise happy scene was Sadie, who sat under a tree, glaring at each group of students. Pretending not to notice, the three boys continued their trek onto the castle grounds.

Past the grand courtyard and the greenhouses, Griff and his friends stepped into the stands overlooking the Altar Storm arena. A cool autumn wind rustled Griff's hair as he silently admired the battlefield. The late afternoon sun cast a long shadow across the entire stadium. Perfectly manicured soft green grass lay two stories or so from the bottom row of chairs. The stadium sat atop an oblong hole in the ground. Griff imagined the view of each battle would be spectacular—the audience seated safely away from the action—but close enough to watch every adrenaline-filled moment from above. He shaded his eyes from the sun, peering farther into the arena. On either edge of the field, he noticed two empty stone altars that sat atop wide rocky platforms: the goals. This was where the storm orbs would be placed to end each match.

"Nervous? Excited?" Marth quietly asked.

"Yes," Griff answered. "Both."

"You'll love it. It's ... mostly safe. Our professors won't let anything life-threatening happen under their watch. But don't let this peaceful view fool you. This isn't the same field you'll be stepping onto during the battles.

"What do you mean?" Vincent asked.

"I mean that the professors turn this peaceful patch of grass into an extreme magical obstacle course! They might turn the whole thing into a giant body of water, and your team's floatin' on those platforms over there." Marth pointed to the altars.

"They might create mountainous terrain, or portals to the other side of the map. Might have a giant wall you have to climb over or some sort of barrier that only lets you through if you perform the proper spell. King's crown! One time, they brought in nightstalkers. Nightstalkers, for king's sake!"

"No way, they did *not* bring nightstalkers onto the battlefield!" Griff said, his stomach twisting.

"Well, okay, so they were pretty tame ones, according to my sisters. Ya know, slow. No teeth or nails. Just a nasty temper. They looked a lot like cows, but you know, with black scales and all. Apparently, the battlegroups had to get through a herd of them before they could cross to the other side."

"How do they even do all that?" Griff asked. "I mean, building mountains, giant walls, portals?"

Marth turned to Griff and poked his shoulder with every word. "Very. Powerful. Magic. Bergots is home to some of the most powerful mages. When you bring mages with that kind of power together, they can do a lot of really cool things."

Griff took in a deep breath and let it out slowly, trying to calm his racing heartbeat. How could he ever face challenges like that in the arena? Sure, he'd have his team with him, but he was supposed to bring something to the match as well. Although the scene before him was quiet and peaceful, Griff's stomach twisted at the thought of his first steps onto the arena grass next semester.

"You'll be all right," Marth said, breaking the silence. "C'mon, let's check out the rest of the castle."

As the three first years made their way back inside, Griff noticed the game of pass was still in full swing, though a few students sat off to the side, nursing their arms, heads, or knees from apparent falls.

Marth led the way as they continued to wander aimlessly through the maze of hallways, passing storage rooms, offices, and study lounges fit with couches, tables, chairs, and large fireplaces. Eventually, they rounded the corner and found themselves standing before an almost infinite library. Towering bookshelves stretched upward toward the tall arched ceilings, and never-ending ladders sat at the ends of the shelves, ready to assist students with their journey upward.

They walked past a busy librarian who shuffled among the skyscrapers, pausing to float books upward toward empty slots in the shelves.

"Mrs. Finnegan," Marth whispered. "My sisters say she's ancient! There's a rumor that she was the first human to walk the earth. Knows every book in this whole library, too, mind you. So, you don't want to get on her bad side, 'cause you'll need her."

"Shh!"

Griff looked back to see Mrs. Finnegan glaring over her glasses at the three boys.

"And quite the hearing she has too!" Marth added, receiving another shush from the librarian.

Deeper in the library, they found a large spiral staircase that opened into an expansive study area. At the far end of the room, an older gentleman sat behind a bar, preparing to serve tea and light snacks to the students. On the opposite side of the large room, past the many study tables and bookshelves, a door frame was embedded into the stone wall.

"This must be the Lower Library," Griff said. "And that must be the way back to Solastran."

"Yep," Marth said, uninterested.

Griff peered at his friend who was staring in bewilderment toward the study tables. Mira sat quietly off in the corner with a large book opened, furiously scribbling notes onto parchment.

"She's already started?" Marth asked, perplexed.

"Yep," Vincent said.

"She's already started," Griff repeated. "Guys, we've *gotta* keep that girl in our battlegroup!"

CHAPTER 10

Griff's eyes snapped open at the sound of squeaking bats in the distance.

No. He panicked. *No, no, no. This can't be happening!* He reached his hand through the darkness and found the perspiring wall. His head turned toward the sound of the bats and found the familiar haunting orange glow.

He thought his dreams had become a distant memory. He had hoped that by leaving Cordelia and coming to Bergots he wouldn't find himself back here. But there he stood, back in the caverns. Back by the lava pool. Back by the skull.

"Not this time," Griff muttered through gritted teeth. He wasn't going to stand for this anymore. He wanted out.

Heart pounding in his chest, he turned and strode in the opposite direction from the pulsating orange light. Keeping his hand on the damp wall, he fumbled through the dark tunnel, wondering if this would lead him out of the caverns. While the light from the lava had been a welcome severance from the darkness, Griff ventured farther away from it, wishing he knew some sort of spell that would light the path and guide him.

He traveled through the pitch-black tunnel for some time before he noticed a faint glow up ahead. It wasn't orange. It was pale and white. Griff ran, hope racing through his mind. The tunnel curved upward and there it was, he could finally see it—the moon. He was almost out of the cave. Laughter escaped his throat as he sprinted toward the opening. He was finally free. He had made it! He could—*bang!* Griff's body slammed against an invisible barrier. It felt like two powerful hands had pounded into his chest and sent him flying.

Griff moaned as he sat up, the moon staring back at him—so close and yet so far away. Fresh, non-cavern air taunted him from the opening, daring him to try again. He stumbled to the exit, careful to not get too close. It was right there. His freedom from the caverns held hostage by a stupid barrier.

He sat back down, defeated. Why did he keep dreaming about this place? After staring out the opening for some time, Griff decided the only way to end this was to face whatever was in the cavern. So he made his way back down through the tunnel. The darkness swallowed him whole until he neared the pulsing orange light. Quiet squeaking greeted him as he cautiously entered the hot room.

The alligator-like creature peered at Griff from the opposite corner. Realization dawned on him as he stared at the beast. This was another nightstalker. Having just finished another feast, the enormous creature didn't budge from his napping place filled with the bones of his meals, but his devilish eyes followed Griff's footsteps.

The skull was nowhere to be found, the lava bubbling calmly in its place. Griff sat on a large boulder, keeping his eyes on the nightstalker, who returned his stare. It didn't take long for the pool to stir into the dance Griff was all too familiar with. Once the roar had settled, and a tall glowing pillar stood proudly in the center of the pit, Griff stood, fists clenched, ready to face the skull once more.

This time, however, the lava slowly fell back into place, cascading delicately back into the pool, like a gentle waterfall. As the pillar slowly disintegrated, Griff saw the figure of a man floating motionless above the hellish pit. He leaned back casually, his hands together near his chest. When the molten column had vanished, the man straightened up and floated gradually toward his nightstalker companion. His long brown hair floated carelessly alongside him. When his bare feet touched the rocky cavern bottom, he turned toward the creature and smiled. A beautiful, brilliant light shone from his clasped hands, and it radiated on his graying, stubbled beard and a narrow scar on his left cheek. Shadows danced across his face, twisting and distorting his smile. The man opened his hands and held the light out for his companion to see. He chuckled quietly, before he whispered in a deep voice, "Finally."

CHAPTER II

A violent gust of wind hushed the excited first year mages. Shutters forcibly closed against the many windows, immediately darkening the classroom. A small flame penetrated the darkness, which brightened as the fire swelled into a large ball. Professor Hatlen's hands swirled effortlessly as he flew the flaming sphere around the room. Haunting shadows danced across each mage's face as they all looked on in wonder. With a loud clap, the professor's hands came together, and the fire disappeared at once.

Before anyone's eyes could readjust to the darkness, the room lit up in electric blue. The students had to shield their eyes from the strand of lightning Professor Hatlen had produced. His hands were held wide, and one strip of pure lightning flickered and danced between them. With one hand, he brought the lightning up around his head. Then he brought it down like a whip. With each crack of the whip, sparks flew toward the ceiling like shooting stars. Despite his overall plump stature, the professor was a master, commanding the lightning to dance as everyone gawked. His hand shot up, sending the lightning to the ceiling where it hit and multiplied, expanding toward every corner of the room. The students stared as the tall, vaulted ceiling disappeared in a dazzling display of light. Thunder shook the room and the lightning storm in the ceiling disappeared.

The sounds of rushing wind could be heard once more, and the shutters flew open, the morning sun pouring back into the dark classroom.

The students erupted in applause and Professor Hatlen removed his bowler hat and took a bow.

"Welcome to your first class on essence manipulation." Professor Hatlen's gravelly voice was filled with excitement. "And I'm sorry to disappoint, but you will not learn how to do all of that today. Aye, one day you will, but not today. Today, we're going to take baby steps.

"You're all here because you've surfaced, yes? So now, I want you to close your eyes and place yourself back into the moment you first surfaced. Go on, close 'em now."

Griff, seated with the rest of his battlegroup, tried to push aside the previous night's dream. It took serious effort, but with his eyes closed, he focused intently on the night he found himself kneeling in the dark forest: dirty, bloody, and in excruciating pain.

"Now, I want you to remember what was going on in your mind, your thoughts, your feelings, and especially your emotions."

Griff remembered vividly how he had felt that night. Angry. He'd felt anger and frustration and hatred toward the nightstalkers. He'd felt fear and panic, not knowing what would become of him and his dad. His heart beat faster and sweat began to bead up on his forehead at the thought of returning to that moment.

"Most of you probably surfaced during a very stressful or frustrating event." The professor snickered. "Raise your hands if it was a brother or sister that helped you with that."

Griff heard the sounds of soft laughter but kept his eyes shut, trying to stay in the moment.

"Aye, for me, it was my brother. Picked on me incessantly, he did. One day he went too far, and let's just say, Mom and Dad found him hanging from a tree branch by his trousers."

The professor chuckled quietly before continuing, "Now, eyes still closed, find yourself back in that moment when you surfaced. Do you feel it? Do you feel that same power you felt in that moment you first surfaced?"

Griff did. The memory had been seared into him; it wasn't hard to place himself back there. He remembered the power swelling inside him, ready to burst out of his body.

"Now I want you to try to grab that power—mentally, that is—and see if you can channel it into your hands."

He felt an energy residing in his chest. It pulsed and grew, and, using all his effort, Griff tried to direct it toward his right hand. Surprisingly, he felt the energy move. It slowly crawled through his chest and down his arm until he could feel it in his clenched fist.

"Now, if you've got that power in your hands, give me a resounding 'Aye.'"

"Aye," Griff mumbled, trying to remain focused. Neither Marth nor Vincent had responded. Surprisingly, not many students had. Griff's voice was among only a few to respond.

"Good. About what I expected. For those who have it, hold onto it for just a wee bit longer. Now, steady ... steady. I want you to slowly open your hands and hold out your palms, facing away from you. Imagine that there is a stone wall just in front of you. And you need to push against it. When I say when, I want you to push that wall down, but not with your physical body. Release that power from your hands and push against that wall. Ready? NOW!"

Professor Hatlen roared that last word. It startled Griff. In a moment of panic, and with a flash of white light, he released all the power that had built up in his outstretched hand and felt an enormous gust of wind shoot out. He fell backward, knocked his chair over, and tumbled to the floor.

"Atta boy, Driscoll!" Professor Hatlen hollered, after picking up his bowler hat from the floor. The other mages were all roaring with laughter as Griff scrambled to his feet.

"You did it!" Marth said, a look of shock on his face. "King's crown, mate! You did it."

Griff looked over at Vincent, who gave him a smile and a congratulatory thumbs-up.

"Not many mages are able to do that on their first go," Professor Hatlen said, quieting the room and leaning on a table in the center of the room. "But we always have a few who stand out in the first session, and you four did great."

The professor pointed to Griff, Tyrell, Finn, and Sadie. "Driscoll might've been a little over ambitious, mind you. Trying to conjure up a hurricane. But overall great work, you lot."

Chalk from the front table rose in the air and scribbled against an old chalkboard on wheels. Professor Hatlen twirled his mustache with his fingers as it wrote the words: *The Colors of Magic.*

"Now, for most of you, this is as elementary as learning your ABCs. However, many mages have decided to ignore the wisdom of the colors, and I'm here to make sure that doesn't happen with you lot.

"Sometimes spells produce a color. Essence crafting is ultimately an expression of the one casting the spells. As such, it can display, through color, the mage's state of mind. We had four students successfully cast the wind spell so far. What colors did you see? Yes?"

He pointed to Finn who pointed to Tyrell. "R-red."

Tyrell glared at the boy.

"Ah, yes, red!" Professor Hatlen chuckled, his rosy cheeks glowing brighter. "The color of anger."

The chalk transcribed the professor's words: *Red: Anger.*

"Aye, and what else?" He scanned the crowd and continued to twirl his mustache.

"Yellow."

"Hmm? Who said that?"

Tyrell raised his hand, his eyes never leaving Finn's before repeating: "Yellow."

"Good! Very good." The chalk was a blur of motion: *Yellow: Nervous.* "And? Did we see any other colors?"

"Oh! Blue!" Marth said, waving one hand in the air and pointing at Sadie with the other. He clearly had a death wish.

"Blue! Very, *very* impressive! What's your name, miss?"

Sadie looked around the room. All eyes were on her and no one made a sound. She glared at Marth for pointing her out in front of everyone before she crossed her arms on the table and buried her head in them.

"Her name's Sadie, sir. She's shy. OUCH!" Marth rubbed his shin under the table, and Sadie smiled.

"Well, Miss Sadie, we are all very impressed. Let's talk about the color blue."

Professor Hatlen turned to face the board. The floating chalk rose to the top, above all the other words it had written, and started writing.

"Blue is the *goal* of good essence manipulation. While red shows that the caster's state of mind is angry, and yellow shows nervousness, *blue* denotes that the one casting the spell is in charge—not their emotions. That is to say, the person's emotions are controlled, not swaying too heavily one way or another."

The professor faced the class. "You see, class, we need mages who are tempered. Who are in control. We don't want spells that are unruly and unmanageable.

"Now, to be fair, emotions are *very* complex creatures, and I'm not here to say that all emotions are bad. To say that anger or excitement or even fear is either positive or negative is too simplistic. There are times where it is absolutely appropriate to be angry at something. Take injustice, for example. And there are times where fear keeps us from doing something irresponsible, like touching a hot stove. But when it comes to casting spells ..." He snatched the chalk out of the air and rapped it against every word it had finished writing. "*You. Need. To. Be. In. Control.*"

The room was silent, save for the intense scratching sound of Mira's pencil against her notepad. The professor scanned the rows of his students, allowing the brief silence to carry the weight of his words. He tossed the chalk back into the air and it resumed writing.

"Not every mage abides by this, but this is how you know that you have truly mastered a spell. When you can *intentionally* change colors like Headmaster Aldamund with his multicolored sparkles and such, you will know that you have mastered not just the spell, but yourself.

"So, besides blue, red, and yellow, we also have green for extreme excitement or mischievous intent. I see that a lot around here. And purple is for sadness. Now, it's understandable that first years will—"

"Professor? What about white? What does white mean?" Marth asked, waving his hand wildly in the air again.

"I'm sorry?" He turned to face his student.

"White, sir. What emotion does that symbolize?"

Professor Hatlen chuckled. "I'm afraid there's no such thing as 'white' magic. Perhaps it was a very pale yellow."

"Sir, Griff's spell was white. As true as my sisters are annoying, I tell you it was white."

Several other classmates nodded in agreement. After a long pause and many twirls of his mustache, Professor Hatlen finally said, "Well, Griff, you are a mystery."

The rest of their essence manipulation class was spent working on the same wind spell. A few more of Griff's classmates successfully cast it, including Marth and Vincent, though blue was noticeably missing from everyone's spells. Sadie surprised the whole group with each perfect blue spell; her signature scowl replaced by a look of cool confidence.

Mira was the only one in the group who was unable to conjure wind. The harder she tried, the harder she ground her teeth and furrowed her eyebrows in frustration. Griff wanted to console her and tell her she'd get it eventually, but he was having his own problems. While he was able to consistently produce a white wind spell, he couldn't control its power or its color. He eventually had to stand up and position one foot behind him, just to keep from falling over, which made him quite the spectacle.

"Now, most of you are still holding onto moments of fear or anger to generate your power. Your colors don't lie! Fear and anger *are* conduits for energy, but over the next couple of weeks, I'm going to teach you how to use joy and love instead. Living in fear and anger as the basis of your power is debilitating. I will not have my mages dwelling in fear and anger when true power lies in love and joy.

"So," the professor continued, walking back and forth among the rows of students, "your homework over the next couple of weeks is to search for and list everything and everyone and every memory that brings you joy and love."

Griff heard a sigh from Marth before he grunted, "I don't think he realizes how hard this assignment is gonna be. He doesn't know my sisters."

"See you all tomorrow and come back with that list!" Professor Hatlen called, dismissing the class.

CHAPTER 12

"Mate, that was amazing," Marth said as they sat down for their first essence crafting lesson. They were back in the room where orientation had been held. The neat rows of five chairs had been cleared out, making room for desks that encircled a large table covered with a sheet.

"It was hilarious," Vincent chuckled, sitting down next to Marth.

"It was both," Mira said, her long hair falling over her face. She brushed it back behind her ears, looking curiously at Griff. "Coming from the guy who couldn't even tell his trunk to go down yesterday, I'd say it was amazing and ironic. Have you been hiding your true powers from us this whole time, Griff Driscoll?"

"I wish!" Griff laughed nervously.

He was as surprised as everyone else that he had actually cast a wind spell. Sure, it may have been hard to control, but he *actually* cast it. He felt both proud and afraid. Proud that he was one of the first in his class to conjure wind. But afraid of the power he was unable to control.

Just then, Professor Coen waltzed through the large double doors in his usual cheery state. He strode to the front of the room, the sun gleaming brilliantly through the large windows overlooking the castle grounds.

"Welcome to essence crafting!" He flashed a large, genuine smile at his students. "Show of hands, who here knows what essence crafting is?"

Several hands went up, Marth's being the first in the air.

"Lemme guess, your sisters told you all about it?" Griff asked.

"Yep," Marth said, hand still proudly in the air.

"Very good, hands down, hands down," the professor said. "Now, you've all just come from your essence manipulation class, correct?" the professor asked. "Essence manipulation is all about spell casting. It teaches you a whole range of skills; everything from everyday uses like moving or levitating things, creating fire for cooking or heating, and engaging in offensive and defensive combat."

Professor Coen moved to the middle of the circle, facing the covered table.

"Essence *crafting* is all about combat." The professor, still a couple of feet from the table, swirled his hands. The sheet flew off the table with a resounding *whoosh* and folded itself neatly in the corner of the room.

An assortment of weapons and other peculiar items covered the table, but on closer examination, Griff noticed that pieces were missing: a bow without arrows, a long spear missing a point, and a sword without a blade. Professor Coen grabbed the sword handle and walked around the circle for everyone to see it.

"The art of essence manipulation is—just as it sounds—all about manipulating the very essence of life. Energy that can be channeled, controlled, directed. Under the right hands, that energy can be channeled not just through yourself, but through other objects as well."

He grabbed an apple from the table and threw it into the air. Then, with one swift motion, the professor swung the sword handle, and a bright blue light erupted into existence and sliced the apple in half. When Griff's eyes adjusted, he stared from the spinning apple pieces on the floor to the now complete sword Professor Coen was holding. The shimmering blue blade swirling with magical energy looked like a long strand of lightning, which an invisible force had squeezed into the shape of a blade. In some ways, it seemed almost liquid, but the pieces of apple on the ground proved otherwise.

"With essence crafting, almost anything can be a weapon." the professor said, breaking the silence. "Just as a warrior is in complete control of their blade, a mage is in complete control of their magic and can command it to do their bidding."

He swung the sword around masterfully, the magical blade streaking through the air.

"On the battlefield, mages must be ready for any and all possibilities. Sometimes you need a sword, and *sometimes* you need—"

He snapped his wrist. The blade shone brighter before growing longer and thinner. The professor swirled his hand around his head, the blue energy following him in a more fluid motion than before. One more snap of the wrist and the energy flung forward before snapping back with a loud *pop*.

"—a whip." In his outstretched hand, the professor held out his new weapon: a long, deadly whip surrounded by blue fire that now dangled where there had once been a blade.

"Sometimes you need a sword. And sometimes you need something different. In this class, you will learn how to channel your energy into different weapons and use them in combat."

Professor Coen casually twirled the flaming blue whip around as he talked, causing several students to scoot back in nervousness.

"Imagine the possibilities for a battlemage. Regular warriors need to carry a sword, a shield, and a dagger, among other things. Some soldiers carry swords, and others carry spears, but we mages"—he pounded his chest with his fist—"we mages are our own army. Able to adapt to any situation."

An electric hum accompanied the disappearance of the professor's new weapon. Then he held the handle in front of himself, and blue energy whooshed out and grew into a large oval transparent shield. He raised it up for the mesmerized students to see before extinguishing it and placing the handle back on the table.

"Long past are the days where the kings of Oriel had to fight to keep our land, but present are the dangers that still exist. Nightstalkers are, of course, the most prevalent. Those creatures of corruption have a bloodlust that knows no end. But even worse are mages who do not know the integrity we teach and whose moral compasses spin wildly out of control.

"In addition to essence manipulation, you will learn essence crafting. These will give you the tools to defend yourself—whether you find yourself in the king's service or not—from the dangers that are ever-present around you."

Professor Coen casually waved his hand, and a wooden bow from the table glided over to him. Instead of snatching the bow out of the air, he commanded it to hover around his body as he talked.

"Now, not only does this magic apply to melee combat, as I have already demonstrated for you. This also applies to ranged combat. For example ..."

The professor picked up an apple piece and tossed it behind his back toward the large window in the front of the room. As swift and accurate as an eagle, he snatched the bow out of the air, rotated on his heel, pulled back the string in perfect form, and shot a blue energy arrow at the apple. In a dazzling flash of light, the arrow shot across the room, piercing the apple piece before clattering against the stone wall. When the arrow hit the floor, it quietly disintegrated, leaving a hole in the center of the apple.

Before anyone had a chance to respond or applaud, the professor pulled the string back again and again and again in rapid fire motion, each release sending another luminous streak through the air toward the apple. Each time it hit, it disappeared as before.

Only slightly winded, the master of essence crafting turned toward his students and said, "And *that* is how it's done."

Even with real arrows, such a display of skill would have been over-whelmingly impressive. The students erupted in a roar of applause.

The professor calmly set the bow back on the table and picked up a unique metal artifact Griff had never seen before.

"Who knows what this is?" Professor Coen asked.

Marth and Tyrell both raised their hands in unison.

"Ah, yes, you there, next to Mr. Driscoll." The professor pointed to Marth.

"Yeah, um, I've heard of it before. Uh, is it called a ... a goon?"

Tyrell stood and laughed in response and called from across the room, "You idiot, it's not a *goon*, it's a *gun*. My dad used them all the time back in the day."

"While I applaud your correct answer, Mr. Falkenburg, I will not tolerate pettiness in my classroom. Ya hear?" Professor Coen said.

"Yes, sir. Sorry." Tyrell took one last look at his dad's former boss before he sat back in his seat, looking embarrassed.

"Mr. Falkenburg, here, is correct, though. This is called a gun. It is from the world before ours, which means they're not made anymore, and therefore makes them extremely rare.

"When these were still in their original employment, they held small metal capsules called bullets. These guns would shoot the bullets at an incredible speed, able to kill anything in their way. Nasty little weapons, they are. As rare as guns may be, bullets—working bullets, I should say—are even more rare. Temperamental, these bullets are. They also require almost perfect preservation to work.

"But mages don't need to use bullets, just like we don't need to use arrows."

The professor pulled back the hammer at the back of the gun, took his aim, and squeezed the trigger, sending another brilliant flash of light toward the apple with a loud *bang*.

"Poor apple," Marth whispered once the room was quiet, "it never did anything to anyone, and Professor Coen is mutilating it beyond recognition."

Griff would have laughed, but instead, he stared in shock at the place where the apple piece had once been. The only remaining evidence was a smoldering scorch mark on the stone floor.

CHAPTER 13

"I can't believe that after all that, we gotta go to a boring history class." Marth said as they hastily marched from the dining hall through a maze of hallways toward their next class. "You think our next professor will let me take a nap?"

"I dunno," Griff said. "Might be kind of interesting. Coming from the middle of nowhere ... I could use a catch-me-up class."

"Guys! Will you stop talking and pick up the pace! You're going to make us late!" Mira huffed. "And Vincent, next time, just ask for seconds on the first go around so we don't run into this problem again, okay?"

They heard a snicker from behind them and turned to see Sadie, who had silently followed them out of the dining hall.

The battlegroup sneaked into the dark classroom, lit only by candles tucked away in the corners of the classroom. Sadie, who had yet to say another word since revealing her name, plopped into the outermost chair and scooched herself even farther away from the group before kicking her feet up on the table.

"Good afternoon, students." A tall slender man, whose short dark hair was dusted with gray, stepped into the candlelight at the front of the room. His white smile of welcome shone through his thick dark goatee, but the stern eyes that peered over his horn-rimmed glasses seemed to stare into each student's soul.

"My name is Professor Thames Erebus. Welcome to magical history."

With a casual wave of his hand, Professor Erebus extinguished the candles overhead, covering the entire classroom in darkness.

"Not many students like history." His deep voice reverberated off the stone walls. "Why talk about boring stories and dead people? Why talk about civilizations and kingdoms that rise and fall? History, you'll find, is a lot like light. Without it, people stumble forward in the darkness, making all types of silly mistakes that could have been avoided. They can't see where they've come from, and therefore, they can't see where they are going. But when you take the time to *learn* from history—"

A rush of warm air filled the room and the candles burst in a brighter light than before, bathing the students in a warm glow.

"—you will better see where your path forward lies. The most successful men and women learn from the past and use its wealth of knowledge to create a brighter future."

Professor Erebus leaned on the table at the front of the room and held out his hand for a large heavy book that floated from across the classroom.

"You should have your own copies of *Magical, Historical Happenings*. Please turn to page three hundred and ninety-four."

Griff reached down into his bag, pulled out his copy, and hastily flipped to the page. Staring back at him, as though ready to jump out of the book and attack, was a nightstalker. Griff immediately recognized the black, armor-like scales and strange bony spikes protruding from different parts of its body. A chill ran down his spine as he stared at the lifeless, snowy-white eyes and remembered seeing them hovering in the darkness in the Cordelian forest.

While this creature shared certain features with the nightstalker he had faced nearly two weeks ago, it also looked very different from the ones he had encountered in the forest. The nightstalkers he'd battled resembled feline animals like a jaguar or a lynx; this one looked more like a bear.

"You're all familiar with these creatures, yes?" The professor asked.

There was a somber mumble throughout the classroom. Griff looked around and wondered to what extent his peers had experienced these horrific creatures. Some students seemed to be lost in their own thoughts, as if reliving a horrible memory.

"Scores of people through the ages have lost friends and family members to these monsters. Towns and villages without any protections have been laid to waste in the night. These ... nightstalkers ... have ravaged our world for a long time."

He rolled up his left sleeve, revealing long jagged scars that snaked across his pale skin.

"Many of us in this room have experienced their terror. But have you ever wondered where these beasts came from? Have you ever wondered why they are the way they are?"

The professor slammed his book shut, causing everyone to jump.

"Did you know that there was once a time where there was no such thing as a nightstalker? To say the world was once at peace would be quite an exaggeration, but it was certainly more peaceful than it is today."

Professor Erebus straightened up and sent the book across the classroom into an empty space on the bookshelf. Griff's eyes followed the book, but his mind was miles away, thinking about the prospect of a world without nightstalkers.

In a quiet, almost remorseful voice, the professor asked, "What has happened to our world?"

He looked around at the students, waiting patiently for an answer. Griff looked to Marth, the know-it-all of the group, always ready with an answer he had heard from his sisters, but he seemed lost in his own thoughts. After the silence became almost unbearable, Griff slowly raised his hand.

"Name?" Professor Erebus asked.

"Uh, Griff, sir. Griff Driscoll."

"Mr. Driscoll, what has happened to our world to cause such calamity?"

"The Corruption," Griff answered.

"Indeed. The Corruption, a magical plague that haunts our world. And does anyone know how the Corruption came to be?"

He looked around the room for a moment, but didn't allow the silence to grow as it had before.

"I would suspect not. Because *that's* the great mystery of our world. Something happened over five hundred years ago, Day Zero, they call it, for that's when our world started over. Something happened on that day that caused our world to be turned upside-down. And since that day, our world has never been the same. And nightstalkers? Nightstalkers are *symptoms* of the Corruption. Symptoms of this plague that originated a few years after Day Zero, but they aren't the only symptom, are they? Someone tell me another."

Across the room, a curly, blonde-haired girl raised her hand.

"Name?"

"Katrine Penderson."

"Yes, Ms. Penderson, what other symptom of the Corruption are you aware of?"

"Well, just outside of our town is a lake. We call it the Lake of the Dead. Its waters are black, but it's called that mostly because anyone who has ever swam in it or drunk from it has gotten sick, gone mad, or even died. They say nightstalkers dwell at its depths, but nobody has ever proven that to be true. They say the Lake of the Dead is cursed. Could that be because of the Corruption?"

"Undoubtedly so, I'm afraid," Professor Erebus sighed. "That's an excellent example of the Corruption at work. This is a *magical* plague, which means that living things like animals aren't the only victims. All of nature can be affected by this plague: water sources, plants, even weather ... though that is a rare occurrence."

"Remember this moment. Remember all that you see before you. It is important that you do. Professor Erebus will teach you much about what you see here. You would do well to pay attention to him."

Griff remembered the king's words as they sat on the back of the warg staring at the death and destruction plaguing the beautiful countryside. The Corruption had done that. The Corruption was killing the forests and destroying life and beauty. The Corruption had birthed these horrific creatures—these nightstalkers that had afflicted the world and caused so much terror and grief.

"Over the next few weeks, we will learn about the Corruption and its effects on the world. As I mentioned earlier, you would do well to learn from history as it will light your path forward."

And with Professor Erebus's final words, he casually waved his hand, the flames extinguished, and darkness invaded the space once more.

CHAPTER 14

The next few weeks felt like a whirlwind. Every class was filled with new information that fought for the limited capacity of Griff's mind. After a few more lessons on the wind spell, Professor Hatlen had taught them how to levitate objects and heat water. But every time Griff tried these new spells, he would either fling the object with such speed and force that it shattered against the wall or cause the water to explode in a mushroom cloud of steam. And whenever his spell produced a color, it was baffling. His classmates sent red, yellow, green, and purple spells across the classroom. Some, like Sadie and Tyrell, had even reached the goal of conjuring blue spells. But not Griff. Whenever his spells produced a color, they were mysteriously white, which confused even Professor Hatlen.

Each passing class caused his frustrations to grow, and more and more of his peers found ways to steer clear of him—all except his battlegroup who were held captive—at least for this semester. While Marth and Vincent did all they could to reassure him that they were a team and nothing would separate them, Griff feared he would be without a battlegroup next semester.

"I've got to figure this out," Griff said, staring at the rubble strewn all over their bedroom floor.

"Yeah, mate, you do," Marth said, leaning against the doorframe, a tiny tornado in the palm of his hand. "'Cause you're out of rocks, and I ain't goin' rock huntin' with you at this hour and in this weather."

As if on cue, lightning lit up their window, followed by a loud thunderclap that shook the floor.

"Oh, don't be such a showoff," Griff said, eyeing his friend's newest trick with jealousy.

Marth shrugged casually, "What can I say, I've found my niche."

He closed his fist, smothering the miniature cyclone. Griff walked over and sat on his own bed and listened to the sounds of the rain pitter-pattering against the windows, hands clenching his black hair.

"Every. Time. Every time, Marth! I can feel this ... power, this intense power inside me, and I ... I can't control it."

"Well," Marth sat down in his own bed across from Griff, "I mean, at least you're not *not* doing magic, ya know? Like at least you're doing something. And even if ya can't control it ... it's strong, whatever it is. You just need more ... practice." He looked at the chunks missing from the stone wall where Griff's rocks had crashed against it.

"And maybe practicing with, oh, I dunno, feathers or pillows might be better. King's crown, mate, you would be *deadly* in a pillow fight!"

Marth snatched his pillow and threw it as hard as he could at Griff, who simply leaned to the side, allowing the pillow to soar past him and land on the wooden floor next to Vincent's bed.

"Sorry, Marth." Griff said. "Not interested. Plus, I figured you wouldn't want to see your pillow explode into a thousand feathers."

Vincent picked up Marth's pillow, and sat next to Griff, the bed groaning in complaint. After tossing the pillow back to its owner, he turned to Griff and said, "We'll figure it out. *We* ... will figure it out. Together."

"Thanks," Griff said, wishing he could absorb his friend's optimism.

"There's gotta be something in a book somewhere that talks about this," Griff said, pulling open his trunk and foraging through his supplies.

His friends waited patiently, listening to the rhythmic rain and thunderous booms outside as he pulled out his trunk's contents and started reading off titles of the different books he had bought.

"You think any of those have something to say about my ... condition?" Griff asked.

"I dunno about that ... but what's this?" Marth asked, holding up an object wrapped in brown paper.

"Oh, yeah! That's my birthday present. My dad and I were working on it the day before I surfaced."

Marth carefully turned the sword handle over and over in his hands, admiring the work. The metal gleamed in the candlelight, and every intricate detail shone with perfection. Marth handed it to Vincent, whose enormous hands made it seem like a child's toy.

"Beautiful," he whispered.

"Yeah, Griff, that's a piece of art right there," Marth said. "And what's the deal with these wings?" He pointed to the cross guard.

"It's a Nightflame dragon," Vincent answered before Griff had a chance to explain.

"Aye, but how'd you know that?" Griff asked.

The giant shrugged, "I read a lot."

"I knew that too," Marth said.

Griff rolled his eyes. "'Course you did, Marth. You know everything."

"I do." He shrugged before jumping onto his bed and conjuring another mini tornado in his palm.

"I guess my dad wanted to add some extra flair to my birthday sword," Griff said.

"Well, your dad is the best blacksmith I've ever seen. And ... Griff ... you know what this means?" Marth suddenly jumped to his feet, extinguishing his pet tornado immediately. "You know what this means, right, Griff?"

"No ..." Griff answered, all of a sudden becoming very hesitant.

"It means we can practice essence crafting!" Marth said.

"But we're not supposed to yet. We're 'just learning theory for now.'" Griff gave his best imitation of Professor Coen.

"Yeah, but think about it. Imagine the professor's face when we *do* start essence crafting, and we can already do it perfectly. C'mon, it can't hurt to try!"

"Well ..." Griff looked around the room at the shattered rocks.

"Okay, well it *might* hurt to try, but we should do it anyway! May I?" Marth said, looking toward Vincent who looked tentatively at Griff.

"Oh, all right, fine. But don't break my stuff. It's very important to me."

"I'll be careful, I promise." Marth said, grabbing the handle as though it was a precious artifact.

He let out a whoosh of air and said, "Okay, stand back."

Marth closed his eyes and held the handle out. He settled his breathing and spread his feet into a battle stance. He stood silently for several moments, a rare and difficult feat, before his face clenched in effort and he let out a loud, "Hiyaah!" Nothing happened. He grunted with effort and swung the piece around. Still nothing.

Finally, as Marth's face grew redder and darker with each flimsy attempt, Vincent reached out with a hand and settled him back down.

"You're gonna hurt yourself or us," he chuckled.

Marth sighed and ran a hand through his sweaty blond hair, "Yeah, you're right. Here you go." He held the handle out to Vincent, who refused it.

"No, thank you. I'll wait for class."

"All right, then. Griff, your turn."

Griff stood and gently took the handle, holding it in both hands. A swarm of memories flooded through him as he reminisced about all the time he had spent with his dad. Hours upon hours spent in the heat of the forge, carefully crafting it. Pain hit him in the stomach as he thought back to his family. He missed them greatly. He missed his dad's strong presence and wisdom. He missed his mom's firm but fun and loving demeanor. How he wished they were closer, so he could visit. Especially given his recent difficulties with his classes.

He grasped the leather handle that was made just for him, and it felt perfect. The weight, the design, every inch of this handle—no, not *this* handle—*his* handle, felt exactly right. Griff felt a calming presence come over him. The son of the blacksmith spread his feet and held out his hand. He felt power generating in his chest like the onset of a summer storm. It was strong and intense. But as he stood there, with *his* sword handle in *his* hand—remembering his family, remembering the weapons training his dad had given him—for the first time since setting foot onto Bergots' grounds, he felt ... right. He felt comfortable. Natural. With hardly any effort, Griff took control of the power flooding through him. He pushed it through his body, past his hands and into the handle. A bright blue light flared into existence, illuminating the entire room. Griff Driscoll, the son of Gaelic Driscoll, the great blacksmith of Cordelia, stood tall, staring calmly at his newly formed sword. Its flaming edges swirled and danced with power, casting a flickering light on the surprised faces of his friends.

"Whoa ..." Marth gasped.

"There you go," Vincent said with a smile.

"Griff ... Nightstalker's fury, Griff! Ha-ha! You did it!" Marth jumped high and pumped his fist in the air.

Like an expert swordsman, Griff swung his blade around, mimicking the moves he had learned throughout the years. His sword felt weightless, and like the lightning that streaked through the night sky outside, it moved with ease, leaving bright blue streaks where it had once been.

"Wait." Marth stopped his dancing. "How did you do it?"

Griff paused, thought for a moment, and then said, "Well, my dad is a blacksmith. I've been around weapons all my life. It's all I've ever known.

Soon as I held this in my hand, I didn't feel like a stranger in my own body anymore. Maybe that's why?"

"Well, how about this," Marth said. "How about I continue to help you practice your wind spell"—he slowly took the sword handle from Griff's hands and watched the blade quickly extinguish—"and *you* can help *us* learn how you just did that."

Griff laughed before he said, "Well, my help will probably be about as good as my wind spell, but I'll take what I can get."

"Vince, you in on this deal?"

The giant shrugged and Griff's bedframe sent out another groan of complaint, "Sure."

"King's crown, the ladies are gonna get a kick outta this when we show 'em what we can do! Everyone's gonna want us in their battlegroup after that!" Marth said, swinging the handle through the air.

"Yeah," Griff laughed, "I'm sure they will."

The next morning, the dining hall was filled with contagious energy. It had finally come, the first day of Altar Storm. Not a single conversation could be heard about anything else. Heated debates arose as people speculated on which groups would come out on top.

"My eyes are on Milo's group," Griff said, munching on his breakfast sausage, the warmth of his savory meal rising up to greet him. "He sounds like one nasty spell slinger."

"Don't put it past Erian's though," Mira joined in. "Her group's never lost a match!"

"Yeah, but don't forget, it all depends on the arena," Marth chimed in. "Wonder what crazy things they've come up with this time. Sadie, you got any guesses?"

"No," she mumbled before taking an enormous bite of peach.

"Yeah," Marth sighed. "Me neither."

Milo walked past Griff at that moment and slapped him on the shoulder, "Get ready to see some real action today!" the second year called.

"Yeah, okay. Good luck, Milo!" Griff said.

After breakfast, the whole academy thundered down to the arena, chanting and cheering, yelling and singing the entire way there. Even the professors were laughing and having a good time. Despite the cold morning breeze and soggy conditions, the air was electric. Griff had never experienced such a spectacle, but was quickly caught up in the festivities. Even Sadie's sour demeanor wavered under the overwhelming positivity. She was like an excited child in a new place. Her head, which normally hung low, was held high and bobbed this way and that as she gazed on the joy of others and stretched to get a better view of the arena.

When the battlefield finally came into view, Griff's group paused and peered down into the pitch. The grass that was once manicured, soft, and flat had been replaced by rocks and boulders that climbed at a steep angle to the top of the arena walls. It looked like a large, rocky funnel. Because of this, the action would have to occur in the middle, where two stone pillars stood proud and tall. Between them, strands of lightning arced dangerously, splitting the narrow stone field in half. At the mid-point, just underneath the lowest strand of lightning, was a deep pool of water. And, as usual, at the far end of either side were the stone altars housing the glowing orbs.

Finally, once everyone had taken their seats, the crowd was quieted by the booming sound of Professor Coen's voice echoing from the field.

"Welcome to the first Altar Storm matches of the semester!"

A deafening roar erupted from the crowd as students stood and cheered with gusto. The professor laughed, waiting for the thunderous screaming and chanting to stop. His voice resumed its elevated volume so he could talk above the masses.

"Yes, yes, we're all excited for the action to begin, but as this is the first Altar Storm match of the semester, and our first years have yet to learn how these matches work, let me explain the rules. As you know, there will be multiple Altar Storm matches throughout the semester, and each match will be between battlegroups of your own experience. First year groups will take on other first year groups and so on. The goal of each match is to bring your storm orb to your opponent's altar. Each battle brings with it new challenges to test your skills and abilities.

"Today our arena has unique obstacles. There is limited space to work, and the lightning wall in the middle is no small complication either. There are ways to reach the other side, but make no mistake, there are no easy solutions here.

"First years, pay close attention," Professor Coen paused until there was complete silence. "While we work hard to ensure that Altar Storm is safe, let me make it clear that it can still be dangerous. As such, all mages who step onto this battlefield *must* wear their battle clothes to ensure it softens the power of any magical attacks. Additionally, we always have our judges"—he bowed his head in the direction of a group of professors on the side of the field—"who will watch closely to prevent any serious harm.

"And finally, before we bring out our first two groups"—he picked up two long wooden poles, one in each hand—"for today's matches, each group will be given one wooden pole as an essence crafting accessory to aid them. Use it to craft whatever weapons or tools you might need for this match."

He tossed both poles out; they glided across the field and leaned against the hard stone of each altar.

"All right! That's enough of that, let Altar Storm BEGIN!"

Another thunderous explosion of cheers and applause shook the floor under Griff's feet. Celebratory music blared from the musician-less instruments at the top of the arena as the first two groups of second years marched onto the field.

"There's Milo's group!" Griff called, pointing to the far side of the pitch.

"And look! There's Erian's," Mira said. "Looks like we're going to get quite the show."

Each group huddled around their altar to talk strategy as they waited for the battle to begin. *BOOM*! A giant explosion of multi-colored sparks burst above the field, as Headmaster Aldamund signaled the start of the match. The crowd roared as the two groups sprinted toward the middle. Milo and another bulky fellow from his group veered off toward the rocky terrain on the side. When they reached an area that had multiple boulders jutting out from the wall, Milo's partner held up his team's wooden pole and crafted a large blue mallet head at the top. He lifted the giant hammer high and swung it hard against the rocks. Again. And again. The mage hammered away until he had knocked off two large boulders, which Milo levitated toward the middle of the field.

Of the other team, Erian was first to the center. She rushed toward the pool at the base of the lightning wall and swirled her hands to form an orb of wind around her. Two of her partners dashed in and followed suit, each making their own sphere. The fourth member joined, storm orb in one hand, the other a blur of movement identical to his teammates.

In a diamond-like formation, the group walked carefully through the water, kept at bay by the wind. Before they could reach the other side, Milo's group had reached the wall and worked together to turn the pool into ice, trapping their opponents underneath.

"Looks like Milo's group is going for the all-out attack!" Marth yelled. "Nobody's guarding their altar!"

Griff nodded, then looked at Erian's side, where one lone mage guarded it with vigilance, the long wooden pole gripped tightly in her hands. Milo and his partner reached the center with their boulders. Carefully, Milo levitated the first boulder in front of him until it was in the midst of the lightning. Then he placed the second one several feet away from the first, interrupting the flow of electricity to create a small opening for his team to walk through. Since the pool was now solid ice, Milo's battlegroup had no problem crossing the center.

"Shouldn't she have helped her teammates?" Griff asked, pointing to the lone guard on the other side.

"Not yet," Mira said. "You've got to trust your teammates."

"She's right," Marth responded. "Just watch."

Just when Milo's team had passed through the lightning wall, a bright red light radiated from the ice, and large cracks appeared on the surface. Suddenly, the base of the lightning wall became an explosion of ice as the mages trapped underneath waved their hands in unison, breaking it apart and sending the frozen chunks toward the other team. With a nod from Erian, two of her teammates climbed out of the pit and headed back toward their altar, while she and the orb carrier climbed out on the other side.

Milo and his comrades staggered up from the ground, wiping away bits of ice and dust from their clothes. When they had regrouped and encircled their own orb carrier, they pressed forward in a confident sprint, barely slowing down as they approached the lone guard. Milo stretched his arms out, preparing to cast a spell, when the guard struck the ground with her pole and sent powerful waves of wind and sand at the oncoming assault.

"Well, I see now why they left that girl to guard their side!" Marth laughed, watching Milo and his teammates flip through the air.

Milo sprung from the ground, red energy flaring from his fists. He looked back at his teammates, who were all focused on Erian's reinforcements that had doubled back. It was down to him and the guard. With one swift motion, a fireball barreled toward her, but it fizzled against the blue energy shield she had crafted from the pole. Back and forth they fought in a blaze of spectacular light, casting spells, dodging, and defending. Milo bellowed and rushed the guard with all his might—but was cut short by another burst of brilliant fireworks above the field. Everyone on the pitch stopped and looked to the other side, where Erian and her teammate leaned against the altar, wearing proud, confident smiles. The match was over.

CHAPTER 15

"Oh man, it feels so good to have a little break," Griff sighed, his warm breath greeting the crisp, cold air in a dense cloud. Two months had passed since the first Altar Storm match and winter had finally decided to stay, but that didn't stop the battlegroup, save Sadie, from making a weekend trip to Solastran.

"You think she'll stick with our battlegroup next semester?" Griff asked as they trudged down the street.

"I don't think she'll stick with the *school*," Marth said.

Griff turned to Mira. "Does she ever say anything to you in the dorms?"

"No," she sighed. "Not for lack of effort on my part, though. She's one tough book to read. Plus, she's hardly there when I am. Once it's free time, she's gone. And she's never in the library, I can tell you that."

"Are you sure about that?" Griff asked. "I've seen how you read. And when a book's in front of your face, not even a rabies-ridden warg could get you to put it down."

Mira reached over and shoved Griff, forcing him to yank his hands out of his warm pockets to steady himself.

"My gut says she likes to skulk in the dungeons underneath the school. Vince, any idea what that girl's up to? You're the only one who's had any sort of luck with her," Marth said.

"No idea. But she's ... nicer than you give her credit for."

"Okay, big guy, I'll believe it when I see it."

A ringing bell announcing their entrance into the Whimsical Warlock was barely audible over the crowd of other students looking for something fun to bring back to the castle. A hidden treasure in Solastran, the Whimsical Warlock was located farther down the cobblestone street, past the inn and the busy town center. It was a small shop that only got traffic from the students from Bergots. The group did their best to wander through the tightly packed store, but they were barely able to squeeze down the aisles past the floating fancies and shimmering statues without bumping into someone. When he thought he would suffocate from the crowd, Griff asked, "How about a nice hot cup of tea instead?" He received relieved nods from his friends, and they fought their way back out into the cold.

Griff shivered against the wind and tried to shove his hands deeper into his coat pockets. A hot drink sounded perfect. He wished that he could have his favorite drink from Talley's again. A cup of Dragon's Beard would do wonders right about now, but something from Solastran Inn would have to do.

They didn't talk much as they slowly strolled through the streets of Solastran. The professors didn't teach first semester students to conjure fire, so the battlegroup couldn't warm themselves. Instead, they bundled close together and walked in silence.

Suddenly, flashes of light exploded from an alleyway up ahead, followed by a thundering *crack*. The lights and sounds from the alley would have gone unnoticed to most people since it was a considerable distance from the town center. Without a word, Griff and his friends took off at a sprint, thunder rumbling the ground with every bounding step they took. Griff was the first to the alleyway but skidded to a stop just short of the entrance as a bolt of lightning shot out from it. Then he heard screams.

"You think you can jus' do whatever you want 'cause you're so tough, eh?"

Griff's eyes widened. While he had rarely heard that voice, he still recognized it.

"Well, if you're so tough, why you gettin' beat by a little ol' girl, huh?"

Hearing a pause in the commotion, Griff jumped into the alleyway, paused for a split-second, then sent an uncontrollable burst of wind into the fray. While he still hadn't been able to control the power of his abilities, he was getting better at aiming, and his spell hit Tyrell perfectly, sending him flying. Sadie whipped her head toward Griff, eyes as wild as her hair and hands ready to sling another spell. When she recognized him, she lowered her guard, turned around, and helped Finn off the ground.

"There," she mumbled.

The mousy first year dusted himself off and said, "Th-thanks."

"Yeah, whatever. Don't ... don't mention it."

Cradling her left arm, she turned to look at her battlegroup at the entrance of the alleyway.

"Nothin' to see here! Go on an' get outta he—" *WHAM!* A large chunk of ice hit her in the back, knocking her to the ground. Griff raised his hands to cast another wind spell, but Vincent was already moving. As large as he was, he moved with surprising speed and agility. He marched up to Tyrell, whose hands were still raised from the previous spell, and grabbed him by the center of his coat, slamming him into the alley wall.

"No. More." Anger flashed across his face. "Only the weak attack an enemy's back." He threw Tyrell toward the other side of the alley, away from Sadie and the rest of the group.

"Weak?" Tyrell jumped to his feet, bright red energy swirling about his hands. "You think I'm-I'm *weak*? C'mon, I'm not afraid of you, giant. I'll take you on too!"

"You'll take us *all* on then, Ty." Marth stepped in front of Sadie, arms crossed. "You really wanna try your luck there, friend?"

Griff and Mira quickly joined the group, creating a wall in front of a distressed Finn and an injured Sadie whose left arm was covered in scratches and gravel.

"C'mon mate, why would you wanna fight us? There's no need for that," Marth said, taking another step forward.

"None of this is any of your business! This is between me and *him*." He pointed past Griff toward Finn, who looked down to the ground, ashamed.

"Finn?" Griff asked, "What'd Finn do that would make you wanna fight him?"

"Like I said. None of your business," Tyrell spat.

"It-it's my fault, really. Wasn't payin' attention and bumped into him. Made him drop his flowers a-and then I accidentally stepped on 'em." Finn turned and pointed to a bundled mess behind them.

Underneath the tattered wrapping and broken collection of stems and leaves, Griff saw a dim pink light radiating from the most beautiful flowers he had ever seen. Mira quietly gasped and whispered, "Those are so pretty."

"Not just any flowers, you moron. They were the last of the twilight roses. Got them ... for my mom for winter break," Tyrell said quietly. He passed through the group and knelt next to the contorted bouquet. The boy who always tried to act tough reached down and tenderly touched the roses.

"They're dying," he said. "The magic's almost gone now."

For a brief moment, everyone stood in silence, as if they were at a funeral. And also like a funeral, no one seemed to have the right words to say.

"Ah, hello, students." The group looked up to see Headmaster Aldamund standing in the opening of the alleyway, his beaming smile a stark contrast to their gloom.

"What have we here?" he asked kindly. He knelt down next to Tyrell and saw the dwindling glow of the twilight roses.

"Twilight roses," he said. "Extremely rare. And they only grow in the wintertime." He delicately placed a hand over them.

"It's too bad to see them like this. They are truly magnificent flowers." He paused, allowing silence to fill the air.

"Well, I guess we should do something about this, don't you think, Mr. Falkenburg?"

"Sir?" Tyrell asked.

Headmaster Aldamund smiled at him, then turned his attention back to the roses. A faint blue light emitted from the headmaster's palm. The broken stems flinched and rolled until they were back with their missing counterparts. Petals that had fallen off floated through the alleyway and reattached themselves to the body of the flower, began to glow pink again. Leaves twirled through the air as though carried by a gentle breeze until they found their place as well. Broken parts healed, missing pieces reattached, even the torn and tattered wrapping was mended until the entire group stared at the twilight roses in all their glory.

"Th-thank you, sir!" Tyrell said, eyes as wide as the moon.

He grabbed his mother's present, then stood up along with the king's son. Headmaster Aldamund laid a hand on Tyrell's shoulder and smiled at him.

"What's the point of magic if we can't use it to do good? Why don't you run along now and find a secure place for those special flowers before another unfortunate event befalls them."

Tyrell gave Finn a glare that Griff was almost sure would summon lightning, before he stepped onto the street and into the cold, wintry breeze.

"Well, then. Ms. Trygg, I was wondering where you had gone off to." Headmaster Aldamund looked past the group to Sadie, who continued to nurse her arm. "I became worried when you missed our meeting.

Looks like I was right to be concerned. Let's take care of that injury, shall we?"

The hard-headed, independent, calloused girl stepped forward obediently, and for the first time since Griff had met her, the permanent look of defiance was surprisingly absent. The headmaster placed an arm around her and together they stepped out of the alleyway.

"Sadie ... Trygg?" Marth asked in bewilderment once the two were gone.

"Those are your first words after all that?" Mira asked. "How about the fact that she took on Tyrell Falkenburg all by herself?"

"Yeah, it was amazing," Finn added. "She was casting lightning spells and shooting this bright light out at him an' everything!"

Mira held out a hand toward Finn as if to say, "See?"

"It sounds to me like we have an expert spell slinger in our battlegroup," she said.

"Yeah, you do," Finn said, in awe.

"Well, we do for the next couple of weeks ..." Griff sighed. "I'm not so sure we will next semester, though. The way she looks at us and treats us? King's crown! Either she sees us as her enemies or she's really bad at this whole friendship thing. C'mon, it's freezing. Let's get to the inn. Finn, care to join us?"

"No, thanks. I think I've had enough fun for the day. I'm gonna head back to the castle."

Once they were nestled next to the fireplace inside the inn, each holding a hot cup of tea, Griff let out a long relaxed sigh. He had been so busy studying and practicing essence manipulation that he hadn't taken the time to visit Solastran. For the past two months, he had reserved a training room every weekend to work on controlling his power. Despite all his hard work, his aim only improved slightly. He was glad he had decided to go today. He had needed to push aside his thoughts of frustration and inadequacy, even if it was just for one day.

Nyall was as cheerful as ever, waltzing back and forth with hot plates of food from the kitchen. While the warm cinnamon spice aroma of Mira's pumpkin soup was intoxicating, the guys all decided to pile their plates with meat. The table was quiet, save for the munching sounds and the random bursts of "mmm" coming from Marth.

Griff sat back in his chair, a hand on his happy stomach, and allowed his thoughts to drift back over the past semester. Three months. It had been three months since he had last set foot here. Three months since he'd sat here, eating dinner with Professor Coen. In some ways, it felt like yesterday; in other ways, a lifetime. He had learned so much, and he had grown in his abilities—even if he couldn't control them yet. His skill in essence crafting continued to impress his battlegroup, and it seemed as though that was enough for them to keep him around.

A burst of giggles pulled Griff out of his food coma, and he stretched his neck in the direction it came from. Across the room in a worn leather loveseat sat Milo and Erian. Milo was laughing as Erian playfully slapped his shoulder. The second year met Griff's eyes and gave him a wave, which he returned.

"So, I guess they're a thing now?" Griff asked.

"Yep," Marth said, slurping the last bits of his tea. "So long as they're not in the arena, I guess."

"I think they're a cute couple," Mira added.

"You mean *power* couple. Those two on the same side would destroy any opposing force, trust me," Marth said.

"You're not wrong. Erian is as tough as they come," Mira said before leaning back in her chair. She opened a newspaper she had retrieved from the entrance of the inn and started thumbing through it, ignoring the guys' conversation.

"Speaking of power couple ..." Marth said, leaning over the table. "When're you gonna ask out Katrine Penderson?"

"Katrine Penderson?" Griff said, bewildered. "Why would I ask out Katrine Penderson?"

"Are you kidding me? She's been giving you the googly eyes all semester! You haven't noticed it?"

Griff paused and thought for a moment, remembering the blonde girl from his classes. "No. No, I hadn't noticed, I guess."

Vincent let out a low grumble of a laugh. "It's been pretty obvious. Don't think she's trying to hide it."

"You should go talk to her! Twenty silver pieces says that she'll melt into a puddle right there because you're giving her any bit of attention."

Griff caught himself staring at Mira, whose bright green eyes intensely followed each line in the paper, and pulled his attention back to Marth.

"Yeah, I-I'm not really interested in Katrine. She's not really my type."

"Well, your loss then, mate!"

"*My* loss? Whatd'ya mean, *my* loss?"

"Hey, she's about as pretty as they come! And if she's pining for *your* attention, I say that's about as good as you're gonna get! She must be blind as a bat, so ask her out before she gains her sight!"

Before Griff could find a snappy response to his friend, Mira straightened up, cutting him off.

"Hey! Did you guys see this?" She set the paper on the table and pointed to an article: "Attack on Shimmerstone."

"Attack on Shimmerstone? What does that mean?" Griff asked.

"Shimmerstone's on the far east of Oriel," Marth said. "It's a small coastal town, 'bout as far east as you can go."

"Well, who attacked it then?" Griff asked.

"No one knows." Mira said. "There weren't many survivors. And they're asking anyone who knows anything to report to the nearest authorities. They say the king is putting all his resources into this investigation. Must be pretty big."

Just then, the door to the inn opened, sending a chill through the tavern. Sadie walked over and grabbed a chair from a nearby table, pulling it between Vincent and Mira. The four mages looked at each other and then back to Sadie, not sure what to say.

"I ... I just wanted to say thanks for havin' my back out there," Sadie said. Griff imagined that thankfulness probably tasted bitter to her but was glad she tried it anyway.

"Yeah. You bet," Griff said.

"You're part of the team too," Mira added, "and when one of us needs help, we're supposed to be there for each other."

"And king's crown! After what you did out there, we'd be crazy if we didn't make sure you were on our side!" Marth added.

Mira shot him a look that could have melted metal, but to everyone's surprise, Sadie laughed.

"Yeah, well, he deserved it," she said.

"He usually does," Marth said.

"Is your arm okay?" Vincent asked.

"Yeah." Sadie lifted her arm up and bent it back and forth. "Alexander fixed me up."

"Alexander? Who's Alexander?" Griff asked.

"Wait ..." Mira said. "You mean Alexander Aldamund, don't you? You're on a first name basis with the headmaster?"

"Oh, there's definitely a story there." Marth said, rubbing his hands together.

"Listen, just because we're friends doesn't mean I'm gonna tell you my whole life story, got it?" Her eyes had narrowed at Marth, but for the first time since meeting Sadie, Griff knew there was no real threat of injury.

"We're friends?" Marth asked, excited. "Yay! We're friends. No take-backs!"

Sadie slumped back into her seat and crossed her arms. "Shut up."

CHAPTER 16

Bright lights sparkled and danced amid the never-ending strands of holiday garlands that lined the long hallways. The countless galaxies of light slowly swirled around the thick green strands, almost smothering them in brilliant displays of green, red, and gold. In the long hallways, like guardians standing between each of the many stained-glass windows, were several holiday pine trees, meticulously decorated with shapes of ice that never melted. The twinkling gold lights within the trees reflected off each icy shape, radiating against the dark green branches.

Griff and Professor Coen walked down the hallway in silence, waiting until they were clear of the dining hall and any possible eavesdroppers who might have left dinner early. He was embarrassed enough to ask for a private conversation with the professor. He didn't need other people listening too.

They came to the large archway that opened into the grand courtyard. Night had fallen, but the cover of darkness was alleviated by even more bright and festive decorations. In the center was a large fire pit, its flames dancing provocatively against the crisp winter air and falling snow. Griff dusted off the fresh snow on a wooden bench near the fire and sat down. He stared at the opposite corner of the yard, where the most magical of all decorations stood: a thick, never-ending trail of snow that cascaded in an ever-widening spiral to the ground, forming the shape of a large holiday tree. It was as tall as the courtyard ceilings and the galaxy of lights embedded in the falling snow bathed the courtyard in a shimmering glow.

"So, you're still having a hard time controlling your powers, huh?" Professor Coen asked, breaking the silence. "Is that what you wanted to talk to me about?"

Griff stared into the flames, his mind drifting away from the courtyard and into the training room where he spent countless hours trying to do just that.

"I am," he said at last, feeling as though he were admitting defeat. "I can't do it. I don't know why, but I can't seem to get control. Every spell I cast goes wrong somehow. Something either explodes, goes flying, or throws me to the ground causing new scrapes and bruises."

Griff sighed and held out a hand. The snow fell into his palm and immediately melted against its warmth.

"As far as I can tell, no one else seems to have this problem. Almost everyone can cast even the simplest of spells by now. But me? I can't. Is there something wrong with me, Professor? Something ... broken?"

Professor Coen laughed for a moment, then stopped and gave Griff a sympathetic smile. "No, Griff ... no." He paused.

"Your situation is unique, I'll admit. I've been teaching here for quite some time, and in that time, I've had lots of students, many of whom also struggled with their powers. Most students that do struggle, though, struggle with beginning—with casting the spells. You, on the other hand, are different. I've never seen a student who can immediately cast spells with such power.

"But Griff ... let me tell you something that you need to hear more than understanding the secrets to controlling your powers." Griff saw the kindness in his eyes, but heard firmness in his voice. "Being different doesn't mean you're broken. Being different just means you're human. We're all different in our own unique ways."

He stretched out his arms, smiled widely, and said, "Embrace your differences, Griff! Don't flaunt them, mind you, but embrace them! Part of growing up is learning what makes you uniquely you. Your friends tell me that while spell casting has been a challenge, essence crafting has not." He glanced at Griff with a mischievous smile, "Is that so?"

"Well ..." Griff reached into his pack and pulled out his sword handle. He looked around to make sure everyone was still at dinner, then ignited the end of the handle with a burst of energy, generating a small dagger-like blade. The blue energy pulsed and glowed with power. Power that was deliberate and tamed by the first year wielding it.

"*That* ... is impressive," the professor said, his voice conveying a sense of amazement. "I'm going to overlook the fact that you're not supposed to be doing essence crafting yet. You're clearly beyond theory at this point."

Griff smiled sheepishly, then extinguished the blade and placed the handle in his bag before anyone could see it.

"Now," Professor Coen reached up and brushed the snow off his hair, "you *do* still need to learn to control your spell casting. And even though I've never dealt with this specific issue, I'd be happy to help you. How about you and I spend some time together over the holiday break to see if we can't figure it out, eh?"

Griff smiled; the feelings of defeat were starting to drift away, and a sense of hope filled him instead.

"That would be great. Thanks, Professor."

Griff paused for a moment, remembering there was something else he had been meaning to ask Professor Coen all semester.

"Professor, can I ask one more question?"

"Answering questions is what I do best! Please, ask away."

"During orientation, you whispered something to Headmaster Aldamund. And you looked really upset. What was that all about?"

"Ah," he laughed, his breath visible in the snowy air. "Alas, you ask the one question I cannot specifically answer. All I can say is that while I may not be part of the king's guard anymore, my duty to the king still finds me. And when I hear something of interest, I report it."

Before Griff could ask any more questions, a series of shrill screeches cut through the still, snowy silence. Harsh guttural snarls and growls joined the shrieks, creating an otherworldly chorus that filled the hallways. Then came the screams. A look of horrific realization dawned on Professor Coen's face. He stood abruptly and stared in the direction of the commotion.

"No," he whispered, "it can't be." He whipped around toward Griff. "Get your sword out. Now!"

"Professor, what's goin—"

"No time! Follow me!"

He rushed across the grand courtyard, not waiting for Griff to respond. Griff yanked the handle back out of his bag. With a thought, he crafted it into a long blue sword bursting with energy. By this time, Professor Coen had started a full-on sprint that Griff was barely able to match. They ran down the long hallways, its once festive lighting now emanating a haunted glow. The two mages ran toward the screams until they reached the grand foyer.

Griff's eyes fought to adjust, but the pandemonium made it nearly impossible. Students and faculty were running, screaming, and fighting. Fire shot through the air. Lightning flashed intensely. Stones flew in all directions. Furniture levitated and flew across the room. Dazzling lights threatened to blind nearby onlookers.

Then Griff saw them. Nightstalkers. Everywhere. They came in many different forms that loosely resembled other animals: birds, snakes, wolves, bats, otters, spiders, alligators, and monkeys among others. And while they had different shapes and sizes, they all shared the same scaly black armor and lifeless white eyes. His heart jumped to his throat as one of them veered off from the group and aimed toward him. It resembled a black armored goat except its extremely long tail had spikes jutting out in every direction. Its head, which had just lowered toward Griff, was covered with multiple jagged horns that curled toward the front. And they were all aimed at him.

He jumped to the side just in time, the edge of his blade slicing the side of the beast. Its roar of pain was cut short as Professor Coen lifted it high into the air with his magic, and slammed it back down to the ground. Without a second look, the professor sprinted into the fray and out of sight.

Griff quickly scanned the chaos. Milo and Erian fought back-to-back, fending off a small group of dark infernal monkeys. He wielded a fireball in one hand, and in the other, levitated one of the large antler chandeliers from the dining hall. Erian held a broken chair leg, from which she had crafted an electric whip that sizzled with yellow energy. Farther into the chaos, Griff saw Finn on the ground, clutching his side. Professor Hatlen stood his ground next to the first year, an electric cage warding off hordes of nightstalkers. Vincent and Sadie had cornered a giant armored spider and were clearly in no need of help.

A familiar cry broke Griff from his petrified state. He spun his head in the direction of the noise and saw her: Mira. She had a bloody arm and was trying to fend off a large demonic falcon. Its four wings beat the air in rhythmic fashion, then tucked them in to dive for another attack. Its shrieks filled the air with every strike, but each one was unsuccessful as Mira dodged to the side or deflected with a burst of wind. Griff dashed through the battle, sidestepping swipes from nightstalkers, and jumping over the contorted, corrupted bodies of their fallen comrades. He reached an open stretch and watched as the falcon reared back for an attack. Mira tripped over a large rock and was on the ground, defenseless.

The look of fear in her eyes fueled Griff even more. Adrenaline pumping through his veins, his heart on the verge of explosion, he roared as he took his final steps toward Mira. His handle exploded in a bright blue light as he transformed his sword into a large shield. The nightstalker, now directly above Mira, dove for the kill, and was met by the unforgiving protective magic.

It let out a distressed shriek, and its massive wings flapped as it attempted to reposition for a counterattack. But Griff was too fast. He moved his shield out of the way and sent an overpowering burst of wind directly up at the beast, which was immediately flung to the ceiling. There was a sickening thud as its head met the hard stone above. Before its body could hit the ground, Griff crafted another sword blade and swung with all his might.

"Griff!"

The two halves of the nightstalker couldn't even hit the ground before he was moving again. He whipped around and ran toward Mira, who had been pinned to the ground by a leopard-like monster. He held out his hand and let out another unruly burst of wind, sending the beast through the air. It writhed in pain as it soared over the battlefield, and as it reached the top of its arc, a stone spike shot out from the wall, impaling the creature.

"Marth!" Griff yelled.

"You're welcome!" he said, running over to join the two mages.

"What's going on?" Griff yelled over the sounds of battle.

Mira, in too much pain to talk, pointed across the foyer to the front doors. They were open. Endless waves of nightstalkers poured in from the night. Any sign of hope of winning this battle faded at the sight. But Griff wasn't about to go down easily. He would take out as many of these corrupted creatures as he could. He would kill them all if he could. Rage filled him, and he stood with purpose.

"Let's kill as many as we can," he said to Marth through gritted teeth.

Marth nodded, and they stood to either side of Mira. The nightstalkers surrounded them—their lifeless, soulless eyes fixated on Mira, who remained on the ground. The circle drew closer. Each nightstalker taking one slow step after another. They growled. They shrieked. They snarled. But their threats fell on deaf ears. Griff was ready. He could feel the power swelling inside his chest. One more step. One more step, and he would unleash it all.

A swirl of vicious fire spun along the top of the ceiling. It covered every stone and spread down nearby hallways. A deep voice thundered throughout the castle, halting the battle.

"Stand down! Or this can get worse. Much. Worse."

Griff looked toward the entryway. A row of nightstalkers had paused and waited obediently by the door, watching as men and women in identical black battle clothes walked through. They marched forward in complete unison, then abruptly stopped, crossing their arms and creating a wall between themselves and the entry doors.

A man with long brown hair casually walked onto the Bergots grounds as if he owned the place. His hands in his pockets and his relaxed smile seemed almost comical given the scene before him. When he moved close enough for Griff to see him clearly, his stomach lurched. The man had a scar on his left cheek. It was the man from his dreams. The man from the cave.

"Well, then." The man with the scar floated above his guard and over the now less-than-grand foyer. All eyes were on him. Nightstalkers who hadn't pinned down a faculty member sat submissively on the stone floor or perched on chandeliers or crossbeams in the ceiling.

"Thank you all for joining me to discuss this ... important matter," he said. "I have gathered all of you here to extend an invitation—"

"YOU!" Headmaster Aldamund burst into the room. His bright blue eyes were alight with fury, and the power that surged within him was almost tangible. Mages and nightstalkers alike parted as he stormed across the foyer.

"That fake intel came from *you*!" he roared.

"Now, now. Hold on there, nephew. I come bearing news that you will all want to hear. Please allow me this request."

"I will do no such thing." The headmaster leaped into the air, and hovered toward the man, a fire in his eyes and crackles of red lightning surrounding him.

"I must insist."

The man with the scar casually swirled his hands and several students floated into the air against their will. They struggled against the unseen force as it pulled them across the room, but it was no use. Within seconds, the students were held captive by the men and women in black.

Headmaster Aldamund paused in the air. "Don't do this, Korrun. You're better than this."

"I *am* better than this, nephew. Look around you. Notice that none of your teachers or students are dead! I did not come here to kill. I came simply to inform. Now, it is up to *you* which of those two will happen here tonight."

Seconds ticked into eternity while the entire room waited for Headmaster Aldamund to silently weigh his options. Griff's muscles tensed. Should the headmaster choose to fight, he would be ready.

"There will be no death tonight. Yours will come soon enough, but for now, say your piece and leave."

"That is all I have come to do," Korrun said. "Thank you, nephew. You are too kind."

He turned his attention to the rest of the room and addressed them from the air.

"Power is shifting in Oriel. Our world is broken. The Corruption grows and infects it, and your king is no closer to bringing peace to our land than you are.

"I, on the other hand, offer hope. I am on a quest to rid the world of the brokenness and corruption that plagues us all, and I want you to be a part of it. As you can see, I am stronger than your king, and can promise you results that he cannot offer.

"Consider my friends, here." He motioned to the nightstalkers. "Creatures of the darkness, they say. Maybe so. These creatures are known to fear the light. As their new king, however, I have alleviated those fears, and now they stand proudly in the presence of the very thing they most feared. Indeed, they are not as strong in the light, but what they lack in their strength, they make up for in loyalty to their king."

The man paused to allow the weight of his words to sink in. Nightstalkers were no longer bound to the night under the command of Korrun Aldamund. He was their king, and they did his bidding.

"Join me in my quest of healing, and when we succeed, we will have a new land ... a better land. And we will also have a new king. A better king."

Korrun flew across the room and landed in front of his followers, who were still holding the squirming students.

"All I ask is that you think about it. Would you rather continue to be complacent toward the brokenness and corruption, or would you rather take a step of courage and fight for something new and better? Should you choose to side with me, you only need to leave Bergots and whisper my name in the night. My friends here"—he nodded at the nightstalkers again—"will find you and bring you safely into our little family."

The man with the scar clapped his hands twice, and the beasts in the foyer slowly made their way toward the entrance, all but one nightstalker Griff immediately recognized. It was the nightstalker from his dreams; the one that stayed with this man in the cave. Students and faculty were released by their captors, and the army of nightstalkers disappeared into the night. All that remained were Korrun, his pet, and his followers.

"Dad!"

Griff turned toward the sound of the scream.

"Dad? Dad!" Tyrell burst through the crowd, not waiting for anyone to step aside. He stumbled up to one of the men in black and threw his arms around him.

"W-where have you been? Wh-wh-why did you leave? Why did you leave us like that?" Tyrell said, tears streaming down his face and lips quivering uncontrollably.

"Now's not the time, son," the man said indifferently. "Power is shifting in Oriel. Make sure you and your mother choose the right side."

The man halfheartedly placed a hand on Tyrell's shoulder, then turned and walked out the door with the rest of the followers. When his figure disappeared into the black night, Tyrell crumpled to the floor in a muddled ball of tears and despair. Headmaster Aldamund walked to the sobbing boy, knelt on the floor beside him, and embraced him tightly. All of Tyrell's self-confidence and dignity had disappeared with his father, and he clung to the headmaster, his uncontrollable sobs filling the grand foyer.

The headmaster glared at his uncle and said, "Your quest for healing is funded by blood and broken families. You want to heal our land, but it will cost too much. Leave now or I will break my promise to spare you."

The man smirked, then nodded and turned his attention one final time to the dazed crowd.

"I am Korrun Aldamund. Tell this to your friends and family. If you are not for me, then you stand against me. You have until the start of the next semester to decide. Power. Is. Shifting."

CHAPTER 17

Crumpled sheets rustled loudly against the still night, threatening to wake Vincent and Marth. The wood floor was uncomfortable, but that's not what kept Griff tossing and turning. So much had happened in the past few days. Griff's thoughts were like a violent whirlwind that battered his sanity. Try as he might to avoid them, there were still times where he was forced to be alone with his thoughts, and he never knew how to piece them all together.

Why had he dreamt of Korrun Aldamund in the caves? Why was the headmaster's uncle at odds against him? And how could he command the nightstalkers like that?

Although he had more questions than answers, Griff knew one thing. He would never follow Korrun Aldamund and his tainted ideologies. King Aldamund would never invade a school with nightstalkers and mages just to make a point. The king, powerful as he was, would never need to prove his strength like that. No, the only clear choice was to stay at Bergots and remain loyal to the king.

The aftermath of that night in the grand foyer had been almost as chaotic as the battle. Students and faculty worked to help the injured, clear the ground of fallen nightstalkers, and repair broken furniture and chunks of stone that had been dislodged from the walls. The medical ward was full of non-lethal injuries, so the Bergots' faculty spent the night mending small wounds.

When Marth suggested that they all come to his house for the break, Griff had eagerly accepted. As much as he missed Cordelia, it was too far for him to travel—there were no free warg rides home for the break—and he desperately needed something to distract him from the questions that plagued him. Vincent was also quick to accept the invitation, although Mira was more reluctant, since the quiet castle would allow more time for study. Given the earlier events in the grand foyer, though, both Mira and Sadie agreed that time away from Bergots might be best.

Griff stared out the window, the bright stars now dimming with the rising sun. The barely noticeable pink glow was invading the dark sky. He grabbed his blanket and quietly sneaked out of Marth's room. He headed down the creaky stairs, hoping no one would hear him. Cold winter air slapped him as he stepped out onto the large wraparound porch. He pulled his thick blanket around him and waddled to one of the wooden rocking chairs facing the sunrise. The long fields of tall grass seemed to glimmer with the sunlight reflecting off the dew.

Only a few quiet moments had passed before Griff heard a creak and the door to the porch opened. Carrying two cups of hot tea, Sadie sat down next to Griff and offered him one.

"Couldn't sleep?" she asked.

"Y-yeah," Griff answered, surprised. He half-wondered if she had sneaked poison into his mug.

"Me neither."

They sat in silence, rocking in their chairs, and slurping the tea. The tea was sweet. Too sweet, even. It was like a child with a taste for candy was given free rein over the tea kettle and sugar. But Griff was thankful for a myriad of reasons. While it was too sweet for his taste, it was still warm in his hands. More importantly, it seemed like a peace offering from the girl with the permanent scowl. And repeatedly bringing the tea to his lips kept him from having to say anything to the girl he knew so little about. He hadn't spent much time with Sadie, and she had never seemed interested in a conversation with him.

"Ya know… people think of me as mean and selfish. But I just think of myself as being safe. I dislike most people. They tend to be just as self-centered as they think I am, only they cover it up like icing on a rotten cake."

Griff chuckled and said, "Yeah. You're not wrong."

"But you're all right, Griff. You and Mira and Marth and Vincent. You're good people. Took me awhile to see it, but you're all right."

"Th-thanks," Griff said. "Does this mean you're not leaving us for that crazy Korrun fellow?"

She paused mid-sip.

"You know …" she held her cup tightly in her hands, embracing its warmth. "I don't know."

"Really?"

"Yeah. Really." Sadie stared long and hard into her cup as if trying to gather her thoughts.

"That Korrun guy—good or bad—he's strong. I mean, he can command *nightstalkers*? That's impressive. That's power. And, well … power is the real currency of our world. I don't like it, but that's how it is."

"What do you mean?" Griff asked.

"I mean, gold and silver and a big fancy castle are nice, but if you have enough power, you can *take* the gold and silver. You can take the castle. And nothing against the king, but you have to wonder if Korrun might actually be able to take the kingdom from him. Power's what tips the scales one way or another, and I've always been one to make sure I'm on the right side of things."

He shouldn't have been surprised. This was Sadie, after all—the "ginger scowler." But words failed him all the same. She could leave them—leave them to join Korrun on his mad quest.

The top of the sun was now visible, the beams radiating through the sky. They sat in silence for another moment, listening to the chirping birds and their creaking chairs.

"You wanna know why I decided to come here for break?" Sadie finally said.

"Vincent?" Griff asked, slyly.

"Watch it!" she said, but no threat appeared in her eyes.

She stopped for a moment and gazed into the distance, though it was clear her mind was somewhere else.

"Because I have nowhere else to go."

"Really? No parents or ... or other family?"

She shook her head.

"I-I'm sorry to hear that, Sadie. Really."

"I've been on my own for a long time. Stupid thieves came after me and my family. Didn't care what they did or who they hurt, so long as they got money. People say nightstalkers are the enemy, but that's 'cause they haven't taken a closer look at themselves."

Griff thought for a moment, letting her story sink in. He was thankful that she was finally talking to him, and yet his heart ached at her loss.

"Hey, wait a minute," he said. "Then how did you end up at Bergots?"

"Well, when you have no parents, no family to take care of you ... you do what you can to survive. Ironic, isn't it? I became the very thing I hated—a thief. On the streets, there's no rules, just survival. You steal, you fight, you survive. And when you're a mage ... it's a lot easier."

"So *that's* how you got so good at magic!"

"Yep. I've been practicing for years. Didn't know how I could do it, just knew that I could. Sure helped me outta some crazy situations too. Then one day, Alexand—uh, Headmaster Aldamund caught me stealing. I tried to use magic against him, and well, you can imagine how that turned out." She laughed.

"But ... well, he wasn't mad. He didn't try to hurt me. He was ... kind. A lot like you all. He gave me some gold to help me get by and told me about the academy. When I realized he was genuine—and trust me, it took some time for me to see that—well, he became the first person to give me any hope in humanity."

"He has that effect on people, I think," Griff said.

Sadie nodded and looked at the floor.

"What about you? You're out here freezing your tail off. Why can't you sleep?"

Griff sighed. It was only fair to tell her after all that she had shared.

"I ... I've seen him before."

"Who?"

"Korrun. I've seen him before. In my dreams."

He proceeded to tell her about his nightmares. The cave, the lava pit, the skull, the nightstalker, all of it. He even mentioned trying to escape and feeling trapped, and that moment where Korrun held something in his hands as though he had found what he was looking for.

"Is that weird?" he asked. "Like, I know magic exists and the rules of the world are a little less ... structured than I once thought. But it doesn't seem like this falls into a 'normal' category, even for mages."

"Yeah, no. It's definitely weird."

Sadie drummed her fingers on the chair, the rhythmic beat joining in the morning chorus of birds and breeze and creaking chairs.

"You should tell someone about that."

"I just did." Griff laughed.

"Yeah, but not me, you idiot. You need to tell Headmaster Aldamund."

"Oh, I dunno. He ... he seems pretty busy. I don't think he'd have time for my little problems."

"Hey. You're dreaming of *his* uncle, who came to *his* school with an army of nightstalkers. That's not little." She pointed her finger at his chest. "Tell him."

"All right, all right." Griff answered, defensively putting his hands in the air. "I'll tell him when we get back to school."

"Good," Sadie answered, pleased. "Well, I'm gonna go wake Marth up and tell him to make us breakfast. I'm starving."

She stood to leave, but before she could take a step, Griff grabbed her arm tightly and said, "Hey, one last thing." He quickly let go, lest he lose his hand.

"There's something my dad used to tell me. He always said, 'Love is power.' And you know, I never fully understood that until just now. You say power is the currency of this world, but I believe there's different kinds of power. Think about that day in the alleyway. Tyrell was completely bonkers. Sure, we kept him from hurting anyone, but it was Headmaster Aldamund who stepped in and actually fixed things. You saw the look of surprise and relief on Tyrell's face. That's something you don't see every day. *That's* true power.

"Korrun wants to heal the world of the Corruption, but in the process, he's willing to sacrifice the very things that make the world worth living. He's already destroyed towns. He's destroyed Tyrell's family and I'm sure others as well. Who knows how far he's willing to go to bring this ... 'healing'?

"The king and his son are working toward healing as well, but *love* is at the center of their solution. You told me that the headmaster gave you hope in people. Don't lose that hope now. I think we're gonna to need it more than ever."

He stared unblinking into Sadie's eyes as he tried to communicate the weight and truth of his statement.

She paused for a moment, returning the stare, then nodded.

"I'll keep that in mind."

Laughter filled the dining room, drowning out the clinking sounds of forks and knives. The roasted rabbit, carrots, and baked potatoes reminded Griff of home. While he may not have been able to travel back to Cordelia, traveling to Marth's house had been a great second option. They had welcomed the entire battlegroup like long lost friends.

"So, what exactly does a literarian do, Mr. Hayes?" Mira asked.

"Ah, well … it's a simple job really," Marth's dad replied.

"Oh, don't be so modest, Oliver. Tell the girl what it is you do," his wife said, placing a loving hand on his arm.

"Well, as you know, Whisperspell is known for its great library—"

"One of the biggest libraries besides the king's and the one at Bergots, mind you," Charlotte, Marth's oldest sister, said.

"Yes, yes, indeed." Mr. Hayes answered, pushing his glasses back up his nose. "And how do these books come to be? Copying them by hand is much too slow, and the king's desire to preserve history demands greater speed."

"So … you use your powers to wield multiple pencils at once, then?" Griff asked.

"Even better." Griff couldn't tell if his glasses reflected the candlelight or if there was a spark of excitement in his eyes.

"Think about postmen for a moment. What do they do?"

"Postmen?" Griff said. "What's a postman?"

"Seriously?" Alice, Marth's other sister, asked. "Where'd you find this kid again, Marth? Buried deeeeeeep under a rock?"

Griff blushed a little. Alice and Marth were a lot alike: both full of energy and both full of questions most people would never ask. Normally he didn't mind, but that was because the questions weren't usually directed at him. Thankfully, the Hayes family was already starting to feel like his own family, so the question didn't offend Griff; instead, it felt like an older sister pinching his cheek saying, "Isn't he cute?"

Marth chuckled and said, "Pretty much. But we're catchin' this middle-of-nowhere country boy up to the big city livin'."

"You say that like I'm your project or somethin'." Griff said. "Like I'm a lost puppy in need of a good bath and a nice home."

"Hey, your words not mine!" Marth held up his hands as evidence of his innocence.

Mrs. Hayes snatched a roll from the middle of the table and chunked it at her son. "You be nice to our guests! Or you can sleep on the back porch."

Griff chuckled, "It's okay, Mrs. Hayes. I've learned to put up with him by now."

"Good," she said. "That makes you the most patient boy I've ever met."

"As you were saying, *Dad*," Charlotte said, leaning forward on the table, giving her brother the stink eye, who returned her look with crossed eyes and a protruding tongue.

"Oh, right, yes. Postmen. So, Griff, how do you send letters where you come from?" Oliver Hayes asked.

"Um, I thought the same way everyone else sent letters ... by hand? Sometimes if we hear about someone travelin' to a town, they'll help a friend or family member by bringing any letters they need sent with them. Or, we'll pay them a little something for their troubles if they deliver a message for us. Is that not how everyone else does it?"

"Well, I suppose it does happen every now and again. But not in most cities. Especially not in cities with mages."

Everyone remained silent as Mr. Hayes removed his glasses, leaned back in his chair, and sighed from the pleasure of a full belly and happy taste buds. Griff eyed all the plates in front of Vincent. The fact that everyone seemed to have eaten their fill was remarkable considering the Hayes family had to feed not just themselves and an entire battlegroup, but Vincent as well. Griff wondered if they would be invited back, or if by the end of the holiday they would have eaten them out of house and home. Mr. Hayes resumed his normal posture, save for a hand that lovingly rubbed his wife's back, much to his children's displeasure.

"This past semester you learned the theory behind essence crafting—embedding your magic into everyday items to make weapons—yes?"

Griff nodded.

"Well, while some may embed magic into items to make weapons, others embed magic into old world technology for other reasons. Take the postmen, for example. They have discovered machines called type-writers. Prior to Day Zero, typewriters were used to *stamp* letters instead of writing them. Now, thanks to essence manipulation, postmen can connect two typewriters together to send a message."

"No need to send a letter with a friend anymore," Charlotte inter-jected. "That takes too long. Now you can send messages through the postmen, and so long as there's a typewriter in the town where you'd like to send your message, it'll get delivered."

"Well, that explains why we don't have a postman in Cordelia." Griff said. "No mages, and no ... writer ... things."

"Isn't magic great?" Marth said, before he casually picked a sliver of meat from his teeth and flicked it at Alice.

"Now," Oliver said loudly as he eyed the look of death in Alice's eyes. "Similar to battlemages and postmen who embed magic into everyday items for their own purposes ... a *literarian* uses their magic on old world technology to make multiple copies of books at the same time."

Oliver Hayes leaned forward and raised his eyebrows at the group.

"Have any of you ever heard of a printing press?" he asked.

"Ok, Dad, *now* you're headed into boredom territory." Alice said. Her whole body jerked as she sent a swift kick underneath the table. Marth yelped and pulled his knee up to his chest so he could nurse the tender spot on his shin.

"He thinks everyone else is as interested in the book copying world as he is," Alice continued as though nothing had happened.

"It does seem fascinating," Mira replied casually. "At least, you're not covered in nightstalker blood. And who doesn't love a good thick book anyways?"

Marth and Alice both raised their hands and laughed.

"Coulda seen that coming," Griff chuckled along with the rest of the table.

It felt good to laugh again. Korrun's proposal had created a lot of unease within the magical community. Word of his attack on Bergots had spread like wildfire. "Throw off your loyalty to King Aldamund and join the new revolution" was a tough idea to swallow. Knowing that Korrun commanded nightstalkers made it even worse. Spending time with the Hayes family had settled a lot of the anxiety that Griff and his group had felt following the attack. Although the holiday decorations created a cozy atmosphere throughout the house, it was the laughter and love that warmed the cold rooms in their home and settled the anxious hearts within their walls.

Organized chaos followed dinner as everyone helped with the evening chores. Some did dishes, while others cleaned the table and wiped down countertops. Animals in the barn needed their evening meals, and the lanterns surrounding the house needed to be lit.

To show their appreciation for the Hayes's hospitality, the battle-group tried to do their part as well. Griff and Mira helped with the dishes, Marth and Vincent fed the animals, and Sadie offered to light the lanterns outside. After he finished, Griff stood by the holiday tree, admiring its glistening lights. It was snowing outside. Watching each falling snowflake that eventually joined the beautiful blanket of white that covered the ground mesmerized him. Suddenly, the pounding sounds of someone sprinting through the house broke Griff out of his trance. He turned to find a breathless Marth standing in the doorway. His eyes were wild, and sweat was forming on his brow.

"Griff, have you seen Sadie?"

"Sadie? No ... why?"

"I-I don't think she's here ..." he whispered.

"She's not he—"

Realization struck him squarely in the jaw. He looked outside. Night had fallen. She'd only need to whisper his name. "No. You don't think she'd ..." He began to panic.

"I dunno, mate. She might."

Just then, Vincent marched past them and threw open the front door, a look of determination painted on his face.

"Umm, okay, okay," Marth said. "You grab Mira and search the south side of the city. I'll catch up to Vince. I don't think she could have gotten past the walls yet."

Griff rushed through the house, grabbing his and Mira's coats. He found her in the kitchen, drying the final dinner dishes.

"Come with me," Griff said, but he didn't wait. He grabbed her arm, which had completely healed from the battle at Bergots, and pulled her out into the snowy night.

"What're you doing, Griff?" Mira demanded, yanking her arm back into her possession.

"It's Sadie. We don't know where she is."

Mira stopped. "What?"

"Yeah. We gotta find her. Before Korrun does."

"No way. She wouldn't do that. She wouldn't leave us like that."

"Actually ... she might," Griff said. "C'mon. I'll fill you in while we look for her."

As they searched the south streets of Whisperspell, Griff told Mira what Sadie had shared with him that morning.

"Poor girl," Mira said, as they stepped out of the local tavern and back onto the cobblestone street.

"I know," Griff answered. "I can see why trust isn't something that comes naturally to her. I did my best to help her see that there's still hope in this world. But … I dunno. Maybe I couldn't get through to her."

Buildings along the side of the street thinned as they moved closer to the south wall. They were running out of places to look. It seemed inevitable that she had made it out of the city and was on her way to join Korrun. Their pace slowed as the night dragged on, and any hope of finding Sadie dwindled.

The pure white snow sparkled brilliantly against Mira's dark brown hair, like the holiday trees that glistened with festive magic. Her bright green eyes reflected the fire of each street lantern they passed. Had they not been looking for their missing friend, Griff would have enjoyed walking in the snow with her. Even the cold winter air couldn't stop his heart from feeling warmer when he was near her.

They walked by a lone house, meticulously decorated with pine wreathes and festive lanterns along the gate. Like a beacon of light against the black night, a large window opened to a living room with a blazing fire in the fireplace. Through the window, Griff could see a young family playing and laughing together. The husband and wife danced merrily to the tune of the inaudible song they sang, as their two young children clapped along.

"Do you miss them?" Griff asked quietly.

"Miss who?" Mira answered, her eyes glued to the happy family.

"Your family. Do you miss them?"

She stood silently for a moment, staring into the window and watching as the father twirled his little girl around.

"Every day," she said. She turned toward him, those bright green eyes magnified by the tears threatening to fall. "It's so hard being this far from home. And with everything else going on, I can't even visit. It's not safe to travel alone, and even if it was, it's too expensive. My family doesn't need any more financial stress ..."

His eyes met hers, and he stared for a moment, allowing himself to forget everything else. The snow, the wind, the night—it all disappeared. Griff had always known that boldness and bravery on the battlefield was a risk. You could be bold and brave and win the war. Or you could lose your life. He wasn't sure the cost of bravery in this moment, but it was a risk he had to take.

He walked forward and gently wrapped his arms around her. "It'll be okay, Mira."

He felt her arms tighten around him; her head lay across his shoulder. For a moment, Mira's muscles relaxed as she leaned into his embrace. The pounding of his heart reached his ears, and his pulse beat harder against the veins in his arms. He wished those five seconds would last an eternity. But they didn't. She quickly dropped her arms and took a step back.

"A-and it's *because* of my family that I-I'm here. I'm here to focus on my studies so I can make a better life for them. Which means ... which means ... no distractions." Her eyes lowered to the ground. She turned and continued walking down the snowy street.

Griff's heart sank. He didn't know what to say. He thrust his hands into his pockets and trudged through the snow, not sure if he wanted to catch up to her or not. They walked in silence, the feeling of disappointment almost tangible. There was no sign of Sadie and no chance of a relationship with Mira.

Suddenly, she stopped. Lost in his own thoughts, Griff almost ran into her. She stared at an old, abandoned stone building with a tall steeple ahead of them. All the other houses and buildings looked like bright stars in the night sky, lit with festive decorations. This building, however, was dark and almost unnoticeable. A single set of footprints veered off the snow-dusted cobblestone street and up to the wooden front doors. One of the doors stood slightly ajar.

Griff and Mira locked eyes for a moment, then he nodded and started forward. There was still a chance. Maybe not for him and Mira, but a chance to save Sadie. With Mira close behind, her breath warm on the back of his neck, Griff slowly opened the door and stepped inside.

He heard her before he saw her. While his eyes fought to adjust to the almost utter darkness, his ears were on high alert. Sniffling sounds echoed throughout the large room. Past several rows of wooden benches, Sadie huddled like a child in a corner. They ran to her, their pounding footsteps disturbing years of dust.

"Sadie! We've been looking everywhere for you!" Mira said, falling to her knees and wrapping the girl in a tight bear hug. For once, Sadie didn't resist.

Smeared tear streaks across her face shone in a single strand of moonlight. Griff sat on the other side of Sadie, but remained silent so Mira could continue to comfort her. The tough never-back-down-from-a-fight mage allowed herself to be held by her friend and did nothing to keep the tears from falling.

"It's ... it's not *fair*," she said. "I grew up *fighting* to survive. I-I grew up fighting *alone*. But not you," she said looking at Griff and Mira. "Not you. Not Marth. Not Vincent. You all had family. You had friends. I had nothing. I *have* ... nothing."

"Sadie ..." Mira said, stroking her messy red hair. "Griff and I ... well, we can't change your past. We would if we could but ... we can't. Still, if there's one thing I believe in this world, it's that your past doesn't define you and it doesn't hold you back. You may have grown up alone. But you're not alone now. And as far as what happens next, well, I believe you have a choice. That's what motivates me. I'm not leaving my family's future up to chance. I believe I have a say in my family's future. And you have a say in yours."

Sadie wiped a tear, smudging dirt across her face.

"You guys just need a fifth person for your battlegroup. That's why you're here, isn't it?"

"We could probably find another person to join us," Griff said. "I'm not convinced Tyrell's group really enjoys him bossing everyone around."

Sadie snorted.

"Plus, you'd have to be a pretty special person for me to spend hours searching for you in the snow with *that* girl over there," he jabbed his finger in Mira's direction, and she gave him a playful glare.

"Shut up," Sadie said. "Everyone knows you like her. It's annoyingly obvious."

"Moving *on*," Mira interjected. "As Griff has so cleverly explained, we actually *are* your friends. So, will you come back with us? Marth and Vincent are out searching for you as well."

"Well, Marth's probably stopped searching by now ... but not *Vincent*," he winked at Sadie.

Griff received a second glare. Sadie paused for a moment, then stood up, wiped off her face as best as she could, and dusted off her clothes.

"Well, if you guys want me to stay *sooo* bad, then let's get going."

She took a step and paused, then turned back to her friends.

"And ... thanks, you guys."

CHAPTER 18

The crunching snow under Tyrell's boots might as well have been hammers on rotten wood. Careful as he was, every light footstep risked waking his mother. He had to hurry before she noticed his absence. Still, it felt wrong to leave her this way, especially after all they had been through.

He turned, the snow groaning loudly underneath him, and took one last look at his house. It was brightly decorated; the festive, colored fire swirled inside lanterns that hung on the front porch. The holiday tree glistened from the living room window, beckoning him back inside. Just that morning, he and his mom had sat by the tree with his little brother, enjoying fresh eggnog and opening presents. Their fun had almost removed the weight of duty he felt in his heart. A tear began to form but Tyrell wiped it away before it froze against his face.

I have to do this. He gritted his teeth and marched forward, the small survival pack bumping against his spine with every step. As his house disappeared into the distance, his footsteps quickened; he marched ahead with purpose. He didn't dare conjure a light, lest anyone see him leave.

In the distance, he heard yelling. There were two distinct voices, both shouting the same word. Tyrell paused, not wanting to be seen, but also needing to get as far away from his house as possible. Like a leopard targeting his prey, Tyrell's movements were deliberate. Intentional. He moved only when they yelled so his footsteps wouldn't be heard. He dipped farther into the shadows every time their light turned in his direction. But they continued to move closer. When their faces became clear, Tyrell let out an aggravated sigh.

It was Marth and his friend Vincent. They were looking for that red-headed girl. The one from the alleyway. He'd almost rather stumble into his mother than meet those two fools. Of course, he could always take them right here and leave them dazed in the snow. They wouldn't die, but they would always remember that he was to be taken seriously. But no. Now was not the time or the place. He had more important matters to deal with. And if he was successful, they would respect him and his family name. Just not now. Now, he couldn't be seen by anyone, not even two dumb mages looking for their friend.

When he could no longer move forward for fear of being seen, Tyrell stepped into an alleyway and hid behind a brick pillar. Away from his house, he appreciated how loud footsteps in the snow were. Even when the two dummies weren't yelling their heads off, he could hear their crunching getting closer and closer. He hated the racing of his heart, as though it were a sign of weakness or fear. He wasn't afraid. He was Tyrell Falkenburg—the son of a battlemage. But he couldn't steady his breathing. His desire to remain hidden was so strong that every crunching step closer made his heart beat faster.

A light shone down the alleyway, but he remained in the shadows. He tried to stay still, but his hands were shaking uncontrollably.

Curse these hands! he screamed in his mind. *Obey me!*

He shook his hands to try and get them back under control. As he did so, he grazed the metal pipe that drained rainwater from the rooftop into the alley. A small thump echoed in the night. His heart stopped. Maybe they didn't hear it. There was silence. Not a crunch in the snow, not their stupid voices yelling in the night. Nothing.

And then, he heard a sigh from Marth.

"She's gone, mate. I'm sorry."

Tyrell heard the snow groan as Marth turned to leave, but the silence was shattered when a large icicle broke from the gutters above. The sound of breaking glass echoed through the night as the icicle hit the cobblestone street.

"Hey! Who's there?" Marth yelled.

The light grew in the alleyway, and Tyrell knew it was no use. He bravely stepped into the light. He was going to face them unafraid and remind them who they were talking to.

"Put that light out, Hayes," Tyrell commanded Marth.

"Tyrell? Is that you?" he asked. He commanded his light spell to grow brighter.

"Of course it is, you idiot. Now, stop trying to blind me with your light spell, or I'll find a way to put it out myself."

Marth lowered the intensity but refused to extinguish it. Tyrell decided not to waste his energy on the mage. He was going to need it later.

"What're you doing here, mate?" Marth asked.

"Doesn't matter," Tyrell stated matter-of-factly.

"You seen Sadie?" the giant interjected, his deep voice filled with concern.

"No. But even if I had, I wouldn't tell you. I'd have finished that little conversation she started back in Solastran."

Marth paused for a moment, then said, "Let's go, Vince. Clearly, he's not gonna help us."

They took a step back into the street before Marth turned around to Tyrell and said, "Tyrell ... I dunno why you're out here at this hour. But ... just don't do anything stupid, okay? Just ... don't."

That only made Tyrell angrier. He revisited his idea of fighting them and showing them who the stupid ones were, but he was a man of discipline. And he wouldn't let them stand in the way of what really mattered.

"Mind your own business, Marth," he said. He stormed out of the alleyway, without waiting for a reaction.

They resumed calling for their friend, but in a matter of minutes, their voices had faded into the night along with the rest of Whisperspell. Now, he only had to get past the gate. He tossed his pack to the other side, and then used a trick he had picked up years ago, back when he and Marth were still friends—wriggling the chained gate so there was just enough space for him to slip through.

From there, it was only a ten minute walk to the forest. Still refusing to conjure a light, Tyrell took the most traveled path into the woods. He kept waiting to hear nightstalker footsteps, but there were none. Just the rhythmic crunching of his boots on the snow.

Tyrell stepped into a clearing. Moonlight poured down through the opening and engulfed him. This time, he was afraid, and there was no convincing his heart otherwise. But his duty lay before him, and duty was the antidote to fear.

The son of the ex-battlemage cleared his throat and whispered boldly and defiantly into the night:

"Korrun Aldamund."

CHAPTER 19

The old, wooden chair creaked, breaking the awkward silence that hung heavy in the air. Griff fidgeted against the ancient leather that was worn and cracked. Headmaster Aldamund and Professor Coen's mouths weren't moving but Griff could tell their minds raced to make sense of the story he had just shared with them. As the silence settled deeper into the headmaster's office, the crackling of the fireplace grew louder. The sound reminded Griff of snapping frozen tree branches over his knee when he used to gather firewood back home. Try as he might, he couldn't read either of their expressions. Were they disappointed? Were they angry at him for not telling them sooner? Were they shocked or scared or ... anything? Anything at all?

"I see," Headmaster Aldamund said at last. He stood and walked around his large ornate desk, sitting on it and facing Griff.

"There ... is a lot to unpack there, Griff. And with it, a mystery that needs to be solved. My father, the king, has shared with me your dream from the night you surfaced. And Professor Hatlen has made me aware of your white spells. However, the fact that you have had *three* of these dreams, with the last one revealing my uncle, whom you have never met, is new.

"This is a very peculiar situation, and while I certainly have my guesses, I must investigate this further before I make any assumptions."

"Please, sir," Griff responded, desperate for an answer. "What's wrong with me? Why did I dream those dreams? What connection do I have to your uncle?"

The headmaster calmly stroked his chin and said, "My boy, there is nothing *wrong* with you."

"That's what I said as well." Professor Coen leaned back in his chair, folded his arms, and gave Griff a look that said, "Told ya."

"You have unique gifts and talents, Griff. And a gift, if not taken out of the box and used, merely sits on a shelf collecting dust."

The headmaster walked past his student and stopped in front of the fireplace. He glanced at the flames, which immediately dwindled. Above the mantle sat a brilliantly decorated sword. Headmaster Aldamund reached out his hand, and the weapon floated from its mount and into his hands. Adorning the handle were emerald, sapphire, and ruby gems that would have sparkled in the light of the flames, if not for the layer of dust that smothered their glow. The short, curved blade ended in a sharp point. Headmaster Aldamund gently blew on the sword, dislodging dust from every surface, before he handed it to Griff.

"This sword was given to me when my dad named me headmaster of Bergots. With it was a letter he had written, describing how proud he was, and that I had a great purpose ahead of me. That letter"—he walked back around his desk, opened the top drawer, and pulled out a worn piece of paper—"has yet to collect dust. I read it weekly to remind myself of my father's love for me and the importance of my role in his kingdom. However, that sword has yet to be used."

He sighed, and his eyes glazed over as if reliving a distant memory. The worn leather chair groaned with age when the headmaster plopped back down and began lightly drumming his fingers on the desk.

"For years, the kings of Oriel have only ever wielded their army as a shield, never as a sword. That is changing now, I'm afraid. You are powerful, Griff. You are strong. You have a unique gift that is meant to be used rather than sit idly by collecting dust. When the time comes, your gifts and talents will be needed."

He carefully placed the letter back into its drawer before motioning to Griff's teacher.

"Professor Coen has told me about your arrangement to receive extra training."

"Well … yes, sir. We did have an arrangement, but that was before the attack, and it was supposed to be during the break."

"I dare say that there's even more reason for you to learn to control your powers now. Professor Coen has graciously agreed to train you after hours, provided you do your best to learn and do not waste his time."

"O-of course, sir. That would be great."

"In the meantime, I will see what I can find regarding these … prophetic dreams of yours."

"Thank you, sir," Griff answered. The silence that followed his answer implied that their conversation was over. Headmaster Aldamund had nothing else to say, and was probably waiting for Griff to leave so he and the professor could talk about what he had told them. But Griff didn't budge.

"Is there something else, Mr. Driscoll?" the headmaster asked.

"Yes, sir. I … I was wondering about your uncle. He … he can control nightstalkers? How is that possible?"

The headmaster and Professor Coen locked eyes for a moment before he finally spoke.

"We don't know."

"You don't?"

"No. You see, Griff, essence manipulation is a fickle thing. Much like the ocean. The closer something is to the surface, the more we know about it. The deeper you go, though, the less we know. So I'm afraid I don't have an answer for you."

Griff nodded in understanding. "Thank you, sir." He turned to leave.

"And Griff, one more thing."

"Sir?"

"Please be careful. Remember, you have unique and special gifts. And where there are gifts of great value, there are thieves who would like to take those gifts for themselves."

A chair flew wildly across the training room and smashed against the hard stone wall. Tiny bits of wood sprayed the air like the snow falling outside.

"That was a close one!" Professor Coen said as he stood back up and shook the wood shavings from his hair.

"I'm so sorry!" Griff called from across the training room.

"All part of the job, I'm afraid. Now, remember: focus. Feel that energy, but don't lose control of it. Feel it, and then immediately grab it before it has a chance to take off on you like that."

Griff nodded and readied himself. His mentor stood to the side and created a shield in front of himself.

"Okay, *now* I'm ready," he said.

Griff sucked in a lungful of air and concentrated on the energy swelling inside his chest. He could feel it, an endless ocean held back by a wall of twigs. This was the moment. The energy was building and threatened to crash through the flimsy failsafe inside Griff's mind. He focused on the new chair in front of him, his eyes flickering to the red *X* across the room. Slowly, the mage allowed the power to flow through him and toward his hands.

But then, the energy released on its own. The chair whizzed through the air and smashed against the wall as it had in all of his previous attempts.

"Urgh!" he groaned. "Why. Can't. I. Do. It!" Every stomp of his foot placed emphasis on each of the words he yelled. He plopped down on the floor, defeated, disregarding the wood shavings underneath him.

"I would *love* to be able to cast anything beside a wind spell."

"Is that all you've been doing?" the professor asked, taking one of the remaining chairs and sitting backward so his hands rested across the top.

"Yeah. At least I can aim it ... even if I still can't control its power. Worst thing that usually happens is I go flying backward. But better that than trying fire or lightning or levitating something ..." He eyed the dismembered chairs across the room.

"Well, I can appreciate your wisdom there, Griff."

Professor Coen paused for a moment and cocked his head as though an idea had just hit him. He stood quickly.

"Hey. Grab your handle. You brought it with you, yes?"

"Yeah, right here."

Griff walked the short distance to his bag, but as his fingers grasped the familiar leather handle, he heard a loud grunt from his teacher. Out of the corner of his eye, he saw a brown blur fly right toward him. Without a thought, he snatched the handle out of the bag and conjured up a long two-headed axe with blades the size of his head. In one breath, he turned on his heel and swung the axe with all his might, chopping the chair aimed at his head in two.

"What in nightstalker's fury was that for?" Griff asked.

"Oh, quit your whining," the professor said. "It worked, didn't it?"

"What worked?"

"You used your magic to conjure up an axe in the time it took for that chair to come at you!"

"Okay ... and ...?"

"*And* you know that there are third years who *still* can't do that?"

"Okay, so ... I'm good at essence crafting, but I might as well be a warg under water when it comes to spell slinging. How does that help me?"

"We need to figure out *why* you can do one, but not the other. I mean, sure, most people excel in one or two areas of magic, but they can usually at least fumble through the others."

The professor walked over and stood in front of his student with his arms crossed.

"Why is it, Griff, that you excel in essence crafting?"

"I-I don't know," he lied.

"Oh, c'mon, yes, you do. I know you do." Professor Coen's eyes narrowed and peered into Griff's as though searching for the truth in them.

"Why?" he asked, getting closer.

"I ... don't ... know." Griff grabbed his matted black hair in frustration. He had to be strong, right? If he was going to be a good mage, a strong mage, he would have to bury these feelings that lurked in the shadows of his mind.

"Yes, you do, Griff! Yes, you do! Now's not the time for humility, now's the time for honesty! Think! Why?"

"B-be-because!" Griff cried. "Because it's the only time I feel like my-self again. Because ... because when I hold that weapon in my hand, I don't feel like a stupid child who lost his mommy in the town square. Because it's the only time I feel like I belong here."

Big fat tears forming at the base of his eyes threatened to fall. He quickly wiped them away with his arm.

"Everyone else here *knew* that they were coming here. It was expected of them. Everyone else here grew up with magic around them. Not me. My entire life changed in one night, and now ... now I'm a thousand miles away from home, in a place I've never been to before, learning things I'd only heard whispers about. My battlegroup's first Altar Storm match is just weeks away, and if I don't do well, I dunno if I'll have a battlegroup next semester.

"I feel like … like I'm completely out of my depth. I feel lost and alone and … and … and I don't know what in the king's crown I'm doing."

"Look at me."

Griff did.

"I am not a figment of your imagination."

Professor Coen backed up, allowing Griff space to breathe. He remained silent, waiting for understanding to dawn on him.

"You are not in this room alone. You are not in this school alone. Where did you go during break?"

"To … Marth's house."

"I see. And did he pay you to go there?"

"No."

"Did you sneak in, uninvited?"

"No."

"Did you have fun?"

"Yes … I did."

"See?" He threw his hands in the air as if he had just won an Altar Storm battle.

"You have friends and allies within these walls! You are not alone, Griff Driscoll! You belong right here alongside these mages who are *all* struggling to find their place in this world! They have some advantages over you, sure, but you have some advantages over them! King's crown, boy, I've never seen such skilled essence crafting at your age! And from what you tell me, you have a family who loves you and cares for you and misses you when you're gone!"

"Yeah … that's true, but why does that matter?"

"Professor Hatlen's been teaching you why that matters. Think about it. When you first learned of your abilities, you used them out of fear and anger. Remember?"

"How could I forget?" Griff mumbled, his mind racing back to the Cordelian forest and his battle against the nightstalkers.

"But that's not how he has been training you to manipulate essence is it? Not with fear or anger but ..."

"Love," Griff said, understanding finally dawning on him.

"Love," his mentor repeated. "Love is powerful stuff, Griff. And when you draw your power from that ... I think you'll start to find your control. *That's* why it's important you remember that you are loved. *That's* why you need to understand that you do belong here."

He walked back over to the chairs, pulled another one out, and sat on it like he had before.

"I can see that, right now, you're still pulling from your anger, your frustration, and your insecurities. You're drawing from a place of discomfort. But you don't draw from there when you grab your sword and remember where you came from."

Professor Coen held out his hand and beckoned one of the chairs forward. It hovered dangerously over him, but he ignored it.

"So, from now on, I want *that* to be your focus when you cast your spells."

Griff's mentor casually set the floating chair in front of his student, and said, "Let's keep going."

CHAPTER 20

There should have been excitement radiating throughout the dining hall, but the empty chairs sprinkled throughout the room were a reminder of Korrun's proposal. Students should have been moving from table to table, placing bets on which first year battlegroup they suspected would shine in the arena. They should have been laughing and joking and telling stories. But Korrun's attack on the school had dampened everyone's enthusiasm. Griff thought back to the headmaster's speech weeks ago at the beginning of the second semester.

Headmaster Aldamund said that things were changing in Oriel and at Bergots. Some of the older students and their families had joined in his uncle's quest, while other students had been forced to stay home by their parents. Returning students must have a renewed sense of focus in their classes; the knowledge and skills they were learning would be useful in ways that they hadn't expected before. Even Altar Storm battles would carry a greater weight.

Griff looked around the dining hall. Those who had stayed—thankfully, the majority—were doing their best to make the most of the day. They tried to joke and laugh and tell stories like everything was normal. But the jokes weren't as funny, and the stories centered on battlegroups scrambling to replace lost members. He was thankful his group remained intact over the break, though it wasn't without some serious work. He was especially glad they'd convinced Sadie to stick around.

"I still can't believe he left," Marth said, jerking Griff out of his thoughts.

"You're sure he went to be with that maniac?" Mira asked, pulling herself out of her history book.

"I'm telling you, Mira. He had his bag packed, it was the middle of the night, and he clearly didn't want anyone knowing where he was going. Right, Vince?"

Mouth full, Vincent nodded and dove back into his second bowl of oatmeal.

"See?"

Mira shrugged and went back to reading.

"I mean … his dad is one of Korrun's followers," Griff said. "Maybe he went to fight alongside him."

"I can see that," Sadie said. "That no good boy-who-thinks-he's-a-man is always trying to prove himself."

"Can't disagree with you there, Sadie," Marth said.

He turned to look at Mira, whose face was scrunched in concentration.

"Seriously, Mira?" he asked. "Why're you doing homework *now*? We've got a match to prepare for."

"*Because*"—she slammed the book shut and glared at him—"as you know, Professor Erebus doesn't give a warg's hind end about everything that's going on. If anything, he's giving us more essays now, and I'm not gonna fall behind like you guys."

"Ouch!" Marth placed his hands over his heart as though she'd just stabbed him.

"You shoulda seen that coming," Griff said to his friend. "You know better than to get between her and her one true love."

Griff reached over and rubbed the book as though it was a pampered puppy. Mira snatched the book away as he pretended to give it a little tickle.

"You're just jealous," she said confidently and then tucked the book away.

Griff felt his face grow warm at the comment, so he fussed over the remaining bites of egg on his plate.

"So ... any guesses on today's arena setup?" Marth asked, coming to Griff's aid.

"Well, it's gotta be based on the things we've been learning, right?" Mira asked.

"Right," Griff answered, digging through his memories to remember which lessons those were.

"So ... no essence crafting then, mate. Sorry." Marth slapped Griff's shoulder.

"Too bad," he responded.

"But ... it could be essence crafting *theory*," Sadie interjected. "Dunno how that would come up in the arena, but who knows? I'm just hoping for a good old-fashioned beat down. Don't get to have many of those here, you know?"

Marth turned to Griff. "How's your training with Professor Coen going?"

"Getting there." Griff sighed. "I'm still having a hard time controlling most spells. But I *can* finally cast a consistent shield spell without using my sword handle!"

"Great. Well maybe you can just shield yourself and run really fast into people on the field," Sadie said.

He readied a smart comment but was interrupted by Vincent's burst of laughter.

"Probably some form of levitating ..." Mira mumbled to no one in particular. Her eyes stared at the ceiling, and she seemed to be talking to herself rather than her group.

"I mean, we *have* been focusing a lot on that spell lately. It's one of the more basic and useful spells ... but then again, we did *start* with a wind spell ... oh, I dunno ... I guess I'll have to just see when I—" She looked at her team who stared back at her.

"—I guess *we'll* have to see when we get there, won't we?"

Griff leaned over to Sadie and whispered, "Does she always talk to herself like this?"

"You don't know the half of it. Pretends I'm not even in the room, and sometimes ... I wish I wasn't."

The buzz of the room slowed as Headmaster Aldamund stepped to the front of the room.

"Today is a special day for our first years. As you know, today you will undergo your first Altar Storm match. Today we will see how much of your lessons you remember ... and how much you left back home during winter break."

A quiet chuckle echoed through the crowd. Curiously, the headmaster was quite cheery despite the ominous pronouncement his uncle had left hanging over the school.

"Now, as I mentioned at the start of the semester ... your classes and training have become of the utmost importance, given the current circumstances in our land. I know many of you feel the pressure that has been placed unfairly on you by my uncle. But allow me to relieve some of that pressure."

He walked through the sea of students until he was standing in the center. He jumped with surprising agility on top of a table surrounded by first years. Their eyes almost popped out of their sockets. The room was quieter than midnight in winter.

"One of the best ways to fight back against the gloom Korrun has left you with"—he swirled his hands together and hundreds of brilliant balls of different colored lights appeared throughout the room—"is to live with a joy that rebels against it."

The orbs grew larger and rose higher. Their lights pulsed brilliantly with every carefully spoken word from their master.

"I want you to tell any sadness, any fear, and any anxiety that you feel, 'You will not have a hold on me!'"

His voice grew louder, reflecting his passion. Even his muscles appeared tense with enthusiasm.

"You will not let some unworthy person like Korrun Aldamund steal your joy. No! You will rebel *with* your joy! Today, we will do what we always do, and we will do it the way we've always done it. Today is Altar Storm day, and I will not let my uncle sully what all of us enjoy so much. So, pick up your heads, students! Laugh! Sing! Dance and be merry! And let's depart to the arena and rebel against my uncle and his dark ways!"

At his last word, the orbs exploded in brilliant light. Multicolored sparkles rained down on the cheering students. The energy that had been drained by thoughts of Korrun Aldamund's pronouncement had returned a hundredfold. Students of all ages jumped and shouted and sang as they exited the dining hall and headed out toward the battlefield. Cheering and laughter echoed through the halls of Bergots again. As Griff passed the beaming headmaster, their eyes locked for a moment, and he nodded toward the young mage as if to say, "I hope you were listening."

As the stampede of excited mages approached the arena, Professor Coen separated the first years from everyone else. When he saw Griff, he motioned for him, yelling over the singing and chanting.

"Your group is going first. So, head down to the field and await your instructions."

The excitement and joy Griff had felt leaving the dining hall had been slapped out of him by the professor's words. First? They were going first? He had hoped to watch at least one other group, so he and his team could be better prepared. His shoulders slumped in frustration, and Griff lumbered behind his team as they trudged down to the pitch.

"Oh my, this ought to be fun! Look Griff, it's your girlfriend!" Marth said as they stepped onto the field and noticed Katrine Penderson's group making their way down the stairs on the opposing side.

"Not my girlfriend," Griff retorted.

"Well, if you play that card now, we might have a better chance, mate."

Griff shot him an annoyed glare.

Marth shrugged his shoulders, "Just sayin'."

The rest of the battlegroup remained quiet as they stared across the grassy field. Standing two stories tall and meeting the top of the arena walls, a barrier of crushed metal stretched across the entire center of the pitch. In Griff's history classes, they had learned that the building blocks of this wall were once known as vehicles called cars prior to their compacting demise. Pure adrenaline pumped through his body, but there was no outlet for it. Yet.

Professor Coen walked down the arena stairs, past the frenzied mass of students and onto the top of the vehicular wall. He turned to address the crowd.

"Welcome, everyone, to Altar Storm!"

Griff didn't think the crowd could have gotten any louder but was proven wrong as the stands erupted in a roar.

"For our first year students, we have prepared a simple layout. We have our wall of cars here," he stomped on the crushed metal barrier. "Which will require some ... heavy lifting ... to get past. Additionally, you will notice the storm orbs are missing from their altars."

Griff's head perked up. He had been so focused on the wall of cars he hadn't bothered to look at the altar. Sure enough, it stood empty.

"Now, if our teams would like to find their orbs—and they will 'cause it's part of the game—they only need to look inside this box near the wall."

The enormous wall of cars made the wooden box sitting a vehicle's length away from its base almost invisible.

"Our other first year students won't get the pleasure of seeing these matches as we don't want to ruin the surprise for them. Now, the objective remains the same. Find your storm orb and place it on the other team's altar before they do. Teams, I will give you a few moments to come up with a strategy. Headmaster Aldamund will give the signal when it's time for the match to begin."

"Okay, guys, what's the plan?" Griff asked as they huddled together.

"Well, first things first," Mira said, "We need to get our storm orb."

"And ... it wouldn't hurt to start making a path to the other side either ..." Marth said.

An idea struck Griff. "Hey, where's their box?"

The group did their best to peer through the small openings between cars.

"Over there!" Mira pointed to the left side of the arena. Just past a rusted blue car, Griff could see a box identical to theirs.

"What if we could distract the other team as they try to find their orb?" he asked.

"Hmm," Vincent grumbled in agreement.

"What if ... what if two of us made a path through the wall where the other team's box is?" Mira said. "If you can get through the wall, then you find ways to keep them busy. Use a wind spell ... or ... Marth, you're good with levitation spells, too, right?"

He stood up tall, "The best."

Mira rolled her eyes, "Of course you are. If you can get across, maybe you can pull some parts from the cars and throw it at them or something."

"I can find a way to distract them, too, you know," Sadie said. Her smile frightened Griff.

"Ummm ... without killing them?" he asked.

"I have my ways." She crossed her arms.

"Sadie knows more spells than the rest of us … could be good to have her out there too," Mira said. "Could you guys lift those vehicles together, maybe? They're pretty heavy, but that's probably the best way through."

Marth looked to Sadie who wore a confident smirk, "Yeah, we can do that."

"Okay, good. So, who's going to defend?"

Everyone looked to Vincent, who smiled.

"Yeah, that's a good call," Marth said. "Vince, no offense buddy, but nobody's gonna come within a mile of our altar with you on guard. Is that okay with you?"

"Just fine," he answered.

"So, I guess that leaves you and me to find the orb?" Mira asked Griff.

"Yeah, guess so. So, we'll open the box, grab the orb, then meet up with Sadie and Marth? Any idea what—"

BOOM. Multicolored sparks zoomed through the air. The crowd roared. The match had begun.

"Let's go!" Sadie yelled with a little too much enthusiasm.

Griff and Mira sprinted to the right, while Marth and Sadie ran to the left. The chanting and singing from the crowd drifted into the background as they approached the box and Griff's focus narrowed. It was a plain wooden box made of thick planks. Mira grabbed the top and tried to pry it open but was unsuccessful. They walked around each side but couldn't find a handle or a knob or anything. There was no way to open the box. Unless …

"We need to check the bottom," Griff said, trying to sneak his fingers underneath. Thankfully, the grass was thick and left just enough wiggle room for him to get a firm grip. But it wouldn't budge. Mira joined him and together they strained but made no progress.

"We've gotta levitate it," Mira said.

"I ... I can't," Griff said. "I don't think it's a good idea for me to do that."

"You've got to, Griff! We need to get this box open."

"I can't ... I'm afraid I'll hurt someone. I might hurt you."

"Well, it's too heavy for me to levitate on my own!" Mira argued.

Just then, the wall ahead groaned.

"Looks like they had the same idea," Griff said, looking at the curly blonde hair on the other side.

"Hi, Griff!" Katrine called in a singsong voice. "I'm coming for you!"

He tried to ignore Mira's snickers behind him. The wall groaned again as Katrine aimed a weak wind spell at the top car. It teetered dangerously back and forth, which gave Griff an idea.

"Stand back," he called to Mira. "Katrine! I'm only going to warn you once. Get away from the wall!"

"Oh, sweetie, you'd like that, wouldn't you?"

Griff shrugged his shoulders. He'd tried. He would have to hope her battle clothes protected her.

"Griff ... what're you doing?" Mira asked.

"The only thing I can."

He stood in front of the box, the tall metal wall looming over them. Holding one hand in front of him, he readied his feet for the coming power. He summoned a wild gust of wind, and this time, he did nothing to try and hold it back. He commanded the vast ocean of energy directly at the box, causing it to whiz through the air and smash against the barrier of cars. Just like the chairs in the training room, it became an explosion of splinters against the unforgiving wall.

The impact sent a tremor through the vehicles, the top swaying most dangerously. It tilted toward Griff and Mira, then started to slide. The piercing metal-on-metal screeching was painful, as though needles were being shoved into his ears.

"Wind spell! Now!" Griff shouted to Mira.

Without a word, she raised her hand and sent a blast to the top car right before it could come crashing down on their side. The vehicle disappeared, now falling in Katrine's direction. Her yelp came just before the crash, and Griff peered through the smashed windshields to see her on the ground, several feet from the car.

"You okay?" Griff called, knowing she was, but feeling it polite to ask anyway.

Mira ran over and searched through the remains of the box. By the time she came back, Katrine had stood and was dusting herself off.

"Where's the orb?" Griff asked.

"No orb." She held out a piece of paper. "Only this."

"What's it say?" he asked, reading over Mira's shoulder.

She read aloud:

> *My history is bathed in mystery,*
> *A malady of unknown origins.*
> *I terrorize the whole wide world,*
> *With no measure to my portions.*
> *You may know me as a plague, a virus or a curse,*
> *You can name me if you must.*
> *But how I spread is what you're searching for.*
> *Without that word, you're dust.*

"A riddle?" Griff asked. "Seriously?"

"There's more on the back," she said.

> *I'm friend to all, both day and night,*
> *Without me, you would lose your sight.*
> *One beast sees me as their enemy*
> *A wild creature you hope not to see.*

"Great," Griff grunted. "Just what we needed. Something else to slow us down."

"Actually ... I don't think it's that bad," Mira said, studying the paper. "Let's focus on the back part. It's shorter."

Griff nodded and continued to read over her shoulder. Even in the chaos of battle, her flowery fragrance floated toward him. For a second, he allowed himself to forget everything else and enjoy the moment.

"I'm friend to all, both day and night ..." she muttered.

"Without me, you would lose your sight ..." Griff continued.

Mira remained silent, her eyes quickly scanning each line. As she did, Griff scanned the battlefield. Marth and Sadie had pulled two cars down onto their side and were levitating a third. They were using the cars to make steps. One on its own, and the second and third now stacked together. From the looks of it, there were three people from Katrine's group over by Marth and Sadie. One was staring at the box, still trying to find a way to open it, and the other two were scaling what remained of the wall. If the third person abandoned the box to focus on Griff's teammates, they would be in trouble ...

"Got it!" Mira said. "Light."

"Light?" Griff asked.

"Yes! Light," Mira said, sounding impatient. "Without light, you wouldn't be able to see. And nightstalkers are the beasts that find light as their enemy."

"Makes sense," Griff said. "How does that help us find our orb, though?"

"Well, we still have the other side to figure out ..." Mira said, staring across the field at Marth and Sadie who were now climbing their makeshift stairs. A loud *crack* echoed through the arena.

"Okay, let's do this. I think they've gotten the box open," Griff said.

They turned their attention back to the longer riddle and quickly scanned it, their lips moving as they silently read.

"Umm ... okay, okay," Mira said. "You may know me as a plague, virus, or curse ..."

"That's gotta be the Corruption."

"Yeah. But look"—she pointed to the next to last line and read aloud—"But how I spread is what you're searching for."

"So ... the answer isn't the Corruption ... it's how it spreads? How does the Corruption spread?"

"And this is why you're supposed to do Professor Erebus's homework! He just assigned us an essay on this very topic."

"Yeah, but it's not due till next week." Griff answered defensively.

"Well, aren't you glad I've already started studying."

"Okay ... but are you gonna tell me the answer or are you gonna continue telling me how smart and proactive you are?"

"Exposure, Griff. Exposure. The Corruption spreads the longer something is exposed to it."

"Oh ..." Griff paused and thought for a moment. "Yeah, I hadn't read that chapter yet."

Mira rolled her eyes. "I know."

"So ... exposure and light," Griff said. "Light exposure? That's gotta be it, right?"

"Yeah. It's got to be. But how does that help us?"

"Well ..." Griff looked around the battlefield. Marth and Sadie were holding their own with the other two mages. The third, along with Katrine, had scampered back to their altar. The two of them huddled with the altar guard around their paper. Vincent stood at attention, his eyes locked on the battle with Marth and Sadie.

"We *have* been learning light spells, right?" Griff asked.

"True. But how does a light spell help us now?" Mira asked.

"I dunno. But if the answer is light exposure, maybe we have to use a light spell ... to *expose* our orb?"

They looked at each other.

"The altar!" they shouted in unison. They dashed back to where Vincent stood. He stared at them, a look of confusion on his face.

"The orb never left the altar! It was here all along!" Griff said breathlessly.

They surrounded the empty stone structure. Vincent positioned himself at its front so their opponents couldn't see what was happening.

"Just a small one," Griff said to Mira.

She nodded and held her hand out. A small light emerged from the palm of her hand, and she waved it over the top of the altar. It was like the moon had stepped out from behind a veil of clouds. When the boundaries of Mira's light touched the storm orb, it glimmered into view, but when the light was gone, it was like clouds had covered the moon again. Mira kept the light on the orb, and Griff grabbed it. When he pulled it out of the light, he expected it to disappear, but it didn't. He clutched it protectively against his chest and Mira's light vanished.

"Okay," Mira said. "Let's head ove—" *WHOOSH!* A strong gust of wind hurled Mira through the air. While they had been preoccupied with masking their activities, the guard from Katrine's group had slipped over the wall opposite Marth and Sadie. Katrine must have traded places with him. His wind spell was significantly stronger than hers. Vincent and Griff locked eyes for a moment before Vincent said, "He's mine."

He stormed off the stone platform and marched toward the guard, whose eyes immediately filled with dread. Griff clutched the orb tighter and ran to help Mira. She dusted herself off and paused when she noticed Griff holding the storm orb out to her.

"You take it," he said.

"No. You should take it. You're stronger and faster than I am."

"But *you're* the one who needs to shine in these matches if you're ever gonna be in the king's service. Take it and place it on the altar. I'll be right beside you."

Her eyes shot from the orb to Griff, then she stared at him. But he could tell she wasn't just staring at his eyes. She was staring *into* them. She was staring into *him*, as if really seeing him for the first time. But there wasn't time to take advantage of the moment. They had a match to win. And she needed points in her favor.

"Let's go," he said. "I've got your back."

They sprinted across their half of the battlefield, past Vincent and the guard who was very much on the defensive against the giant. Mira tucked the orb under her arm as they climbed the vehicular steps and met their two other comrades who had gained control of the top of the wall.

"'Bout time you two made it here!" Marth said as he used his levitation spell to rain car parts down on the other mages.

"Ran into some complications," Griff muttered.

"Excuses, excuses," he said before he turned to Sadie. "You ready?"

"Always," she said, a hint of excitement in her eyes.

"Protect Mira!" Griff called. "Get her to the altar!"

Sadie jumped down first and slowed herself with a wind spell aimed at the ground. She turned to the opposing mages, both hands extended in front of her, and blasted them with light. It radiated intensely, giving her the extra time she needed. Without missing a beat, she swung her hands wildly, and conjured a dense, dark-blue fog. It floated menacingly in the air but seemed rather harmless. But then the thief from the streets spread her hands wide, and slowly closed them together. The fog followed her movements, compacting into a large rectangle. As it compressed in on itself, dark blue wisps that had once floated and swayed listlessly with the wind now turned nearly black and almost ... solid? It looked like a mass of dark cotton that had been stretched and frozen. Griff could see the swirls of dark clouds twirling inside, but the boundaries of the fog remained firm and intact.

Like a ghost of death, the thick dark shape hovered in front of the opposing mages whose eyes were starting to recover. With a final yell from its commander, the fog whooshed through the air and collided with the students making a loud *THUD* that could be heard across the entire battlefield.

Katrine's comrades soared through the air, but weren't thrown as far as Griff expected. The impact of something that big and fast ought to have sent them flying much farther. Sadie turned to her friends and yelled, "C'mon! What're you waiting for?"

One after another they jumped from the wall. Each time, Sadie broke their fall with a levitation spell.

"What in the nightstalker's fury was that?" Marth said as they circled around Mira.

Sadie shrugged. "Dunno. Came up with it myself one day. Looks scary, and usually sends people running. If that don't work, it hits like a thick mattress. Sends the message, but I don't gotta worry about cleaning up after it."

Griff did his best not to imagine what past circumstances might have caused Sadie to have to "clean up."

As one unit, the battlegroup marched forward to the platform where Katrine had retreated. Griff followed a few yards behind Mira, while Marth and Sadie marched in front of her, the dark wispy wall at Sadie's side like an obedient pet.

It was just Katrine, now. She stood frozen in a defensive stance just a few yards away. Sadie smiled and flung the wall of fog in her direction. Katrine dodged at just the right time. Her spells might be weak, but king's crown, she was *fast*. Marth and Sadie advanced on her, and Mira stepped forward with the storm orb under her arm.

To the right, Griff heard a creaking sound. There was barely any time to react. He saw the crushed car flying through the air toward Mira and did the only thing he could. He ran ahead, casting a shield spell over himself, then leaped between her and the car. The car was fast, but Griff was faster. With only a moment to spare, he threw out a hand and sent a wild wind spell in its direction. The car slowed but didn't stop. It hit Griff with immense force, knocked the breath out of him, and sent him skidding across the grass. As thankful as he was for the shield spell and battle clothes, pain still erupted from every part of his body.

He looked up to see the three mages who had recuperated from Sadie's spell and collectively used their levitation powers on the car. With Marth and Sadie battling an elusive Katrine, Mira was alone, trying to find a way to the altar, and had no idea they were coming for her. Griff wanted to shout for her to watch her back, but there was no air in his lungs. He could only gasp from the ground and watch as the three mages walked past him.

They closed the gap and readied their attack, but the sound of thundering footsteps caused them to hesitate and turn. They were too late. Vincent had already jumped high into the air. He had taken a play out of Sadie's book and reversed it. While she had used a wind spell to slow herself, the giant aimed his spell at the ground, perfectly timed with his jump to send him higher and allow him to close the gap faster. Seeing Vincent soaring through the air was enough to paralyze the three mages who watched the seemingly impossible feat.

The ground shook when he landed, and his hands were faster than theirs. He sent powerful wind spells in all directions, and for the second time, the three students flew across the field. Vincent joined the others from his battlegroup who were surrounding Katrine. One of her mages was incapacitated and the other three were recovering from Vincent's wind spells. The match was clearly over. Mira confidently stepped forward and placed their storm orb on the altar.

CHAPTER 21

It felt good to have his father's arm around him again. Tyrell stood taller and felt a sense of purpose bursting inside him. It didn't matter that something was off with his dad. That he seemed more distant, smiled less, or rarely showed any emotion. He was just happy that his dad was alive and they were together again.

The son of Randolph Falkenburg scanned the crowd of black cloaks. Joining Korrun Aldamund's cause seemed to require the proper attire. But he didn't care about any of that. He wasn't here for the fancy battle clothes; he was here for something bigger, something better. He didn't wear the black with the same pride as the other black cloaks, because he didn't need the clothes to make him feel like he was a part of something important. He already *knew* he was a part of something important.

He noticed some familiar faces in the crowd. Some of those faces had sat across from him at Bergots. He had known some of their names but hadn't bothered to get to know them personally. It had always seemed like a waste of time. Day after day their camp had grown as nightstalkers of all sorts brought in new recruits. Tyrell had been carried off by an enormous raven nightstalker the night he whispered Korrun's name. The large blanket it carried in its jagged claws had been comfortable enough, but eight plus hours of travel in the bundle had left Tyrell feeling like an old man whose muscles and joints had betrayed him.

Korrun and his followers had stationed themselves in one of the many towns they had conquered. It was a town that would have been very similar to Whisperspell, prior to Korrun's attack anyway. Rubble and trash lined the streets. Smoke hovered menacingly in the sky. Many buildings were nothing more than smoldering embers, but some were still standing, or at least functional. Some houses had nothing but a roof left. Signs about a future sale hung crookedly on a broken store window. Korrun had, of course, taken the largest home that was still standing. Having been born into the royal family, he was probably used to such luxuries.

It felt strange walking through the war-torn town. Nightstalkers roamed freely at night, but there were no attacks. During the day, teams of black cloaks left to hunt while the nightstalkers slept. At night, the opposite took place.

Seeing nightstalkers out during the day was even more unusual. It was one thing to see them inside the grand foyer at Bergots. That alone wasn't normal. But seeing them out in the daylight like this was beyond strange. Tyrell didn't understand how such a thing was possible, but his dad had told him that these monsters were stronger at night. Something about the darkness gave them more power. In the presence of light, these creatures lost that power, so they grew to fear the light. But under the command of Master Korrun, their fear was no longer present.

Day after day, the black cloaks huddled by the fire and took turns training. There was a training area for mages outside of town with more room for spell casting. And inside the gates they had built a training area for the non-magical black cloaks. But there was no daily agenda. It seemed as though they were waiting for something.

A few weeks passed, and Korrun's ranks continued to grow. With the brunt of winter behind them and ever increasing numbers in their camp, his new followers finally gathered in front of their master. Had it not been for the torches and hovering balls of fire crafted by the higher-ranking black cloaks—the ones whose armament had white stripes down the middle—Tyrell wouldn't have been able to see at all.

Now roughly two hundred new recruits marched behind Korrun. They had been walking for several hours, and in that time, no one spoke a single word. Nightstalkers guarded their sides. The recruits trudged up a steep hill that overlooked a small, sleepy town. Lanterns hung outside rickety houses, and two guards kept watch at the north and south gates. Windows were dark, and not a soul moved through the narrow cobblestone streets.

"These people have been told of my quest. They have received an invitation to stand right where you are, on the winning side. Not all of them are mages, but all of them were given the same opportunity. They have, however, declined my generous offer, and now we must show them what happens when you stand between us and a new and better world. We need to show all of Oriel what happens when you choose *not* to side with me. You're either with me ... or against me." Korrun's voice echoed through the night. He didn't sound angry or have a vengeful tone. He was simply stating a fact.

"You have decided to join me in my quest for something new, something better. But are you willing to give everything? Are you willing to fight for a better world?"

Tyrell's heart thumped loudly in his chest. He was afraid his dad would notice. He did his best to quiet the beating, but the adrenaline in his body knew what was coming, and it would not allow his heart any tranquility.

"Tonight, you recruits must show me that you have what it takes. You will prove your loyalty by sending a message to the world that no one turns down my offers."

Several shouts of approval came from the crowd of recruits. Energy pulsated through the group. A small knowing smile appeared on Korrun's face. The next word out of his mouth was a whisper. But somehow, it was all they needed.

"Attack."

A roar erupted from the crowd as mages rushed to the gates. Tyrell hesitated for a moment, but quickly followed. The nightstalkers that had marched beside them stayed back. This was not their fight. The guards stood no chance against the wave of black cloak recruits. Tough as they may have been, they were like twigs against a raging wildfire.

Pure chaos filled the night. The light of fire pierced the darkness. Lightning sizzled through the air until it found its mark. Screams echoed from every direction, but they were all cut short. Mages used their weapon handles to craft swords and spears and maces and ... worse. Those that weren't mages relied on their own steel.

Tyrell joined in the chaos, but their numbers greatly outmatched those in the tiny town, so he was more of an onlooker than a soldier. The flow of rushing black cloaks into the narrow streets pushed him past battle after battle and home after burning home. He dodged a clumsily thrown kitchen knife and barely took notice of the nightgown-clad woman who had thrown it. Her screams told him all he needed to know about what happened next.

He was pulled farther in, passing by the town square, which was only marked by a small community well. Brilliant lights danced in the night sky from the battle below. In any other circumstance it would have been a wonder to behold. Tonight, though ... tonight was a different circumstance.

Tyrell continued his jogging, adrenaline still coursing through him. The crowds thinned out, his feet slowed, and he paused to look around. He was close to the far side of town. The guards had left their posts and probably run to be with their families. He could run ... he could leave now while everyone busied themselves with combat.

He stood there paralyzed. A battle raged in his mind. It was a battle of right versus wrong. Good versus evil. Duty versus honor. He hadn't realized that while his focus had drifted toward his next critical decision, he had been staring into a dark alleyway where a woman clutched her two young children for dear life, as though letting go would be an immediate death sentence. They stared wide-eyed at him, doing their best not to move or make a sound.

Then out from the shadows stepped a wiry boy, maybe a year older than Tyrell. He had seen this boy walking the halls of the academy alone, but never knew his name. He had been rather unimpressive in the few Altar Storm matches Tyrell had seen. Whenever his group took the field, he remained behind or had been given a smaller, more menial task. Now, however, this boy was no longer bound by the wishes of his battlegroup. The wild look in his eyes and the swirling green energy in his hands told Tyrell that this boy felt free, and that he would use his freedom in ways he hadn't been allowed to at Bergots.

The young family trembled at the sight of this ... uncaged beast of a boy. Their tearful eyes bounced between Tyrell and this other mage, as though the two mages were on different sides. Whenever they looked at Tyrell, he saw a plea for help, a plea to save them from this untamed monster that stood before them.

But he didn't come here to be a hero. Not this way, at least. He still had a purpose. He had a mission, and nothing was going to get in his way. The battle in his mind raged on as he stared at the wild eyes taking pleasure in the fear of those who cowered before him. Within less than a second, the internal struggle was over. He wouldn't run. His mission was too important. And with any mission worth pursuing, there would always be danger. There would always be a cost. He took one last look at the family, then sucked in a lungful of air. This mission was no exception. So, he leveled his hands, aimed, and conjured the most powerful fire spell he had ever crafted.

CHAPTER 22

Griff punched Marth's leg under the table. His eyes sprang open, and he let out a small yelp that stopped Professor Erebus mid-lecture.

"Everything all right, Mr. Hayes?" His eyes narrowed at his student.

"Y-Yes sir! Ev-everything's ... all good over here, sir." He wiped the drool from the corner of his mouth.

Professor Erebus allowed the silence to grow until it was almost unbearable. His knowing eyes never left Marth's sleepy ones.

"Very good," he said.

His point was clear. Sleeping in his class was unacceptable.

When the professor had turned back to the board to write more notes, Marth glared over at Griff before whispering, "Next time, how about a gentle pat on the shoulder or somethin', okay?"

Griff rolled his eyes and tried not to look at Sadie, whose muffled laughter was about to become contagious. Contagious to everyone except Mira, whose nose was so close to her notes, Griff was afraid she might mistake it for her paper and write on it. How could she scribble so furiously like that without getting hand cramps? And what could possibly be so important in this lecture on old world technology anyway?

The technology that had survived Day Zero was almost always useless. Most required things called "batteries." Batteries had either been destroyed long ago or were no longer usable because the energy had been drained out of them or something Griff didn't really understand. The only time it ever seemed to be useful was for the people like Mr. Hayes, who were extremely specialized and could use essence manipulation to run the machines for things like book copying.

In either case, Griff didn't blame Marth for dozing off like that. After the increase in their homework and their practice time, they were all exhausted. Even now, as he rested his chin on his hand, and his elbow on the table, Griff sensed the warm and pleasing call of sleep beckoning him as well.

A hand shot into the air, interrupting Professor Erebus yet again. This time, it was Finn. Interrupting the professor from his droning was completely out of character for him. Griff had never seen the boy act so boldly. The call of sleep faded as Griff's eyes darted from Professor Erebus back to Finn. Whatever question he needed to ask must have been important. He refused to lower his hand until the teacher acknowledged him. Even the professor was baffled, as though he wasn't used to students asking questions in the middle of class.

"Yes?" Professor Erebus asked.

"P-professor, sorry. I just ... I just have to ask something."

"I know. That's why your hand is raised, yes?"

"Oh ... yes." Finn put his hand down. "Sir ... is it true that Korrun Aldamund's army marches north?"

Silence. The professor looked around the room at all the eyes staring back at him. Even Mira had stopped scribbling and placed her pencil down on the well-marked parchment.

"I don't see what that has to do with our lecture on the rise of the internet and its impact on historical inaccuracies."

The gentle spring breeze rustling the tree branches outside sounded like a hurricane compared to the silent classroom.

"W-well ... it's not, sir. But ... but my family lives north, and the articles I read in the papers say he's moving that direction, looking for followers."

Griff had never paid this close attention to his history professor before. He'd heard of Korrun's attacks, and while the last reported one was still far away from Cordelia, should he continue north, it would only be a matter of time.

"Well, as I am here, I have not found the time to ask Korrun Aldamund what his plans are ..." He stared at his student whose tear-filled eyes followed his every movement. "However, when you look at his pattern of attacks, it does seem that he is moving north, I'm sorry to say. You have every right to be concerned about your family, Mr. Wilson, but I'm afraid we must let the king do what he does best: ruling and protecting the land. That is why it is crucial for you to stay focused on your studies, so you can join in the efforts should your king have need of you."

Finn silently nodded, keeping his head down to try and hide the tears streaming down his cheeks.

"Now, as I was saying ..." Professor Erebus turned back to the board and continued writing. "The availability of information was incredibly high during this time, but so was the ability to provide your own information. This created a disturbing amount of misinformation, and people now held the ability to influence others in areas in which they themselves had no real scholarly background ..."

The professor's voice faded into the background and there was a unanimous slump throughout the room, as though the classroom itself were alive and had let out an enormous sigh. Griff looked over to Marth, whose eyelids were already starting to droop again. The only other sound besides the professor came from Mira, whose pencil was once again a blur across the parchment.

An explosion boomed across the training room. Professor Coen was once again extinguishing the flames from what remained of the chairs.

Griff wondered where the professor was getting all these chairs. He had been through so many during their weekly evening practices, and yet somehow, at each new session, there was a new pile of them ready to be blown to bits one way or another.

"Better!" his mentor said. "Fire's still a little too big, but you're getting it, Griff! You're starting to gain control. You're learning to wrestle it and make it obey you. You're still using happy memories, right?"

"Yeah," he said. "That Altar Storm match really helped too."

"Ah, yes. It would. Your first win in the arena always makes you feel ... a little more confident in your own skin, doesn't it?"

Griff smiled. "Yeah, it does."

Professor Coen brought over two unharmed chairs. Break time. The professor sat on it backward, as he always did when it was just the two of them. There was a twinkle in his eyes, but Griff couldn't figure out why. The professor waited for him to take a seat, and when he did, he smiled and spoke softly. "But there's another reason you feel more confident in your skin, isn't there, Griff?"

"What?"

"Oh, c'mon. I see the way she looks at you. And the way you look at her ..."

Griff laughed. He was doing more of that this semester. It felt strange to admit it, given the battle before winter break and Korrun's quest to take control of Oriel. But he felt like he'd finally found his place here at Bergots. His battlegroup was performing well and settling into their unique roles. He was finally starting to gain control of his powers, and people had stopped looking at him like he was a nightstalker or something. And then there was Mira ...

"Yeah, I dunno about that."

"Oh, yes, you do. Your powers tell me you do."

"Whatd'ya mean?"

"The more she pays attention to you, the better you are at controlling your powers! It means that the voice inside you that says you're not supposed to be here is getting quieter."

"Yeah, but nothing's gonna happen there. She's so focused on getting top marks and all. I'd just ... I'd get in the way of that, and I don't want to do that to her."

"Well, far be it from me to get involved in the romantic lives of my students. But I can tell she's helped *you* focus and gain control of your powers, whether she realizes it or not."

He stood up, stretched, and moved to arrange more chairs so Griff could blow them up with another mostly-controlled fireball. Before he could take another step, Griff said, "Sir?"

"Yeah, Griff?"

"That day ... during orientation. You walked up to the headmaster and said something to him."

"Aye, and like I said, it's not something I can discu—"

"It was about Korrun Aldamund, wasn't it?"

"Aye. It was."

The professor met his eyes with an unblinking stare. Curiosity sparked from his gaze, and he eyed his student carefully.

"Well, I-I won't ask what it was about. I just ask because it means ... or, well, I hope it means that you'd have more insight into what he's doing. Really, I'm hoping you have insight into where he's *going*."

His mentor sighed and rubbed his forehead with his thumb and forefinger. Then after a moment of silence, he nodded.

"As the previous commander of the battlemages, word still finds its way to me, even when I don't want it. When that happens, I make sure to bring it to Headmaster Aldamund immediately and let him handle the details of any news I receive."

"So, do you know where he's headed? Have you gotten any news on that? Is it true that he's actually headed north?"

"I'm afraid I haven't any more news than anyone else who has access to the papers."

His mentor plopped back down into the chair and faced Griff, a look of genuine concern covering his face.

"You're worried about your family, aren't you?"

"Yeah."

Professor Coen remained silent. Griff imagined that it would be hard to know what to say. How could he, the ex-commander of the battlemages, counsel his student to "not worry," when in his duties to the king, he had already seen every reason to worry? And how could he counsel Griff to "stay focused on your studies" and "trust the king" as Professor Erebus had said earlier? Errick Coen had probably never had to sit back and trust the king. He'd been the commander in charge of fighting on the king's behalf. So, he wouldn't understand what it was like to sit and wait and read books while battles raged on in the distance. A question struck Griff, one that had been swimming in the depths of his mind since Professor Erebus' class and had just now resurfaced.

"Sir?"

"Yeah?"

"Where is the king? Why hasn't he stopped his brother? Why is King Aldamund allowing Korrun to storm through Oriel like this?"

"That, Griff, was a question I received a lot as the commander of the battlemages."

His hand found his brown and gray speckled beard and absently stroked it as he thought for a moment.

"You know, the king once sent us out to investigate a series of attacks in a particular town. Once a month, a small gang of robbers and thieves pillaged this town. Never on the same day of the month, never the same business or household. Even the description of the perpetrators was never the same. But it always happened at night.

"I thought it was strange that the king would send the commander of his battlemages out with his entourage to investigate something so small. But two things happened that I'll never forget. The first was that I got to see the people who had been oppressed by these thieves. These attacks meant nothing to me. I sat in the king's castle with all the meat and bread I could ask for. But the attacks weren't so meaningless for the townsfolk. They were hungry. Their livelihood was being drained from them. And they were powerless—there was nothing they could do to stop it. That day, I learned humility and the great responsibility of my position. Protecting Oriel meant protecting its people. And every person in Oriel was worth saving.

"But a second thing happened on that trip. While my team and I were investigating the robberies, the king was nearby with another group, raiding the gang's hideout."

"What?" Griff asked.

"I thought the same thing! Turns out he'd had more intel than he'd given me. Intel that would have led us right to the den of thieves. Instead, we were the distraction. When the commander of the battlemages strolled through town, the thieves had to keep a close watch on me—which meant the king had a much easier time swooping in and taking out their leader. Their leader, who by the way, was not only responsible for the robberies in the town I'd been stationed in, but thefts in several other towns as well."

He chuckled before adding, "They never even saw him coming."

"So ... you're telling me that these towns that Korrun is attacking, they're really just a distraction?" Griff asked.

"No." He shook his head. "No, whenever the people of Oriel hurt, your king hurts. Trust me, I've seen it. What I'm saying, Griff, is that the king is always up to something good, even when we can't see it."

"Now"—he stood and walked back over to the stack of chairs and grabbed two—"we're not leaving here tonight until you get control of your fire spell. Outside of levitation, it's the bread and butter of all essence manipulation, and it's time for you to make some toast."

His mind still swimming from the story, Griff nodded, walked to his usual spot, and readied himself. As his mentor positioned the chairs, Griff thought back to his family. He remembered his birthday breakfast, and how happy he was in that moment. His mother's warm and loving smile flashed through his mind. His dad's laughter—loud and filled with joy. His childhood friend, Sylva. Even though they were three years apart, Sylva had always been a true friend to Griff. He clenched his teeth. He would trust the king. But he would also be ready to do whatever it took to protect his family and friends in Cordelia should Korrun continue on his path.

Griff narrowed his eyes and welcomed the sweet embrace of energy in his chest. As soon as Professor Coen was clear, he stretched out his hand. This time, he didn't concede to the ocean of energy like before. Usually, it was all he could do to keep the energy at bay before it crashed through the weak barriers of his mind. But this time, he didn't *allow* it to do anything, he *commanded* it. Still holding onto thoughts of his family and friends and the love and warmth they always provided, he commanded the energy to do his bidding.

An orb of fire the size of a watermelon shot from his hand and struck the first chair at its base, sending the adjacent chair flying. Effortlessly, Griff dive rolled forward and commanded another blast of fire that zoomed through the air until it collided with the second chair. Fiery splinters rained from the ceiling almost like the fireworks at the start of an Altar Storm match.

A wide-eyed Professor Coen gawked as the last of the burning pieces landed on the floor. He looked at Griff, then back at the place where the chairs had been, then back again at Griff. Slowly he nodded in approval, then clapped and said, "That ... that was much better!"

CHAPTER 23

Tyrell watched the smoldering embers of the town that had rejected Korrun's offer. The stories of past skirmishes his dad used to tell him had always seemed exciting and full of adventure. Tyrell used to imagine what it would be like to be right there, in the middle of the action. But excitement and adventure were far from what he had experienced last night. Instead, last night had been full of horror. The screams of the townsfolk would be permanently embedded in his mind.

There's always a cost, he reminded himself. He walked through the singed gates, past black cloak initiates who were telling heroic stories of their deeds in the night, and found his father waiting expectantly for him.

"Well?" his dad asked unenthusiastically.

Tyrell shrugged, not really sure what to say. "It's done."

His dad nodded and started to walk back up the hill.

"Dad!"

He turned as Tyrell closed the gap.

"Yes?"

"Can ... can we go talk somewhere?"

"We can talk here."

"I'd rather go ... somewhere else ... please," Tyrell begged.

Randolph slowly scanned the area before saying, "If we must. Lead the way."

As they walked, Tyrell did his best to make small talk. It felt awkward having to *try* to talk to his dad. They'd never had a problem in the past. Usually, his father would fill the empty space with stories from his career or drill Tyrell on different combat situations to see how he would respond. After several failed attempts at recreating those memories, he allowed the crunching of their feet on the twigs and leaves from the forest undergrowth to be the only noise between them.

Tyrell looked around. Good. They were finally alone for the first time since he'd come to camp. He didn't know where to start. In the hours spent traveling to camp, he'd planned this conversation over and over. Every word, every sentence was meticulously prepared. But as his father stared back at him with that empty expression, Tyrell's mind went blank and his words fled, leaving him speechless.

"Well ...?" Randolph said.

"Umm ... well, there's something I've been wanting to ask you. This ... this is the first time we've really had a chance to talk since, you know. Since—"

"Spit it out, boy," Randolph said.

"Since you left us!" Tyrell said, tears forming in the corners of his eyes. But he didn't care. He didn't think the hollow shell of the person in front of him did either.

"You left mom. You left me. And you never even told us why. We thought you had died! Everyone knew you had left your post, but when you never came back, we convinced ourselves that you had died. And-and here you are, heart still beating and still no answers."

"There are none to give," Randolph said conclusively.

"You abandoned your family, left us to deal with your mess for the last six years, and you can't even tell me why?" He jabbed the man in the chest with his finger. A storm was starting to brew inside him.

"We're the shame of Whisperspell, now. Did you know that? But as horrible as that's been, the worst part was not having you around anymore. And now? Now, here you are listening to your *son* tell you these things ... these horrible things that you've done to him and you don't even care. You don't even care!"

The storm inside Tyrell grew with each word. He pounded on the man's chest. The man who was once his father. The man who sat there and listened to his pathetic story, watching his pathetic tears stream down his face without showing an inkling of sadness or regret.

Tyrell's fist burned with red energy. A fireball begged to be released. Exhaustion and anger replaced what little sanity he had left. He pulled back, ready to strike again. This time it was not to emphasize his words. This time it was to bring justice. The ex-battle mage anticipated the boy's next move and casually held up a hand and generated a thick wall of ice in front of him. Before he could cast the fireball, Tyrell's hand smashed against the cold hard wall with a sickening crack. Was that the bones in his hand or the ice? Pain shot all the way up his arm and he instantly recoiled, nursing his fist with his other hand. He took a step back in surprise. The wall melted and this time Randolph stepped forward. He spoke as though ordering dinner at the tavern.

"Duty always comes first."

Randolph straightened, did an about-face, and started walking.

"If you're going to continue to be a part of Master Korrun's movement, you need to understand that fully," he called back as he marched out of the woods away from his son.

Mind numb after his conversation with ... that imposter wearing his dad's skin, Tyrell meandered behind the rest of the group as they marched back to camp. Exhaustion continued to sink deeper into his mind and body. He didn't know if it was due to his overwhelming disappointment or lack of sleep, but in either case, Tyrell felt it in every muscle of his body. He just needed to keep putting one foot in the front of the other. Right. Left. Right. Left. He couldn't let anyone see how he felt.

Halfway through their march back, they stopped by a lake to rest. Tyrell must have missed it during their night march. The walls of trees on either side of their path opened to an almost beautiful scene, an oasis of peace in the desert of war. The gray rain clouds overhead provided shade to the tired warriors, and a gentle breeze sent ripples across the black waters of the lake. His dry scratchy throat ached for a drop of water. All the black cloaks, including the ones with the stripes down their capes, readily dropped their gear and dashed to the bank for a drink. Randolph walked with more dignity, but he too knelt down, cupped the water into his hands, and sipped. Tyrell stood and watched the soldiers savor every drop and splash the cool black water on their dirty faces.

"Thirsty?"

The voice made Tyrell jump. He turned to face Korrun Aldamund, who was smiling at him. That smile did nothing to ease his troubled mind.

"M-Master Korrun. Sorry. I didn't hear you coming."

"Good," he said. "It's a skill that will prove most useful in the days ahead. So ... are you thirsty?"

He stared at Tyrell, watching his every move and every expression, as if waiting to see how he would respond.

"I ... am. Very."

"Well, have a drink. The water is refreshing."

"Thank you, sir," Tyrell said. His heart was yet again pounding against his chest.

He slowly walked over to the edge of the water, away from the rest of the black cloaks, and knelt. He looked at the distorted picture of the person staring back at him. Through the rippling of the black waters, he saw, not a boy, but a man. A young man, sure, but a man, nonetheless. A man who'd seen and now done terrible things, maybe, but who had done them in the name of duty and honor.

He reached his hands to the waters, but just before they broke the surface, he heard a cry behind him.

"There he is!"

He turned to see another mage, somewhere around his age, walking toward him and pointing.

"Him! He's the one who killed Liam!"

A few other black cloaks followed behind the boy. He marched up to Tyrell and swung wildly, but Tyrell was faster. He easily sidestepped the boy's fist and sent his own fist into the young mage's gut. A knee to the face was all it took to end the confrontation with this boy, but he didn't know what he was going to do with the other followers who were starting to surround him.

"Enough!" Korrun said, parting the onlookers until he reached Tyrell. He looked from Tyrell to the boy on the ground holding his bloody nose.

"What's going on here?" he demanded.

One of the black cloaks who had marched over with the boy stepped forward.

"He killed Liam last night, Master Korrun. That's what Theo says, anyways."

"Is this true?" Korrun asked, looking at Theo who was now sitting up, but still in no shape to stand. Tears streamed down his face mixing with the blood and snot that came from his nose. He glanced up at his master and merely nodded.

"Well?" Korrun turned his attention to Tyrell.

"It's true, sir. It was my fire that consumed Liam."

An outburst of anger came from the onlookers.

"But," Tyrell yelled, silencing their cries, "it was Liam's *pride* that killed him."

"What do you mean?" Korrun asked.

"He got in the way of my kill," Tyrell shrugged. "I think he wanted a higher body count or something. He tried to kill someone that was clearly mine. I shot fire, and he stepped in the way."

"And what of the person you tried to kill?"

"They received the same fate, Master Korrun. If you'd like, sir, I could fetch their bodies and bring them to you. If ... if I could find them with what little remains in that town."

Korrun Aldamund paused, looking from Theo to Tyrell. Silence filled the air as everyone held their breath.

"No need," he said at last. "But I'll not have any more infighting, you hear?" He looked at Theo, who could only nod his head. "And next time you want to make an accusation like that, bring it to your ranking officer."

Korrun turned his attention to Theo's friends. "That goes for the rest of you who tried to support this nonsense as well. Save the fight for those who stand against us. There is still much to do. And you," he brought his gaze to Tyrell, "I'll make sure to keep a close eye on you as well."

"Yes, Master Korrun. As you wish." Tyrell bowed low in respect.

The leader of the black cloaks turned to walk away. As he did, the crowd parted once more, and he called back to those attending to Theo.

"Leave him be. No healing magic. I want him to remember what happens when you start fights within my army."

The crowd left. Theo's accomplices had carried him over to his pack and helped him with his things. Tyrell eyed the army of black cloaks and nightstalkers and gritted his teeth. There was nobody he could trust now, not even his dad. He'd have to distance himself and watch his back. He'd sleep on the outskirts of camp if he had to. Whatever it took. He wasn't going to let anyone stand in the way of what he had come to do.

CHAPTER 24

Large hands reached through the darkness and grabbed Griff. Was this another dream? His eyes popped open, and he grabbed his assailant's arms. Definitely not a dream. A hand cupped his mouth before he could yell. He tried to kick and flail, but he was tangled in his bedsheets. His eyes struggled to focus on the person at his bedside, but the shadows of the night hid their face.

"Shhh! It's me, Griff!" came a familiar whisper. "Stop fighting, and I'll let go, okay?"

Griff nodded, and the hand was removed from his mouth. He rubbed his eyes and did his best to sit up.

"Professor Coen?" Griff whispered. "What're you doing here?"

The professor leaned in and his face, which now glowed in the moon-light, appeared uneasy.

"I've got some bad news. But before I say anything else, I need you to promise me you'll listen to everything I'm about to tell you. Okay? Promise?"

Griff nodded slowly, fear creeping into his heart.

"I just got word ... it looks like Korrun's army is headed toward Cordelia," Professor Coen said.

A surge of adrenaline hit Griff and he wrestled with the sheets once again, but Professor Coen grabbed him with one strong hand and pushed him back down.

"Listen!" he said.

Everything in him wanted to fight his mentor so he could find a way to reach his family. But he had made a promise. Griff sighed and nodded again.

"If I leave right now, I can probably make it in time to warn your family and get them to safety. I just wanted you to know what was happening before I left. If you'd found out on your own, I figured you'd probably try to sneak outta here by yourself and that wouldn't go so well. But now you know. I'm gonna take care of this, so you need to stay put and trust me when I say I'm gonna take care of your family."

"Sir," Griff said. "Please let me come with you."

"Absolutely not. I'm not sneaking a student out of the castle and taking him across the country, you hear?"

"I'm begging you. Let me come with you. I won't be a bother, I promise."

"I'm not worried about you bothering me. I'm worried about your safety."

"I can take care of myself!" Griff insisted. "What's the point of all this training if I can't use it to protect my own family?"

Griff paused, sleep and frustration muddling his mind. There was no way Professor Coen was going to leave without him tonight.

"Sir ... why are you doing this anyways? Why would you help me and my family like this?"

"Let's just say all that time spent in the training rooms has made me a little biased, all right? Let's just leave it at that."

"There's more to it than that, though, isn't there? Why are you helping *me*?"

The professor paused and stumbled over his words for a moment, as though debating what to say next. He heaved a heavy sigh. "I've been in your shoes, Griff. Years ago, while I was out on duty, I learned that my town was under attack. I was too far away, and ...and I couldn't help my wife. She ..."

The professor allowed the silence to say what words couldn't.

"I wish someone who was *able* to protect her ... well, I wish they would have."

"If you were in my shoes ..." Griff started, trying his best to tread carefully, "and it was your wife in Korrun's path ... would you let someone else go rescue her? Or would you do anything and everything to make sure you could be there as well?"

Professor Coen sighed, the shadows from the moonlight making him look twice as old.

"You know the answer to that, Griff."

"Then let me come with you! You've seen me in the training room. You've seen my spellcasting. You've seen my essence crafting abilities. My control has improved so much over the last two months."

"But you wouldn't be going into combat. You would be going to deliver a message."

"True. Then there's no sense worrying about my safety, is there?"

Griff stared into his mentor's eyes, brows furrowed in fierce concentration. His heart was beating like a madman's. He understood that he was in the middle of the most important negotiation of his life, and he wasn't going to lose.

"Fine. But Griff ... you're not ready to fight this army. I'm not offering you an opportunity to battle. I'm offering you an opportunity to help your family get to safety. Understood?"

Griff nodded vigorously. "Understood."

"And"—the professor held up a hand before Griff could jump out of his bed—"you will listen to every word I say on this trip. There's always the chance it could get dangerous, you hear? Do exactly as I say, or I'll turn us around and your family will be left to fend for themselves. Deal?"

"Deal."

Griff looked around the room that he had come to call home. He silently watched Vincent's chest rise and fall. How he wished that it was *his* chest rising and falling and that this really *was* all just a dream or another a strange nightmare. And, like Vincent, he would wake up the next morning with a whole weekend of rest and relaxation before him—his most anxious thought being the Altar Storm battle two weeks away.

But knowing that his family was on Korrun's projected path of death and destruction was no dream. Rest and relaxation were a luxury he would have to reject until the mission was complete. He looked toward Marth's bed and found his friend's eyes open, quietly watching him and the professor. Their eyes locked for a moment before Marth slowly nodded as if to say, "You're doing the right thing."

Like a thief in the night, Griff quickly and quietly snatched the bare necessities for his trip while Professor Coen left for the stables. Glancing at the nightstand next to his bed, he saw his handle in its special holster. Griff stopped and stared for a moment. There wasn't supposed to be a fight, but ... he had to be prepared for anything. He grabbed it and gently placed it in his bag before he could change his mind.

Griff continued to tiptoe around the room, pausing for a moment to meet Marth's eyes again. "You heard all that, right?"

Marth sat up and whispered, "Yeah, mate. I did."

"So, you'll tell our group?"

"You know I will. Hey, Griff"—he reached out his hand toward his friend and shook it—"be safe out there, all right? We need you in the next Altar Storm match."

"I'll do my best. See you in a couple of days ... hopefully."

The hinges of the door creaked as it opened and shut, causing all of Griff's muscles to tense. He sneaked past the dark common room and out into the castle before anyone else could see him. The lifeless hallways were as silent as death, which made Griff's pounding heartbeat sound to him like a giant's footsteps. He generated a small light to guide him through the dark castle, snuffing it out at the smallest noise. Should any of the professors catch him out and about, he'd have no excuse for wandering the castle with a large pack. It would probably look like he was off to become one of Korrun's followers.

As he passed by the study lounges, all but one were dark. Orange, flickering light lit the last doorway and Griff paused for a moment. Only one person would be in the study lounge at this late hour.

He extinguished his light spell and stepped into the room. The large fireplace crackled and popped, its flames illuminating a large open book and the beautiful girl thumbing through its pages.

"I should've known you'd be up this late studying," Griff half whispered.

Mira smiled up at him. But when she saw his pack, her smile disappeared, and she furrowed her eyebrows.

"Where are you going so late at night?" she demanded.

Griff quickly told her everything. Her face fell when he finished and she looked at him quietly, her eyes staring into his. After taking a moment to process, she closed her book, ignoring its loud *thud*, and walked over to Griff. His heart jumped to his throat when her arms slid around him and squeezed tight. At first his arms didn't want to move; he was too stunned by her sudden boldness. But then he commanded them, and they wrapped around her as well. She rested her head on his shoulder and they stood in the common room, momentarily forgetting everything around them. Mira pulled back and gazed into his eyes.

"Come back to me, Griff Driscoll."

She brought her head close, her face nothing more than a silhouette against the bright backdrop of the crackling fireplace. Her sweet jasmine scent danced before him like dandelion seeds in the spring wind. She gently placed her warm lips on his. Electricity sparked through his body, and he felt invincible, as though nothing in the world could ever tear him from her. The magic that swirled inside his body was nothing more than a drizzling rain in comparison to the waterfall of love that he now felt.

His hand lightly caressed the side of her face, and he felt a tear slide down her cheek. He pulled away and wiped it with his thumb.

"I'll be back, Mira. I promise," he said. "We'll beat him to Cordelia, and there'll be nobody there when he comes."

"You'd better."

She gave him one final embrace, an embrace that Griff never wanted to abandon. But his family needed him now more than ever.

"I'll see you soon," Griff said, his heart demanding he stay, his mind demanding he go.

As he walked the rest of the way to the stables, his heart swelled with joy and ached with pain. His mind reeled to grasp the reality of what had just happened. It felt like a dream, but her lingering jasmine scent assured him that it had been real.

"Finally," Professor Coen said as Griff entered the stables.

He tightened the remaining straps on the warg in front of him and stroked its spine. It closed its eyes and rumbled low with approval.

"Sorry," Griff mumbled. "I had ... something to take care of first."

Professor Coen paused and looked intently at his blushing student.

"Don't wanna know. Not gonna ask," he said.

Griff eyed the two wargs that were packed and saddled.

"Am I riding on one of those things by myself?" he asked.

"Yep," the professor answered as he threw a piece of raw meat in the air. The warg snagged it and swallowed without chewing. "This one here's Magnus." He pointed to the other, slightly smaller one whose fur was more of a tan in comparison to Magnus's darker gray. "And this one is Kindra. She's a real sweetie. Until she's not."

"Uh ... Professor, I don't know how to ride a warg."

"It's easy. If she allows you to jump on her back, then you're golden. Magnus here is the pack leader," he said, patting his warg on the head. "All you have to do is stay on."

"If she allows me on her back ..." Griff said. "That's all?"

"Aye. Just walk up to her and stroke her fur. Don't show any fear, but don't show any aggression either."

"Right ..." Griff said, watching as the two wargs ate their meal. "Are you sure we can't just portal to Cordelia?"

"Sure would be a lot easier if we could. Unfortunately, that's not how it works."

"Why not? We walk through the portals from Bergots to Solastran all the time. And it only takes you and Professor Strickland to open it."

"Yeah, but we're only opening the doors to a hallway that's already established. The amount of magic it takes to open the door is tremendous. Can you imagine what it would take to establish a hallway in the first place? And that's just down this mountain. I'm sorry to say, but it's impossible to craft a portal that could reach all the way to Cordelia."

Professor Coen reached down into a large wooden bucket. "Here," he said, handing him a slab of meat. "Food always helps."

Griff's shoulders sank in frustration and disappointment, but he grabbed the food and slowly walked up to Kindra, whose head was now buried in a large water trough. When he had gotten close enough for her to smell the meat, she pulled her head out and stared back at him with curiosity in her eyes. Considering she was almost as tall as him, and her fangs were the equivalent of an arsenal of daggers, Griff doubted if he could withhold his fear and hoped the peace offering would be enough.

"Here you go," he said, fighting to keep his voice from trembling. "Kindra, right? Let's be friends, eh?"

She stared at his outstretched hand and the bloody meat inside his clenched fist, then looked back to Griff. It took all his might to stand still when the beast took a step toward him and reached down and gently took the meat out of his hands. Griff let out of a whoosh of air that he didn't realize he had been holding in.

"See? You're all right. Now, let's go. We've got a long flight ahead of us."

The professor hopped on Magnus's back with ease, placed his feet in the stirrups, and grabbed the reins, while Griff attached his pack to the back of the saddle. Slowly and awkwardly, he placed one foot in the stirrup before swinging his other leg across the deadly beast. It missed the stirrup and he slid to the side, grasping Kindra's fur for support. The mistake could have ended him, but she merely rumbled in annoyance, allowing Griff to steady himself.

Ignoring Professor Coen's amused look and pretending nothing had happened, Griff asked, "It'll be about ... what, ten, eleven hours or so?"

"Nine," the professor answered.

"Nine?"

"Aye, that's what I said."

"But it took the king and me almost eleven hours to get to Solastran."

"Aye, but we'll be taking a different route. One that's ... well, one that's more dangerous. I imagine the king was trying to avoid that particular ... obstacle, when he was carrying you with him."

"What obstacle is that?" Griff asked.

"You'll see soon enough. Time to go."

CHAPTER 25

The cool spring wind whipped through Griff's hair as they launched into the clear night sky. The stars twinkled brightly and the moon shone proudly, bathing the ground below them in a pale glow. Griff bent low against his warg, hands tightly grasping the leather straps around her side. The last time he had ridden one, he'd had the king to steady him. This time, however, he was forced to learn on the fly.

When Kindra had reached a high enough altitude, her wings stopped their fierce beating and shifted to a smoother rhythm to maintain their elevation. Griff's breathing normalized as he grew accustomed to the gentle ups and downs with every flap. He turned and looked back at the Bergots castle atop an enormous mountain and the beautiful town of Solastran that grew smaller with every passing minute. Most windows in the castle were dark, save for a few that flickered with the light of candles or fireplaces. Griff imagined that one of those rooms housed Mira, who would have faithfully returned to her studies.

His heart sank with longing, reliving every second of their last meeting. How he longed to stay in that room with her. How he longed to be with her every second he was awake. *I'm coming back, Mira.*

Eventually, the castle and the mountain faded into the distance. Thankfully, Griff didn't have to worry about steering his warg or figuring out which direction they were going. He merely needed to stay on the flying beast while she followed her pack leader. Professor Coen periodically glanced back to make sure Griff hadn't fallen off and would give him a nod or a smile to reassure him that everything was all right.

Slowly, the bright twinkling stars began to dim, and the dark night sky lost its battle to the growing sea of orange that radiated from the rising sun. The vast stretches of land, valley, forest, and farmland continued to amaze him. His head swiveled, his hungry eyes insatiably ingesting the beautiful landscape in every direction. Since they were taking a different route to Cordelia, Griff saw magnificent scenery he had never seen before, as well as parts of the land that had been scarred by the Corruption. Rolling fields of bright green grass marred by deadly black streaks. Forests containing dark and disfigured trees and bushes that looked like angry shadows. Ponds whose black surfaces seemed to soak in the light rather than reflect it.

Rarely did they fly close to civilization, but whenever they did pass a town that was near areas marked by the Corruption, they found it abandoned. In most of those towns, the traces of buildings once inhabited were now nothing more than large pieces of rubble. Still, Griff noticed remnants from life before Day Zero and the plague. Rusted swing sets gently swayed in the breeze, waiting for children who would never return. Dirty cars sat on flat stretches of concrete in front of destroyed homes. Shops and taverns that were once filled with customers were now dark, save for the patches of sunlight streaming through the broken windows.

Griff grieved for the buildings and homes that remained intact, left to watch the world pass them by. He wondered about the stories, experiences, and histories each of those buildings must have had that would never be told, since there were no inhabitants left to share it. He was flying over history that had been silenced.

As midday approached, the sun blazing hot, Professor Coen and Griff sought a brief refuge under the canopy of a large oak tree. The narrow spring next to it was crystal clear, its waters gently rippling over a bed of smooth stones. Magnus and Kindra rumbled in pleasure as they dipped their snouts into the cool water; Griff could understand why. Riding had taken a toll on his body already. His joints and muscles were stiff. He imagined even well-trained beasts such as these enjoyed a break after traveling.

Knowing it was just a matter of time before they continued their journey, Griff paused to lie on the soft undergrowth of the oak tree. Feelings of guilt flooded him as he welcomed the break. *You're not gonna be any help to the professor or your family if you don't rest*, he thought.

After Professor Coen had finished munching on an apple, he stood up and looked north.

"Look," he said, pointing toward the sky.

Griff stood, stretched, and walked over to his mentor.

"See those dark clouds up ahead?"

"Yeah," Griff answered.

He'd almost missed them. Barely above the horizon was a point in which the sky darkened. It was like a long, thin, stretched-out shadow with no end.

"A ... storm?"

"Aye, but not a normal storm. A corruption storm."

"Corruption storm? I don't understand."

"Well ... remember, the Corruption is a magical plague that infects all of nature. *All* of nature. That's where the nightstalkers came from. That's why we see those black marks in the forests and fields we flew over. Well, weather is not exempt from this curse either. They're rare ... but corrupted storms do exist."

He walked over to the stream and splashed cool water on his face.

"So, this is the obstacle you mentioned earlier, huh?" Griff said, trailing behind.

"Aye."

"Well ... what's a corruption storm like?"

The professor wiped the water off his face with his sleeve and said, "Well, each one's different. *This* storm has been here for a very long time. Dunno how long, but it's stayed in this region causing all types of trouble ever since its corruption. Its lightning is unpredictable; its rains acidic. There's a tornado at the center that acts as if it's almost alive. And that's just the start."

"How do you know all this?" Griff asked.

"I traveled much of Oriel in my days," he said. "I've experienced a lot of things. Some good. Some bad."

"So, I take it you know how to get past this ... obstacle, then?"

"I've done it before. Plenty of times, actually. But like I said, it's unpredictable. If we do what I've always done, which is to stay high above the clouds, I think we'll be just fine."

"You think?" Griff asked.

"Aye. I think."

"What happens if you're wrong?"

He shrugged, "Well, then we gave it our best shot, I suppose."

Griff paused, allowing the reality of the situation to sink in. He was going to have to fly a warg *over* a corruption storm and hope he didn't die.

"Just so you know, Griff, it's okay to turn back now if you don't want to risk it. I mean, don't get me wrong, I'll be barking mad that I wasted my time bringing you out here, but I will take you back if you want. However, if you want to try and get to Cordelia before Korrun does, this is the only way."

"Now," he patted Griff's shoulder as he walked by and began packing up their scattered supplies. "Which direction are we headed?"

Griff sighed. "Well ... King's crown! I guess we're flying over the stupid storm or whatever."

The professor smiled, "Thought so."

The long shadow grew with each flap of Kindra's wings. After an hour of flight, the black clouds seemed to have risen higher and stretched even farther; its churning mass was like an impassable wall of storm. Griff watched purple lightning zip in and out of the black wall as though it was a hand snatching something out of the sky. The booms of thunder echoed for miles. It was an ominous scene that only grew more intense as they flew closer.

To Griff's relief, they finally began their ascent. They were close now, and the looming corruption storm produced a growing fear in his heart. The thundering grew louder, and amid the crash that followed the bright purple light, Griff heard it. It was faint, but inside the boom was a strange sound. They continued their climb, but he shut his eyes and listened intently to the thunder. Bright purple flashed across his dark vision, and the sound that came after it filled him with terror. Crackling, sizzling sounds joined in the chorus of the crashing thunder followed by the unmistakable screams of a woman. Chill bumps erupted all over his skin. Another flash of light and a man hollered as if in excruciating pain.

High above the acid-rain-stained earth, Griff's eyes darted back and forth, searching for the sources of those screams. They hadn't quite crossed the threshold of the storm ... were there still people on the ground who needed help? Ahead, Professor Coen turned to face his student. Their eyes met for a moment, and Griff must have communicated his thoughts in the look he gave his mentor. The professor, unable to speak due to the deafening noise, shook his head, pointed forward, and mouthed, *Keep going!*

Guilt flooded Griff. If there were people who needed help and he passed them by, he might as well have discarded his honor. But he was unable to control Kindra, and the furious sounds of the storm grew louder, making it impossible to argue his case with Professor Coen. So he gripped the reins of his warg tighter and allowed himself to be carried high above the storm, helplessly listening to the screams and pleas of the men, women, and children that accompanied the lightning.

Just before the ground was completely veiled by the clouds, Griff looked ahead and saw where the chaos was strongest; in the middle of the storm, where the lightning strikes were most prevalent, was a spinning column of storm clouds. A fierce tornado that churned and spun with grace and horror, like a dance of death. Black clouds swirled with blinding speed. Every now and again, purple lighting would strike the deadly column, sending flashes of light spiraling down the eerie funnel. It looked as though the years of a corrupted tornado swirling in place had created a large hole. It was as though it were digging itself into the ground, searching for more debris to add to its never-ending spiral.

Soon, the clouds overtook his view of the storm, and the two mages continued to fly high above the black canopy. The air was thin, making the very act of breathing a chore. As if in open rebellion, the sun shone brightly overhead, but its rays were swallowed by the darkness and corruption below. From this vantage point, Griff could see a pattern to the clouds. They swirled gently in a circular motion, as though the tornado was pulling the clouds into its dance, only to send them back out to the edge again. And, as promised, though they were high above the storm, lightning would burst from the clouds, like deadly crooked hands trying to reach them. Thankfully, their arms were too short.

Professor Coen and his warg paused, waiting for Griff's warg to come beside him. They were close enough now to have a conversation, but Griff didn't wait to hear what the professor had to say.

"What in the nightstalker's fury was that?"

The professor nodded. A look of sadness filled his eyes.

"Were there people down there? People who needed our help? Why didn't we stop and do something?"

"Because they were already dead, Griff."

Griff shook his head. "No, I won't believe that. We could've saved them!"

"No. You don't understand. They were already dead, Griff."

Griff opened his mouth to speak, but nothing came. Confusion had paralyzed his tongue, and silence took the place of his words.

"Many people have died in this storm. And when they die, this corruption robs them of their final farewells."

"You ... you mean ...this storm stole the screams of those it killed?" Griff asked.

The professor nodded sadly. "Aye."

"Oh ..." Griff said. Chill bumps crawled over his skin once again.

"The dead's final moments are relived in the storm's thunder. They speak to us of its terror. The sad part is"—he looked around at the endless ocean of black clouds below them—"The sad part is how many different voices you hear speaking of its terror. We would do well to listen."

The constant booms of thunder that had echoed in the background of their conversation suddenly started to swell in volume. The clouds that had once drifted gently toward the center started to rise and fall like waves in the ocean. With each passing second the storm waves swelled higher, growing more intense. The lightning, as if sensing its opportunity at the peak of every wave, shot out into the bright sky, grasping for its prey.

Fear overtook the professor's sad demeanor. His eyes grew wide, and he yelled, "We have to go! Now!"

Magnus spun and darted upward. Kindra followed without warning. Griff's body jerked in response, and his hand tried to grasp at the reins but slipped. The next second felt like an eternity, trapped in time without any chance to respond. Griff felt his body slide across the saddle. The shift in his weight dislodged his left foot from the stirrup. A scream escaped his throat. He was falling. For a moment, he felt weightless as his body flew through the sky. His scream was cut short when his body jerked again, and he dangled by his right foot, which had been tangled in one of the straps.

The clouds continued to churn. The waves reached higher and higher. The booms of the thunder and the cries of the dead were intensifying. Griff tried to reach for the saddle, to grab hold of anything he could, but Kindra was trying to stay out of reach of the lightning, making it near impossible to climb back on. A bolt of brilliant purple shot just past them. The flying beast darted to the side to avoid a second strike, but in doing so, freed Griff's only remaining connection.

Fear consumed him as his body fell uncontrollably through the sky. The dark clouds were ready to swallow him whole and unite his screams with those of the dead. He saw Kindra turn and dive toward him. Hope tried to convince him that there was still a chance, but reality told him that the beast would be too slow. The warg beat her wings furiously, dodging streaks of purple along the way, but Griff was falling too fast.

Suddenly, a shadow appeared. For a moment, he thought the clouds had finally taken him. Then he felt a hand grasping one of his, slowing his fall. Professor Coen pulled him onto Magnus, and the beast climbed back into the sky.

The storm grew angrier and swelled with ferocity. Lightning continued to flash toward them, but the professor steered his warg with precision and mastery, Kindra following obediently behind. Griff stayed low against the mount and held tightly onto the reins, vowing to never let them go again. His heart beat hard against his chest, a rhythm of gratitude and fear.

"Up ahead!" Professor Coen growled.

Griff sat up and looked. There it was … the other side of the storm. They were close to the edge. He looked back at his mentor, whose eyes were locked on the boundary of the storm.

"Let's go!" he shouted at Magnus.

They flew with speed and agility, swaying right, dodging left, and climbing higher. Up ahead, Griff could see the green grass that the corrupted storm and its acid rain hadn't touched. The chorus of booms and screams from the thunder continued to grow. It was as if the storm was chasing them, getting angrier with every second they remained in flight. Closer … they were getting closer. *Almost there. Almost there!* Griff gritted his teeth.

Then a large bolt of purple lightning burst through the clouds and hit Magnus's wing, followed by a crack of thunder so loud it seemed to split the very sky. The warg roared in pain, and they dropped several feet before he regained control. Griff struggled to hold on as Magnus fought to stay airborne. With every awkward flap, the warg groaned, as though pushing through the excruciating pain.

"You got this!" the professor screamed to his beast. "C'mon now, Magnus! You can do this! Get us to the other side!"

The warg continued to slowly dip closer to the storm, but its boundaries and the lush green grass on the other side crawled nearer and nearer. With a final growl, Magnus closed his eyes and his head fell forward. Griff's stomach jumped to his throat and he held on tight as the beast fell. Kindra dove underneath and steadied them. She grunted with effort and pushed her way forward, but the immense weight she carried pulled them closer to the ground.

"Hyah! You've got this! You've got this!" the professor screamed in encouragement as they descended into the black clouds.

Fear gripped Griff when the storm overtook them. He felt the burning of the rain on his skin and swirled his hands around to cast a protective wind sphere around them. They were falling. Slow as it might be, they were locked in a controlled fall that would probably send them to the ground under the Corruption storm.

They passed an old tree whose thick black limbs reached up and smashed into them, dislodging Magnus and his riders from Kindra. They all fell through the air, crashed through the final wall of rain and storm, and landed on the grass.

CHAPTER 26

Griff took a step and groaned as Magnus stumbled forward, placing even more of his unwelcome weight on the boy's shoulders. The green grass wasn't as lush as he'd expected. His aching bones and muscles attested to that fact, though he knew it could have been worse. Landing on grass was better than landing on rocks. But the impact was intense, and the two wargs had taken the full brunt of it. Since Magnus had a damaged wing and an injured leg, the two mages were forced to help him walk farther from the corrupted storm, lest the lightning strikes find a way to attack from the boundary's edge. Kindra, her beautiful tan coat now stained with blood, limped along slowly behind them.

Bent low to support the enormous wing draped across his back, Griff was unable to look back at the storm, but the sounds of furious wails thundered behind them, as though the storm was angry that they had made it to the other side.

By the time the ragged group stopped and collapsed onto the grass, the screams of the dead withdrew back into the distant booms of thunder. No one spoke a word, but each mage savored every silent breath they took, knowing how close they had come to breathing their last. Finally, after staring into the angry storm clouds for some time, Griff sat up and broke the silence.

"We ... made it," he said.

"We almost didn't."

"Yeah. We almost didn't."

Especially me, Griff thought. He knew that the sensation of falling through the sky and the image of the dark corrupted storm clouds raging below him would haunt his dreams for the rest of his life. As if he needed any other nightmares.

"Thanks for saving me back there," he said.

A small grin appeared on Professor Coen's face before he said, "Yeah, well, if you die, I'm in big trouble."

"Gee, thanks," Griff laughed. "I'll try to stay alive just so you don't get fired."

"Perfect," the professor chuckled as he walked back toward the wargs who were recovering in the grass nearby.

Magnus had folded his wing and was furiously licking the enormous hole in it. Kindra lay on her good side with her eyes closed. Her breaths were heavy; she was clearly in a lot of pain. Professor Coen approached her cautiously and very tenderly touched her bloody side. She yelped, and her eyes jerked open.

"I'm sorry, pretty girl. You're really hurting, aren't you?"

Kindra groaned, rested her head on the grass, and closed her eyes.

The professor clicked his tongue. "Thought as much."

He examined her further, this time without making contact, before walking over to Magnus, who barely acknowledged him. The hole in his wing from the lightning strike absorbed most of his attention. Images of Griff's dad on their couch frantically trying to rip the bandages off his leg after the nightstalker attack flashed before Griff's mind. He wondered if the warg was having similar sensations.

"Well, I'm no medic, but I think Magnus's leg is broken. And his wing's not much better either. I'd say he's gonna be out of commission for a while."

"What about Kindra?"

"Well ... she took a considerable blow. That tree got her good, and she crashed pretty hard." He paused for a moment, thinking through their options. "Healing magic's gonna take some time to kick in, but I think we can make it with just Kindra. We'll all rest for an hour or so. That should give her time to heal enough to get us the rest of the way to Cordelia, and Magnus ought to be healed enough that he won't be completely defenseless out here," Professor Coen said.

"You mean, we're just gonna leave him?" Griff asked.

"Time is our biggest enemy right now, Griff. We'll stay just long enough for Kindra to travel, and then we're off. By that time, Magnus's leg ought to be much better, and then he'll be able to stand his ground should he need it. Won't be able to fly, but he'll be able to fight."

"So ... we're just setting him free, then?"

The professor laughed. "He's always been free. Loyalty is at the heart of every warg. Once he's better, he'll find us. Trust me."

"And ... what about my family?" Griff asked, afraid to know the answer.

Professor Coen sighed and remained quiet for a long time, his eyes darting back and forth as if deep in thought.

"It's gonna be close. Groups of people are a lot slower than just two. Rumors say Korrun has a couple thousand following him, but they're not in any hurry. My guess is, they're making camp right now and will attack at night. Seems to be his way of doing things."

He shielded his eyes and looked up toward the mid-afternoon sun.

"Looks like we've got a couple of hours till sunset."

"And how much farther till Cordelia?"

"A couple of hours."

Griff sighed in frustration and pounded his fist into the grass. "We could've taken the normal route."

Professor Coen eyed his student. "Aye. We could have."

He turned to face Griff.

"Knowing what we know now, yes, we should have taken the way around the storm. But *not* knowing what we know now ... which direction would you have chosen?"

Griff thought about it for a moment. It was hard not to feel biased in the midst of his frustration. After a moment of hard internal reflection, he sighed again. "I would've taken this route."

"I know how you feel, Griff," the professor said. "We're so close, and now we might not make it. You've got family on the line, I know. I want to get you there as quickly as possible."

Professor Coen stood and swiped the grass off the back of his legs and stared off into the storm.

"If it makes you feel any better, I've *never* seen the storm do something like that. It was like ... it was *alive*, and it was hunting us. I've flown over that thing more times that I have fingers and toes, and I've never seen the likes of that."

"No. Definitely doesn't make me feel better," Griff said, laying back on the grass and closing his eyes. "Not one bit."

It took two hours before Kindra was finally able to fly again. The professor gave Magnus a gentle pat and said, "Come find us later," before he joined Griff on Kindra's back, and they set off once again.

Though it seemed as if Kindra understood the sense of urgency Griff and Professor Coen felt, she still flew slower. She was recovered enough to fly, but not fully healed. And it didn't help that she now carried extra baggage. Over the next couple of hours, both mages watched the sun intensely as it sank lower and lower toward the horizon. When its final edges could no longer be seen and the last of its orange rays were being chased away by the darkness, Griff perked his head up and pointed.

"There!" he yelled. "There's Porvalla!"

Off in the distance, barely noticeable lights from a town smaller than Cordelia flickered in the direction he pointed.

"Once a year, my dad and I would travel there to sell off his wares. It was a little under a half day's walk from Cordelia."

"Then we'll get to your family in under an hour," the professor said confidently.

Griff's stomach tightened at the professor's response. They were so close. There was still time. His eyes were fiercely trained ahead, looking for any signs of his hometown, but it was too dark, and the moon hadn't risen high enough yet. The final rays of light had finally disappeared over the horizon, and the first of the stars twinkled into existence. His gaze drifted to the sparkling canopy above. Under different circumstances, he would have done anything to stop and bask in the glory of the heavens. Something about the vastness of the sky always made him feel so small and insignificant.

But something was wrong. In front of them, stars that were once present began to disappear, as though something had snuffed out their light. Griff's eyes strained and fought to gain focus. When they did, his heart sank to his belly.

"Smoke!" he cried. "Up ahead! Smoke!"

The professor hollered, and Kindra beat her wings at a pace Griff didn't think was possible given her state. Griff was confident that his worst fears had come true. The scent of charred wood filled the air. Fire shot to the sky as buildings burned. Blue, green, yellow, and red spells flashed across the streets. They flew closer to the edge of town. He could hear screams coming from the people ... *his* people. Professor Coen finally landed near the town's main gates that were broken beyond repair.

He spun to face Griff, and their eyes locked. Griff was ready for him to try and tell him to dismount and stay put while he went inside to help. Professor Coen searched his student's eyes for a moment, his brows furrowed in deep thought. He looked down and huffed before looking back at Griff.

"You promise to do *exactly* as I say?"

Griff nodded, but surprise stole his words.

"I need to hear you say it, Griff!" he growled. "Do you promise?"

"I-I promise."

"Good," he said, pulling out a sword handle and crafting a large, curved blade. "Trust me now, Griff, and *watch your back.*"

Griff set his jaw, pulled out his handle, and crafted a brilliant blue blade, long and deadly. Violence had never been something he pursued, but as he watched the town he had been raised in burn, he silently promised his blade that it would see action tonight. Griff tightened his thighs against the warg as it sprinted toward the battle. One hand wielded his sword, the other remained free to cast spells as needed.

The warg sprinted through the gates, and the sounds of battle overtook them. Screams, laughter, the clang of metal, and the roar of flames filled the air. They sprinted toward a group of Korrun's followers surrounding a man who was trying to protect his family. Those in black cloaks laughed while the man in the middle shook with fear. The professor's hands were a blur of motion, and a powerful arc of lightning struck the group, leaping from one mage to the next, giving them no time to react and leaving the family in the middle unharmed.

Another follower saw his comrades fall, and sprinted toward Griff, hands at the ready. But Griff was faster. With but a thought, he launched a large flaming wooden beam off the ground and slammed it into the man. His stomach lurched as he watched the impact of his magic. Had he just killed a man? It may have been the right decision, but it felt vastly different than killing nightstalkers.

A roar alerted Griff to two small feline nightstalkers sprinting toward them from the other side. The two beasts jumped simultaneously, but Griff sent a wind spell toward one and sliced the other with his blade. The first nightstalker had regained its composure, then readied for another attack, but Professor Coen's fireball consumed it before it could take a step.

"Where's your house?" he screamed over the sounds of combat.

"Keep going, then take a left!" Griff said, extinguishing his blade, sheathing his handle, and sending a blast of wind toward three black cloaks.

He tightened his legs against the warg as it took off down the cobblestone road. Griff marveled at Professor Coen's speed and power. His spell slinging and sword fighting seemed automatic. He shot a fireball on one side and sliced with his blade on the other. He levitated large stones and flung them through the air at the nightstalkers, then leaned over the warg and stole a bow without slowing down. Every magical arrow from his bow was like brilliant blue lightning zipping through the air before it found its mark.

A lightning bolt whizzed past Griff, forcing him out of his daze. He turned and saw a group of black cloaks that had stopped toying with the townsfolk to chase after them. Fire spell, wind spell, levitation spell. Thanks to their warg, they were much faster than Korrun's followers, but Griff made sure they couldn't catch up.

"Up ahead! Take the next left!" he yelled.

Suddenly, Griff's vision filled with black scaly wings and he heard Professor Coen grunt in pain. A nightstalker had attacked from above and knocked the professor off the warg, his recently stolen bow also tumbling out of reach. He sent a quick burst of fire upward, but the beast had dodged and readied for another attack.

"Keep going!" Professor Coen cried, springing to his feet. "I'll catch up!"

Griff hesitated at his words. He couldn't leave him. He wouldn't. The professor sliced the flying nightstalker and sent a lightning spell up at a second one that had joined the attack, then he turned to look at Griff and yelled, "Now! Go!"

In that moment, he remembered his promise to his mentor. *Exactly as I say*. He nodded and leaned over to Kindra, "Let's go," he whispered sadly in her ear.

They took off toward the direction of his house, and just as they turned the corner, Griff's heart sank as he watched more flying nightstalkers swarm Professor Coen.

He wanted to turn the warg around and sprint to his mentor—no, not his mentor, his friend—and help. But he had made a promise. *Trust him and do exactly as he says. Trust him and do exactly as he says*. Griff chanted his friend's words over and over with every breath. In a ferocious rage, he sent fire and uncontrollable bursts of wind on every side; men and nightstalkers all fell in his fury. Tears of anger streamed down his face, blurring his vision. Thankfully, they were in his territory, and he could have maneuvered down the road blindly if he needed to.

"Griff!" A familiar voice cried his name. "Griff! Over here, Griff!"

"Sylva? Sylva! Where are you?" he screamed. He wiped the tears from his face and looked in every direction. A small, bloody hand appeared from behind some bushes next to a fence.

Griff dismounted and sprinted over to the boy. He pulled him and his sister from their hiding place. He wrapped his arms around Sylva and squeezed tightly.

"Oh, Sylva, you're alive. King's crown, I'm so glad you're alive! Are you guys okay?" he asked, looking at the blood on the boy's shoulder.

"We're okay. Could've been worse, actually." His shaking voice did nothing to convince Griff.

"Sylva saved me!" His younger sister, Lilly, cried. Her face was covered in dirt, and her once-bright pink pajamas were now brown. Thankfully, there was no blood.

"Where's your mom?" Griff asked.

"I-I dunno," Sylva said, "we got split up." His lips started to tremble.

Griff placed a comforting arm around his childhood friend. "We'll find her, I promise. Your mom's tough. I know she's still out there."

He quickly eyed their surroundings. Fires lit the streets of Cordelia. Black cloaks stormed building after building, though most were deserted by now. Sylva had found a clever place to hide. Standing in the shadows off the main road and next to the thick bushes almost completely camouflaged them from their attackers. The nightstalkers and mages flocked like hungry wolves to anything that moved or screamed, so as long as Griff and his friends remained quiet and careful, they might have a chance of going unnoticed.

"Okay," Griff said, "we're really close to my house, and it doesn't look like they've made it there just yet. We just need to stay low and stick to the shadows. We'll check there for our parents, and if we don't see them, we'll run to the gates by Talley's."

Griff led the way, with Sylva, Lilly, and Kindra following. They silently crept through the shadows, between houses and yards, freezing at every noise they heard. As difficult as he thought it would be to hide the warg, it wasn't hard at all. Kindra followed closely, heeding every one of Griff's commands.

After what felt like an eternity filled with too many close calls, they finally hopped the fence that led to his backyard. In that moment, Griff paused and looked around. It was strange to realize that he'd been away for such a long time. He looked at the large, familiar yard where he had grown up. The barn and the forge were still intact. No damage had been done to the house. The only difference was the strange silence—there was no bleating from the goat pens or clucking from the chickens in their coop.

Griff quietly rushed to a window and peeked in. Nothing. It was dead silent inside, and the house was completely dark with no signs of life. From the back window, Griff could barely see the front door, but it was wide open. A sigh of relief escaped his mouth.

"No one's there," he whispered to the group. "They must have left."

A look of disappointment appeared on Sylva's face. His sister dropped her head to hide her trembling chin.

"Don't worry," Griff said. "I bet our parents are all together. It wasn't Dad's night to guard the gates. You know he'd do whatever he could to protect your mom and mine. We just need to find them."

Sylva nodded and wrapped his sister in his arms. Griff walked across the yard to the empty goat pen, expecting to see the door wide open, but it was still shut. Yet, when he reached for the gate door, he didn't feel cold hard metal. Instead, it was warm and wet. He raised his hand in the air, the fire from the burning houses down the street lighting his view. His entire palm was coated in blood. His heart jumped, and he staggered backward. This couldn't be his family's blood, could it? He had to know, but he dared not use a light spell and bring attention to their group. He didn't know if, in this state of panic, he would be able to control it anyway.

He took another step and focused his attention on the ground. Just a few feet from the gate, he saw it. Barely noticeable, because it was covered in so much dirt and blood, was a goat carcass. Then he spotted another. And another. The ground was littered with the bodies of his family's animals. He opened the gate and walked inside, wiping the blood on his pants. The goat had been shredded and torn almost beyond recognition. After Griff had taken a few more steps into the pen, he heard a strange crunching sound. He strained his eyes toward the far corner, where the noise had originated. The back of the pen was so entrenched in shadow, it was difficult to see, but something was moving, something big. He squinted and realized there were two of them. And they were feeding on the last of the goats.

He tiptoed backward, step after careful step. Realization dawned on Griff like a slap to the face. Nightstalkers. He reached behind him to feel for the gate, his eyes never leaving the shadowy movement in the corner. With his final step, his foot slipped on a bloody carcass. He tumbled in the mud, his arm banging against the metal gate.

The crunching stopped, and the nightstalkers spun in the direction of the noise. Fighting to gain control of his body again, Griff jumped to his feet and faced the beasts. Fear overtook him as they stepped into the light of the fires. Standing as tall as a grown man were two nightstalkers that resembled stagmoose. But instead of the royally soft fur of a real stagmoose, they were covered in deep black scales. Instead of the many elegant antlers that paraded atop their heads, dark jagged spikes protruded from every angle. Two spikes, one on each side, curved from their heads and hung just past their bloody mouths.

A scream pierced the night, pulling Griff out of his daze. Sylva slapped his hands over Lilly's mouth, but the damage had been done. The two nightstalkers turned their attention toward the young girl and roared violently. Without a second glance in Griff's direction, they sprinted for the gate, heading straight toward Sylva and Lilly.

"No!" Griff yelled and sent a larger-than-intended fireball toward one of the monsters. It grazed the backside of the monster, causing it to topple over the gate, but the second one had jumped the barrier and already reached its full stride. The beast lowered its head and aimed its spikes at Griff's friends, but Kindra slammed into it from the side. Griff sprinted toward them and stepped in front of the group.

"Run!" he yelled. "Inside the house! Go!"

Sylva and Lilly needed no other word of encouragement. They bolted up the steps to the Driscolls' porch and disappeared into the house.

As big as Kindra was, the nightstalker was bigger. As strong as Kindra was, the nightstalker was stronger. Griff aimed his hand toward the nightstalker but in the tangle of the two beasts was afraid of hitting Kindra.

Before he could cast a spell, the nightstalker he had toppled roared and took a few steps toward him. Griff turned and dodged but was too late. A tusk grazed his side, forcing him to cry out. He fell to the ground, a hand instinctively on his wound. He gritted his teeth and tried to stand before the beast could attack again, but it was too fast. It charged, and Griff was sent flying despite his desperate attempt to dodge. This time, a jagged spike clipped his other shoulder. White hot pain seared through his whole body. He lay on the ground and tried to stand again, but his limbs wouldn't cooperate. He pulled his head off the grass and watched in fear as the nightstalker turned and charged again. Try as he might, Griff couldn't force himself back up. He squeezed his eyes shut as the nightstalker closed the gap and bellowed a victorious roar, knowing his prey would die this time.

Lightning arced through the air and slammed into the beast before it could reach Griff. It slid across the yard, kicking up grass and dirt before it finally lay still. But Griff knew better than to assume the beast was dead. Stunned, maybe, but definitely not dead. He looked for the spell caster, and when Griff found him, his mind clouded with confusion. Tyrell Falkenburg stood in the back doorway of Griff's house, hand still extended.

CHAPTER 27

"What?" Griff mumbled, ignoring the ongoing battle cries coming from Kindra and the nightstalker in the distance.

Tyrell walked over to him and extended his hand.

"Wh-what are you doing?" Griff asked.

"What's the point of magic if you can't use it to do good?" he answered.

"But ... but you're on *his* side," Griff said, pointing to the street, as though Korrun Aldamund was standing there.

The nightstalker in front of them grunted and began to stir.

"You want my help or not?"

"Yeah," Griff said, grasping the boy's hand.

After he had steadied himself, Griff reached for his sword which was still tucked into its holster, but the pain was almost unbearable. As though waking from a deep slumber, the nightstalker's eyes opened and its legs started sweeping the ground, fighting to stand once more.

Tyrell placed a firm hand on Griff's good shoulder. "He's mine," he said. Griff let out a pained sigh as he relaxed his grip on the sword holster.

The beast stood and towered over them. But if Tyrell's expression was a weapon, his glare would have sent daggers through the monster. Before the nightstalker could charge again, Tyrell extended his hand toward a large stone in the yard and flung it at the nightstalker's head. The stone connected with the beast's ear, sending the creature back to the ground and giving Griff and Tyrell a chance to back away. The nightstalker quickly scrambled back to its feet and roared, readying itself for another charge, but Tyrell had already crafted a large fireball and sent it spiraling forward. Tyrell sent spell after spell at the nightstalker in a barrage of fire, ice, and lightning, but the nightstalker wouldn't go down so easily this time. It dodged the fire and lightning, and its jagged spikes were a match for the large ice balls flung in its direction. Even when an occasional spell hit, the nightstalker always recovered quickly.

Ahead of them, Griff could see that Kindra was tired. She dodged left and right, raking with her claws when she could. At one point, she rammed the nightstalker and pushed it against the goat pen, giving Griff an idea. He glanced at Tyrell who continued to distract the monster with his onslaught of spells.

Holding his side, Griff trudged closer to the fence and stopped just in front of it. Gritting his teeth and doing his best to push past the pain in his shoulder, he pulled out his handle and with one awkward motion crafted a blade. He swung it between the post and the chain link fence that was attached to it. As quickly as his body would allow, he freed several posts from the rest of the fence, then, with his one good hand, and a prayer on his lips, he reached with his magic and tried to pull the poles out of the ground. His magic had become a rope and his mind was the hand that grasped it. He pulled and tugged and watched as the posts slowly rose from the dirt.

Off to the side, the nightstalker was gaining on Tyrell. It roared as it dodged another fireball and sprinted toward him. With the agility and form of a well-practiced soldier, Tyrell rolled to the side just in time, and jumped back up for another spell.

Griff tightened his fists in hard concentration and continued dragging the posts out of the ground. Just as the nightstalker prepared for another charge, Griff gave a final yank, freed the posts from the ground, and flung them at the beast with incredible power. It happened so fast that the nightstalker had taken several more steps toward Tyrell before it realized the posts had penetrated its body. It crumpled to the ground, this time for good.

Tyrell wiped the sweat from his forehead and looked at the battle Kindra was still waging with the other nightstalker. Deep wounds bled from the warg's chest, and her left wing was covered in gashes, but she continued to fight.

"Thanks," Tyrell said as Griff approached.

Griff nodded as he watched the battle, unsure of what to do. He couldn't leave Kindra. She'd been through so much to bring Griff to Cordelia.

"Look," Tyrell said, touching the razor-sharp tips of the fallen nightstalker's spikes.

The two mages locked eyes with understanding and Griff crafted his brilliant blue blade once again. With one slice, he managed to sever multiple spikes, which Tyrell immediately levitated.

Griff whistled as loudly as he could then screamed, "Kindra! Get back!"

Tyrell barely waited for the warg to break away before he hurled the spikes with ferocious force toward the nightstalker. A loud roar exploded from the monster, and it fell over, motionless. Griff breathed an enormous sigh of relief and turned to Tyrell.

"Thanks. You saved us."

Griff's heart skipped a beat. *Us? Us!* Where were Sylva and his sister? He cried out, "Sylva! Sylva! Where are you?"

"Here," came the timid reply. Sylva stood in the doorway, Lilly clinging to him tightly.

Griff let out a whoosh of air and turned to Tyrell.

"Thanks again. We'd be the ones on the ground right now had it not been for you."

Tyrell turned and stared long and hard before he spoke.

"I recognized you as Marth's mate. Figured I could help this *one* time. But you never saw me, you hear? I was never here."

The look he gave Griff said there was only one acceptable response.

"Sure," he said. "But ... why, Tyrell? Why are you following him?"

The mage crossed his arms and glared. "I owe you nothing. Especially not answers. But you owe me something. Keep this to yourself, deal?"

He started to walk away, and had moved past Kindra who was on the ground licking her injuries before Griff could even respond. He didn't know what to say.

"Deal?" Tyrell called over his shoulder, without even bothering to look back.

"D-Deal!" Griff called back, wishing there was a way to convince Tyrell to come with them. He could use the extra help now that Professor Coen was gone, but Tyrell had also just proven that there was still some good in him. And Griff wanted to make sure that he didn't lose what was left.

"Okay," Griff said, eyeing Kindra from the kitchen window. "We've gotta get out of here. I dunno where our parents are, but if we want a shot at finding them, we need to stay alive. And that's not gonna happen here, I'm afraid."

Sylva and his sister were tough. They had survived this long, and there was still a chance they could all make it out of Cordelia. While Griff needed time to recover from his injuries, the pain had settled into a more bearable level.

They huddled together in the dark kitchen, sitting on the wooden chairs Griff had grown up with. He looked around the familiar kitchen. Everything was still in place. By the look of the dirty dishes in the sink and the lone iron skillet sitting atop the wood-burning stove, it seemed as though his parents had left just after dinner that evening.

"Looks like we'll have to walk though," he added. "I don't think Kindra can fly quite yet. But if we stick to the shadows like we did before, I think we'll make it. The hardest part will be getting past Talley's. Remember those trees we used to play in over that way?"

Sylva nodded adamantly. "Yeah! The ones with the big bushes at the base, where we used to make really big slingshots and shoot Kaden with tomatoes and hide?"

"Those are the ones," Griff chuckled. "I think we can sneak behind those and skirt around the back of Talley's if we're really careful. We'll have to cross the street, but if we do it right, nobody'll see us."

He placed a gentle hand on Lilly's shoulder when he saw her eyes fill with tears.

"Don't worry, Lilly, you're safe with me, I promise." He knelt and met her innocent amber eyes. "Promise."

She sniffled, then suddenly threw her arms around him, and squeezed tightly.

"Thanks," she whispered before pulling back, leaving Griff's cheek wet with her tears.

He looked back at Sylva who was staring off into the distance at nothing. His knee bounced nervously.

"Once we get past Talley's, we'll go to the climbing trees and over the wall, and then we'll run until we can't run anymore."

"What about the nightstalkers in the forest?" Sylva asked.

"I'm more concerned with the nightstalkers here. I don't think we'll have to worry about running into them out there. We'll just have to find a place to hide until daybreak."

Sylva looked at his sister, his expression of fear transforming into older-brotherly resolve. He clasped his hand in hers and said, "Okay, let's do this."

They slipped out the back door and walked over toward Kindra. Griff ran his hands along the side of the warg's face.

"Thank you for protecting us," he said. She closed her eyes and gave a gentle rumble of approval. "We're getting out of here, and you're coming with us."

Together, the four of them sneaked out the back gate and quietly crept between houses, sticking to the shadows, and using backyards when they could. Thankfully, most of the houses on the way to Talley's were still intact, and offered an abundance of shadows to hide in. Griff supposed most of the black cloaks were still on the other side of town.

After several minutes had passed, and they had made significant progress down the street, Griff saw buildings ahead that were alight with tall flames. As they slowly crept closer, the sounds of yelling and screaming grew louder, along with the sound of roaring fire. Griff peered between the wooden slats of the fence that currently hid them, and his heart sank. Talley's Tavern was filled with menacing flames that reached toward the sky in wicked triumph.

Silhouetted against the blinding light of the inferno, three figures were engaged in all-out armed combat. No spells were cast, just two men against one, each wielding his own sword. Griff realized that Korrun must have recruited non-magical people in his army as well. The lone man was as good, if not better than both of the black cloaks he was up against. In addition to the sword in his hand, the man carried a large hunting bow and a quiver of arrows that bounced back and forth with each careful maneuver. Skill was on his side; numbers were not. Griff didn't have to watch long to know who the lone swordsman was.

Dad. He dared not speak, lest his emotions and adrenaline get the best of him and reveal their location. Griff turned back to the group behind him. He looked each one in the eye as he formulated his plan.

"My dad's out there, and he's outnumbered. I've gotta help."

Sylva's eyes grew wide, but Griff continued before he could say anything.

"I'm gonna go first, and then while the men out there are distracted, I want you three to make a run for it, okay? At this point, your only goal is to get to the climbing trees and over that wall. I'll get my dad, and we'll meet you in the forest, got it?"

Sylva opened his mouth to say something, then closed it and nodded with determination.

"You've got this, Sylva. You're braver and stronger than you think. You can do it."

Griff turned his attention to Kindra and placed a hand under her head. "Watch out for them, will you?"

The warg rumbled again. After giving a final nod to his friends, he slammed open the gate door and sprinted toward the battle. The silhouettes continued to come together and break apart as Griff ran toward them from the side. Adrenaline surged through his veins, determination silencing the pain that coursed through his body. His feet pounded against the cobblestone streets. When he was close enough, he extended his hand toward one of the black cloaks and sent a forceful gust of wind in his direction. The man yelped in surprise and pain as his feet left the ground. Gale and the other black cloak turned in surprise at the new addition to the battle.

"Griff?" his dad called, but there was no time to respond.

Griff continued to run across the street, his attention shifting toward the second man. The other black cloak had turned to flee, but Griff flung a large, swirling ball of fire toward him, ensuring his escape attempt was futile. Griff didn't even bother to see if the spell made contact before he finished his sprint and flung his arms around his shocked father.

"Dad!" Griff cried. "You're alive!"

He felt Gale's arms tighten around him.

"And so are you!"

"Where's Mom? Did she make it out? Is Sylva's mom with her?"

"Look out!" his dad yelled, pushing Griff to the side, and parrying what would have been a fatal blow. The first black cloak had recovered from the wind spell and sought revenge on its caster.

Griff jumped to his feet and waited for the right moment. Now that Gale had only one swordsman to worry about, he clearly controlled the battle, and the black cloak knew it. He turned to run like his comrade, so Griff sentenced him to the same fate, casting another ball of fire. His dad shielded his eyes and watched the flames consume the man. He turned toward his son, placing a firm arm around his shoulder and pulling him away from the scene.

"Oh, Griff. I'm so sorry it came to this. You should never have had to end another person's life." Sorrow filled his words.

"I ... I know, Dad. But I'll do it again if it means saving yours."

"First, it was No Moon Night. And then tonight. When will you stop trying to save my life?" he asked.

"Never."

Gale squeezed his son's shoulder. "The girls are okay. They're hiding in our favorite hunting spot."

Griff heaved a sigh of relief, but it was too soon. Two black cloaks with extended hands approached from a connecting street. In the hand of one, Griff saw lightning crackle, while the other prepared a fireball. They shouted and hurled their spells toward Griff and his dad. In a flash, Griff extended his hand and crafted a large white shield, so the spells veered harmlessly into the night sky.

Gale quickly removed his bow and nocked an arrow in place as Griff maintained the shield. Like a master hunter with his prey in sight, he loosed the arrow on target, but the man casually released a wind spell, and the arrow fluttered to the side. Undisturbed by how easily his attempt had been thwarted, Gale loosed several more arrows. Again, each one was dodged or deflected. Spell after spell, the black cloaks continued their onslaught on Griff's shield as they marched forward. He was amazed that his shield remained intact; it took all his concentration to keep the protection in place, but he was beginning to feel exhaustion wearing down his strength.

Finally, his dad caught one of the men off guard, forcing him to dive to the side. It was the split-second Griff needed to launch a counterattack. He snuffed out his shield and allowed the ocean of energy within his body to come barreling out in an uncontrollable burst of wind. The two men flew backward, surprised by the incredible energy that knocked them off their feet.

"Now!" Griff yelled, drawing out his handle and crafting a large blade.

Without looking back to see if his dad had picked up on his cue, Griff sprinted to the first mage and drove his blade through the man, his look of surprise now permanently frozen. The angry screams nearby told Griff that his dad had in fact understood the plan and executed it swiftly.

They walked toward each other, father and son, both covered with the filth of battle. They embraced again, and a moment of silence hung in the air. Not for these men who had just died, but for the hands that were forced to execute justice.

"That ... was ... impressive." A dark familiar voice called from the shadows, breaking the silence. Gale and Griff spun toward the sound, dread filling Griff's heart.

"The ... *power* ... that you just displayed, boy. You took out two really good mages."

The man stepped out from the shadows, his long brown hair waving carelessly in the evening wind. His brown eyes stared curiously at Griff. The shadows from the blazing fires danced across his face to reveal the slender scar on his left cheek. His nightstalker pet almost seemed to smirk from the man's side. Korrun Aldamund stepped out of the shadows with a wave of nightstalkers at his back.

CHAPTER 28

"You look familiar, boy," the commander of the nightstalkers said. He paused, staring unwaveringly at Griff, who felt his skin crawl at the man's gaze. Then, a spark of realization lit up his face. "You …" he said. "You were in the caves, weren't you, boy?"

Sweat formed on Griff's brow. His hands trembled at the man's words. Fear and anger surged through him. He stood face to face with one of the most powerful mages in all of Oriel. But this time, it wasn't a dream, and the man wasn't in the midst of a floating skull made of lava. There was no sense in running. Even if they could somehow outrun the man, there was no way they could outrun the nightstalkers behind him. The only thing he could do was give his dad the chance to make it out alive and save his mom.

He turned toward his dad, and as calmly and quietly as he could, said, "Dad … run."

Griff screamed at the top of his lungs and lunged forward, calling upon the swelling tide of energy inside him.

"Griff, no!" his dad cried, but his conscience was clear, and resolution filled his mind.

The feelings of death on the horizon had once again flooded Griff. It was as though he was back in the forest during No Moon Night, surrounded by the nightstalkers who had attacked his dad. This time was different, though. His dad was alive, and Griff planned to keep it that way. Anger, frustration, and fear rushed wildly through him. But angry as he was, even afraid as he was, those emotions were not what fueled him. It was love. The love of his family and the overwhelming responsibility he now felt to protect them. A calm look of curiosity appeared on Korrun's face, but Griff didn't care. He would do his best to protect those he loved.

His chest started to burn, and a white light radiated intensely from it. With every step Griff took, he felt the waves of energy rise and fall within him, begging to be released. No. Not begging. *Commanding* to be released. The burning feeling intensified and filled his body. As it moved down his arms, Griff looked, and the white tentacles of light stretched out from underneath his sleeves.

Wind raged around Griff's body, matching the storm within. Like a wild hurricane confined in a protective sphere around him, it grew and became more intense as he sprinted toward Korrun. After he had taken several steps, the nightstalkers tensed, ready to attack, but Korrun held a hand to the side to still them. Griff continued to swirl one hand and maintain the ever-intensifying hurricane around him. With his other hand, he ignited a blazing fire that merged with the wind. The commander of the nightstalkers raised an eyebrow but maintained his calm demeanor as the young mage, surrounded by radiant white light, ran toward him with the orb of wind and fire raging around him.

Korrun Aldamund was only a few feet away when Griff launched the furious fiery gale toward him. The nightstalkers backed away from the incoming threat, but Korrun merely raised a hand with his palm extended outward. Griff's brilliant white light exploded, and a thunderous sound echoed throughout the streets of Cordelia when the spell collided with the man's shield. His smug look of curiosity was immediately replaced with that of shock as Korrun was launched into the air by the spell's power. He landed with a satisfying *thud* and skidded across the grassy floor.

"My, my," Korrun said as he stood to his feet, his eyes never leaving Griff's. "There's something different about you, boy." He took a step forward. "You are no ordinary mage." Another step. "You have something that I need, and I won't take 'no' for an answer."

He raised his hand and Griff felt all his muscles tighten as if a large invisible hand was clutching him and squeezing tightly. Swirling dark energy enveloped Griff—a color of magic he had never seen before, almost invisible against the black backdrop of night. Reflections of the fires of the burning town sparkled within the energy. Unable to fight the invisible force, his body left the ground and he slowly hovered toward Korrun.

"Griff!" his dad shouted. As quick as lightning, Gale launched an arrow directly at Korrun's heart. But even quicker than lightning was the hand that stopped the arrow mid-flight and launched it back at its owner, flinging it straight into Gale's shoulder. With a howl, Gale dropped his bow and fell backward onto the grass, blood already trickling out of the wound.

"Dad!" Griff cried, fighting harder against Korrun's power, but it was useless. He watched helplessly as his dad tried to get back up, only to fall down again.

"He's all yours," Korrun said, turning to the front row of nightstalkers. With a loud roar, they sprinted toward Gale, a look of hungry greed in their eyes. Griff, who was being dragged down the street, screamed at the top of his lungs, powerless to do anything else.

But before Korrun had noticed the threat, a surge of fire flanked the first wave of nightstalkers, immediately turning them to ash. A ragged Professor Coen flung a crackling orb of blue energy at Korrun, knocking him to the ground. Griff felt the invisible hand release him, and he ran past Professor Coen, who was sending bolt after bolt of lightning through the ranks of nightstalkers.

"Dad!" he cried, dropping to the grass next to Gale.

"That was close," he said through gritted teeth.

"W-what do you need me to do?"

"This ... arrow's ... gotta go," he said through pained breaths. "I need you to break it off and pull it out."

"You need me to do what?" Griff asked incredulously.

Gale grasped the feathered part of the arrow and hollered in pain.

"Wait, Dad. Here. Sit still." Griff pulled out his handle and crafted another blade. The sword effortlessly slashed through the body of the arrow, like a knife cutting water.

"O-okay. Now ... we gotta turn you over," he said, grabbing his dad and doing his best to ignore the cries of pain as he positioned him on his belly.

"Sorry," Griff said. He gritted his teeth and yanked with all his might.

Gale screamed at the top of his lungs as the other half of the arrow pulled free.

"Sorry! Sorry! Sorry!" Griff cried, tossing the bloody arrow to the side.

Ahead, the battle between Professor Coen and Korrun Aldamund raged on. There was no denying the professor was strong, but even in his most ready-for-battle state, he would never be a match for this man. He ran between trees, dodging and casting as fast as he could. Flashing lights and thunderous sounds crashed around them with every spell.

"You've gotta get outta here," Griff said. "You need to go get Mom and the Karlsens and head toward Porvalla."

Just then, Griff heard Professor Coen yell in pain. He whipped his head in the direction of the sound, and saw the professor lying on the grass, unconscious. Fear swelled in him as he watched Korrun Aldamund walk toward Griff for the second time, but this time a look of angry determination covered his face.

"You're coming with me, boy. You have something of mine."

Gale roared and leapt from the ground, sprinting toward Korrun.

"Enough!" Korrun boomed. He flung his hand and sent Gale flying. His body hit a tree trunk with a sickening *thud*.

"No!" Griff screamed. He jumped to run, but a wall of nightstalkers blocked his path.

"No more games." A voice spoke from behind him.

Griff turned to meet the gaze of his captor.

"I need you alive ... but only just," he said as he raised a hand full of swirling red and black energy.

And then, the darkness around them exploded in blinding blue light. He heard a loud crash and Korrun cried out in pain. Griff shielded his eyes and fought to regain vision.

"Are you okay, Griff?" The blurry outline of the man standing in front of him was speaking.

"H-Headmaster Aldamund?" Griff asked.

"Indeed. Stay here while I take care of my uncle," he said.

The headmaster marched toward Korrun, who had just jumped back to his feet. The nightstalkers growled as the headmaster passed, but they allowed him through, knowing any efforts to stop him would be futile.

"I told you your death would come soon, Korrun," Headmaster Aldamund said, "and I always keep my promises."

The darkness was once again alight as the two mages fought. Each spell was more powerful than the one before. Dust flew from the ground, pebbles ricocheted in every direction, wind shook the trees, and lightning and fire danced dangerously through the air. Korrun flung rubble from a nearby house ferociously at the headmaster, who caught the stones and sent them back to their caster with equal power. Headmaster Aldamund conjured a giant ball of energy that raced through the air; right before it collided with Korrun, it split into several smaller orbs that curved in different directions before smashing into him. The impact sent waves of blue light bursting outward, but when the light dissipated, Korrun remained standing, having cast a dark shield that covered him completely. Whenever one man cast a spell, the other would deflect or redirect it back with equal intensity. The extreme power displayed between the two mages was almost tangible, as though Griff was back in the middle of the corruption storm.

Griff looked at his dad, who lay still, save for the faint rise and fall of his chest. He longed to rush over and try to wake him, but he knew that the wall of nightstalkers wouldn't allow him through. He eyed his father's bow and quiver of arrows but knew they would do no good against the corrupted army that stood before him. He was stuck, forced to watch the battle ahead.

Underneath the flickering lights of combat, Professor Coen stirred. He raised a hand to his head and rubbed it gently, as though the area was tender. Suddenly, his head whipped around, trying to gather the state of his surroundings. He paused to watch Headmaster Aldamund who was now fighting Korrun mid-air. The two mages were locked in a test of strength. The professor's head swiveled back and forth until he turned to face Griff, who gave him a slight nod, not wanting to draw the nightstalkers' attention toward the professor.

A roar above Griff sent the nightstalkers stampeding backward as Magnus's massive frame landed beside him. The monsters around them scrambled to escape the swipe of the warg's claws. Some succeeded. Many did not. Griff lunged for his dad's bow and once it was securely in his hand, jumped on Magnus's back. The nightstalkers had recovered from the warg's initial ambush and tried to counter, but Magnus's wings, miraculously healed, frantically beat the air, climbing higher and carrying Griff out of the nightstalkers' reach.

"Professor!" Griff called below him, tossing the bow down to his friend. Professor Coen snatched it out of the air, and instinctually fired off several magical arrows. Each arrow connected to a winged monster near Griff. After the professor had brought down several more, the nightstalkers turned to face him, the greater threat.

"Hurry! Let's get my dad while we can!" Griff called to Magnus.

They quickly dropped to the ground next to Gale's motionless body. Griff jumped down and, as quickly as he could, placed his dad on the warg's back. Some of the nightstalkers had noticed him and sprinted in his direction, but Griff flung a fireball at them. Drawing on his remaining energy, he climbed on Magnus, locked his feet into the leather straps on either side, and shot off another fireball, giving the warg time to launch them back into the sky.

Griff clutched his dad's limp body with all his might as Magnus flew. Airborne nightstalkers tried to chase them, but between the warg's claws and Professor Coen's arrows, they stood no chance.

"Go to the forest!" Griff said.

Magnus roared as if he understood and raced past Talley's blazing tavern and over the wall. Griff turned to look back at the ongoing battle. Professor Coen's hands were a blur of frenzied activity as he kept the nightstalkers surrounding him at bay with a flurry of spells and magical arrows. Farther away, the battle raged on between Headmaster Aldamund and his uncle. Now that he was several stories high, Griff was able to see all of Cordelia. His heart sank as he gazed upon the wreckage that was once his town. Even his house was now ablaze, and the shadows of black cloaks and nightstalkers filled every street.

With one last glance back, Griff directed the warg over the sea of trees until they reached one that jutted high above the others. The warg landed gently in front of the large tree with thick bushes in a wide ring encircling it. Apart from being the largest tree in the woods, no one would have given this location another thought. But Griff and his dad had used this tree over the years as the perfect hunting location. They had even dug shallow holes to store small boxes of hunting supplies there.

"Mom?" Griff called quietly. "Mom ... it's me, Griff. Are you here?"

Immediately, he heard the bushes rustling. Leena burst from the one thin spot and pulled Griff into a tight bear hug.

"Griff? Oh, Griff, sweetie! What in the nightstalker's fury are you doing here? Oh, I'm so glad to see you, though! Is your father with you?"

Griff squeezed his mother back while he tried to find the right words. "Yeah, um, he's … he's hurt, Mom. I dunno how bad, but he's hurt."

At that moment, Sylva and the rest of the Karlsen family emerged from the thicket. Kindra also walked around from behind the tree. Her massive frame wouldn't have fit in the space between the tree and bushes, so she must have been lying down out of sight.

"Lemme take a look," Nessa said, marching past Griff until she got closer to Magnus and Gale, who lay motionless on the beast's back. She paused, staring tentatively at the warg.

"It's okay, Mom," Sylva said. He walked confidently forward toward Magnus and reached out a hand. The warg rumbled and gently nuzzled his palm.

Nessa looked at her son, surprised at his confidence before the massive beast, then nodded and began her inspection.

"You made it, Sylva." Griff half-smiled at the boy.

Sylva smiled and nodded in return.

"He's knocked out cold," Nessa said, pulling Gale's eyelids open.

She ran a hand down his back and paused, "Hmm. Could also have a few cracked ribs. And what's this here?" She asked, pointing to the hole in his shoulder.

"Uh, that's where an arrow was before I pulled it outta him," Griff answered.

She turned to look at Leena. "We need to get him out of here."

"I have an idea," Griff said. "I saw Porvalla on the way here, and it looked intact."

"But that's a half day's walk away, Griff," Leena said.

"Not for Magnus. It'd take him less than an hour." He turned toward Kindra, "You're not able to fly, are you, girl?"

The warg lowered her head and rumbled; without Professor Coen's healing magic, her wings were still damaged from her fight with the nightstalkers at the Driscoll house.

"Well, we could send Ms. Karlsen and Lilly along and the rest of us could walk," Griff added.

"They do have a couple of beds at the back of their tavern." Nessa added. "That's probably the best plan we've got."

Leena looked at the group, all eyes on her. "Well, all right. You two jump on and head to Porvalla, and these two knights in shining armor and their valiant steed will escort me there on foot. Take good care of him, Nessa."

"Oh, I always do, Leena. As often as that man has come to see me for healing through the years, I know him nearly as well as you do." She gave Leena a confident wink. "He'll be fine, I promise. It's *you* who needs to be careful out here."

Nessa boosted Lilly onto the warg's back before climbing up herself.

"Uh ... how do I steer this thing?" she asked.

"Um ... right. Hey, uh, Magnus?" Griff asked the beast. "Can you take them to Porvalla?"

The warg snorted in response, which Griff took to mean yes.

Griff, Leena, Sylva, and Kindra watched as the warg gracefully took off and flew through the night sky. Nobody said a word until they were well out of sight.

"Well then," Griff said, "shall we?"

As exhausted as Griff was, he managed to set a quick pace, making sure Sylva was able to keep up. He worried about Professor Coen and Headmaster Aldamund for the entire trip to Porvalla. Things had not looked good when he left. The headmaster and Korrun seemed evenly matched, and the professor had his work cut out for him with the whole army of nightstalkers encircling him. And it looked like more of Korrun's army was approaching as well.

Horrible thoughts plagued his mind, but he fought to repress them and keep moving forward. Griff, Sylva, and Leena kept quiet the whole time. Whenever Griff and his dad had traveled to Porvalla, it had been a fun journey there; they'd laughed and joked and made weird noises along the way. Now, however, Griff was exhausted, having been awake for entirely too long. Fighting had also drained most of his energy, and he was amazed to still be standing.

The hours dragged on without a single incident. It was a long journey, but thankfully, it was also peaceful. By the time they reached Porvalla, the sun had risen, and the little town was bursting with life. Many stopped to stare at the ragged group and their warg when they walked through the gates, but Griff didn't mind. He imagined they looked rather rough, given the night they'd had.

After pausing to check on his dad, who was sound asleep on a bed in the back of the tavern, with bandages wrapped completely around his torso, Griff fell headlong onto another bed in the corner and welcomed the deep and dreamless sleep that awaited him.

CHAPTER 29

"Griff, honey. Wake up, Griff. There's someone who wants to see you."

His eyes popped open, and he bolted upright.

"Hey, relax, son. Relax. It's okay ... you're okay." Gale called from his bed. He was sitting up but still looked rather uncomfortable.

"Dad!" Griff said, rushing to his side. "You're all right!"

"Hey, miracle boy," he started to put an arm around his son, but winced and decided against the motion. "Yeah. I'll live. Probably."

Leena pretended to slap him with the back of her hand. "Don't you go saying that, Gale Driscoll."

"I'm just saying, cracked ribs *hurt*! And this hole in my shoulder ain't no better either!"

Despite the horror of the night before, it was wonderful to be with his family again. Griff probably laughed harder than he should have at his dad's expense, but king's crown, he was so happy they were all alive and together.

"Son, how did you know to come find us?" Gale asked when Leena stepped out into the tavern to fetch them some breakfast.

"Long story," Griff answered. "But the short version is that one of my professors tipped me off, and I begged him to take me."

"I'm familiar with your torture tactics," his dad responded. "You used those many times on your mother and me. Also, speaking of torture tactics ..." he sat up straighter. "What in king's crown are they teaching you at that school? You were shootin' fireballs and using some sort of magical sword …"

Griff walked over to his bed and reached under his pillow. He pulled out his sword handle, dislodged it from its holster, and brought it to his dad.

"Not just any sword, Dad. *My* sword."

Gale's eyes welled with tears as he tenderly ran his hand over the dragon wings on the handle they had worked on together.

"Watch," Griff said, grabbing it and crafting a blue blade.

Gale's wet eyes widened in wonder as he watched energy swirl about the blade.

"Magnificent," he whispered in awe.

So he wouldn't draw too much attention, Griff extinguished the blade, placed it on his dad's lap, and sat down next to him. Gale turned the handle over and over before finally saying, "That was incredible. Well done, son. Well done."

Leena appeared at the door. "Honey, Headmaster Aldamund is here to talk with you. And … he brought another guest as well. They'd like you to come outside."

Griff's heart jumped to his throat. The headmaster was alive! What about Professor Coen? Was he all right? Was that the guest? If they *were* both alive, then he could start to worry about lesser things, like what were the ramifications of leaving Bergots in the middle of the night? Would he be allowed back in? Would he face punishment? His mind reeled with a million unanswered questions as he walked through the tavern and found the headmaster and King Aldamund waiting outside.

"Let's go for a walk, Mr. Driscoll," the headmaster said. It was hard to read their emotions. Headmaster Aldamund stared ahead as they walked, while the king hummed a soft tune.

"Sir ..." One question particularly troubled Griff. He needed to know the answer, and if he had to break the awkward silence to get it, he would. "How's Professor Coen? Is he ... did he ...?"

"Oh, yes," he answered. "He's alive. The beds were full at the tavern, so the owner offered him a place in his own house. Very nice man, by the way."

Griff heaved a sigh of relief. He just had to deal with his punishment then.

"Errick saved the day, as a matter of fact," the king interjected. "Sent an arrow through my brother's side while he wasn't looking."

"Gave me the chance I needed to sway the battle in our favor," Headmaster Aldamund added.

"So ... so he's dead, then? Korrun's gone?"

The king clasped his hands behind his back and bent down to smell some flowers at the edge of a merchant's cart.

"These are lovely, my dear," he said to the seller, before turning back to Griff. "Oh, he and his army are gone, yes. But he is not dead. He's a slippery one, I'm afraid. And alas, I'm sorry to say that the war with him is far from over."

Griff turned to the headmaster. "Sir ... I ... I'm sorry I left the castle. I-I just ... I had to save my family. I understand if that means I'm no longer welcome back. I just couldn't let my family die."

The headmaster nodded but didn't speak a word.

"So am ... am I allowed back, sir? Back to Bergots?

Again, the headmaster remained quiet, and with each passing moment, Griff's heart sank lower, feeling the inevitable truth of his sentence.

"You came to me at the start of the semester telling me about your dreams, do you remember?"

"Yes, sir, I do."

"I had my suspicions back then, but as time passed and the king and I discussed you at length, the more certain we grew about your situation."

"My situation?"

"Indeed," the king said. "Griff, you are more special than you realize."

There's something different about you, boy. You are no ordinary mage. You have something that I need ...

Korrun's words from the night before echoed in Griff's mind, like a nightmare he couldn't shake.

"You have the ability to manipulate essence when your parents cannot. Do you know why?" the king asked.

Griff shook his head slowly.

"As you know, this ability is genetic, and you are part of a family line that has no abilities in this regard."

King Aldamund took two muffins from another cart and handed over a fistful of gold coins, much to the merchant's delight. He offered one to Griff, who readily accepted it.

"The rule is that magic is genetic ... but there is one exception to that rule.

Headmaster Aldamund leaned toward Griff and quietly said, "The orb of essence."

"The *orb* of essence?" Griff asked quietly, taking the cue from the headmaster.

The king nodded, giving himself a moment to swallow a large bite of muffin.

"Indeed," he said, gently wiping at the corners of his mouth. "Legend has it that many years ago, before Day Zero, there was a special orb with limitless magical properties."

They stepped through the entry gates of Porvalla, the shade of the forest a welcome respite from the hot morning sun. Now that they were away from the activity of the town, the king and his son spoke normally, rather than lowering their voices whenever someone passed by.

"Nobody knows where it came from or what gave it such great magical potential," Headmaster Aldamund said.

"But," the king added, "following Day Zero, it is said that the orb was shattered, broken into nine shards that disappeared without a trace."

"That is, except for one shard," the headmaster interjected.

"Except for one." The king looked up and smiled, as if reliving a happy memory. "One shard from the orb of essence remained. It was retrieved by one of my Aldamund ancestors. That shard has been handed down, through each generation of our family, along with the legend of the orb of essence."

"So you have one of those shards, then?" Griff asked.

The king once again smiled, but this time it wasn't a purely happy smile. King Aldamund shook his head and said, "No, I don't have the shard anymore."

He turned, his piercing bright blue eyes locking with Griff's. His long white beard swayed in the gentle breeze that glided along the dusty path on which they stood.

"You do."

Confusion muddled Griff's mind, clouding any sort of understanding.

"Sir?"

"*You* have the shard, Griff Driscoll."

He pointed to Griff's chest. "Right there."

"I-I don't understand. You're saying that I have a shard from the orb of essence in my chest?"

The king smiled. "Your family calls you miracle boy, do they not?"

Griff nodded slowly.

"You were a sick baby. Very sick. I visited your town one night, and as I walked the streets under the cover of darkness, I heard you crying. And your mother too. You see, Griff. I've always been a fixer. If I see a problem, I want to fix it. I saw your mother that night. Tears streamed down her face as she watched her baby boy screaming and crying and was unable do anything about it."

He continued walking, his hands clasped behind his back, and Griff rushed to catch up.

"Healing magic can only do so much, you see," he continued. "Fix broken bones? Certainly. Heal a baby from whatever disease or ailment it was you had? Certainly not. But when your mom fell asleep from pure exhaustion, I slipped in and tried my best to heal you anyway. Nothing worked. Then, suddenly, my pocket glowed brightly, and I pulled out the shard. It was pulsating with bright white light. Now, I didn't hear any audible words, but in that moment, holding the shard of essence in the palm of my hand, I knew what I had to do. I placed that shard over your heart. Light exploded in your room, but when the light disappeared, you stopped crying! And the shard ... was gone. Your tiny little heart glowed right through your chest, and I knew that the shard of essence had chosen you."

Griff tenderly touched his chest, as if trying to remember that moment. As if trying to feel the shard that lived inside him. He thought back to No Moon Night, when he had been surrounded by the nightstalkers, and when his chest exploded in radiant white light. And again, the previous night, when he fought against Korrun. The pieces of the puzzle were starting to come together.

"I ... I should thank you, then, sir," he said to the king, "and apologize too. You saved my life, and I stole your shard."

The king chuckled. "Ah, but you didn't steal the shard, miracle boy. The shard *chose* you. And it saved you!"

"So ... does that mean it was the shard that gave me these abilities?"

The king nodded.

"Is that also why I have a hard time controlling my powers?"

"I think so," Headmaster Aldamund said. "The legend that was passed down our family line says that the orb was what gave people their powers.

It's where essence manipulation originated from. It's more complicated for you, because you are getting your abilities straight from the source, not through a watered-down bloodline, if you will."

"What about the color of my spells, sir? Does the shard have something to do with that as well?"

"Yes, I believe that is the case," the king answered. "Perhaps you are tapping into the power of the shard for your essence manipulation."

"But my essence crafting blades are blue. I don't understand."

"Then that is when you are tapping into your *own* power. While the shard has bestowed on you magical abilities, *you*, Griff, have tapped into the power of mastering yourself. And it shows through your blade's color."

The three mages continued to stroll through the woods, but Griff's feet only moved by instinct as he tried to take in all that the king and his son were saying.

"So, then, why did I have those dreams about Korrun?"

"That," the king responded, "we have yet to determine. Our theory is that the shards are all connected, and since one of them lives in you, it connects you to the others. In your dreams, Korrun was searching for a shard, and was apparently very close. Perhaps you can see anyone who comes near a shard of essence."

"Korrun seeks the shards of essence," the headmaster said. "He wants to try and restore them to their former glory. Consider the power you have, Griff. And that is only from one shard. Imagine what could be possible if the entire orb was intact.

"You asked if you would be allowed back to Bergots. As you can see, you are both an asset and a threat to my uncle. Whether you realized it or not, when you were growing up, you were under the protection of Talley. Now that you are old enough to attend Bergots, you will remain there and complete your training under *my* protection. And your family will be relocated to Solastran, so Korrun won't give you another reason to go sneaking off in the night again."

"Talley was my protector all these years?" Griff asked, astonished.

The king laughed. "Indeed. He is a fierce warrior, and an even better chef. I have the highest confidence in him and sought him out the same night you received the shard, telling him everything."

Griff heaved a heavy sigh of relief. He would get to see his friends again. He would get to see Mira. And his family would live near him. The headmaster's news was a beacon of hope amid the tragic destruction of his hometown.

"Oh, but you *will* find reckoning within your training for leaving the academy like that," the headmaster said.

The beacon of hope dimmed slightly, and Griff nodded in understanding. "And Professor Coen? It wasn't his fault, you know. I begged him to take me, sir. It was all my fault."

"*You* are Professor Coen's reckoning." The headmaster smiled. "He will continue to train you as he has for the past semester."

"And," King Aldamund added, "I have the leverage I need to recruit him when the time comes. He can't say no to me this time, I'm happy to say." The king winked.

The headmaster cleared his throat. "Given the recent events, you are, of course, exempt from the remaining few weeks left of the semester. And your friends will skip the final Altar Storm match. Just know that you will be graded much more severely on your future matches."

"Thank you, sir," Griff said, turning to the headmaster. "And thank you for saving us last night as well. I owe you both a lifetime of gratitude and service."

"Aye," said the king, placing an arm around Griff, "you do. And to start, I would suggest making sure that you make the most of your life, doing all the good you can. To squander such a gift as a second chance at life would be most deplorable."

Over the next few days, news continued to arrive. Not a single building in Cordelia had survived the attack. Talley arrived in Porvalla not long after Griff and the Aldamunds had returned from their walk. According to his stories, he had taken out several black cloaks as he aided families in their escape. Normally, Griff would have said his stories were about as grand as his mutton chops, but considering his profession as a warrior prior to becoming a tavern keeper, Griff was ready to believe him.

Although it shouldn't have been a surprise, Griff was nonetheless shocked to learn that the Horters had become followers of Korrun. He imagined that they leveraged their leather crafting know-how in exchange for their lives. Morality was only necessary when convenient for that family, and Griff was disgusted by how easily they discarded it.

Thankfully, Professor Coen had agreed to stay behind and watch over Griff and his family. Even better, Griff had discovered that there would be no goodbyes to Sylva and the rest of the Karlsens. They would start their new life in Solastran as well. The two families would travel back to Cordelia, escorted by Professor Coen, to scavenge what remained of their belongings, then they would make the journey to Solastran, where a new adventure awaited them all.

EPILOGUE

Towering above the rest of the derelict city, like a king before kneeling servants, stood the building he had been searching for. Nothing, not even the darkness of night, could hide this structure from the man. The once-white stones had faded over the years, but they still peeked out from the mold that now coated its surface. The tall, ornately-decorated pillars stood on either side of the ancient wooden double doors like white knights guarding a castle. Elegant steeples crowned lofty towers that jutted out from the top of the central structure.

Any semblance of landscaping had almost completely disappeared, save for the intentional placement of trees and shrubs on the building grounds. But now, instead of welcoming guests into its elaborate hallways and sanctums, the foliage sent a message of unwelcome.

Overall, the large abandoned building was hauntingly beautiful. Exquisite and terrifying all at once. Frightening though it may have seemed, this man was unphased by such a scene. He had been searching for this place for years, and twigs, branches, and a little bit of mold weren't going to stand in his way. As he neared the entrance, the man launched a fireball at the branches stretched across the door, burning them to ash as he walked the long concrete path toward them. The doors creaked in complaint as the man pushed through them, allowing him access into the sacred desolate building.

His footsteps on the cracked elegant tiles echoed down the hall, and the light he cast sent shadows dancing on the ceiling. The pounding of his pet's feet next to him were much louder than his own. He casually wandered the halls with his fingers gliding along the dusty ornamental walls. He had never been to this place, but he knew exactly where to go. Turning this way and that, the man never backtracked or showed fear, even as he climbed down a winding set of stairs that led him deep beneath the building.

He stooped to walk through a small stone archway that opened to a large room with row after row of identical square holes in the walls. The only other noise that could be heard beyond the echoes of the man's footsteps and the grunts of his excited pet was the sporadic drip, drip, drip of water landing in a puddle at the far end of the room. The man approached the first hollow opening and peered closely at the etchings in the stone underneath it. Not this one. He wandered from one to the next, pausing to read each one. Finally, when he had nearly reached the end of the room, he smiled as he read the name in front of him: *Einar Falkenburg.*

The man pulled out a long rectangular wooden box and carefully floated it to the floor. Without flinching, he pulled open the lid. As he'd suspected, there was no body there, only hay. He then launched the empty wooden casket against the hard stone wall, sending splinters in every direction. Amid the crack of breaking wood, he was satisfied to hear a metal clanging sound. He sent a gentle wind spell over the ground to remove any bundles of hay that lingered until he finally found it. He picked up the tiny metal box and held it in the palm of his hand. There was no lid, no lock, no way inside. At least, no way for an ordinary person to get inside. But he was no ordinary person.

He floated the metal box inches from his face, and, with one finger, sent a tiny-but-powerful bolt of electricity toward a corner. The lightning struck with a satisfying crackle, and the man maintained its position for a moment. It was like performing delicate surgery, and this man was a master surgeon. The power within that single streak of electricity slowly carved through the metal until he had made his own door in the box. The man extinguished the strand of lightning and swirled his finger to force the newly crafted door open. His face, and the narrow scar on his cheek, were lit by the treasure inside.

Korrun Aldamund's deep voice reverberated off the catacomb walls. "There you are."

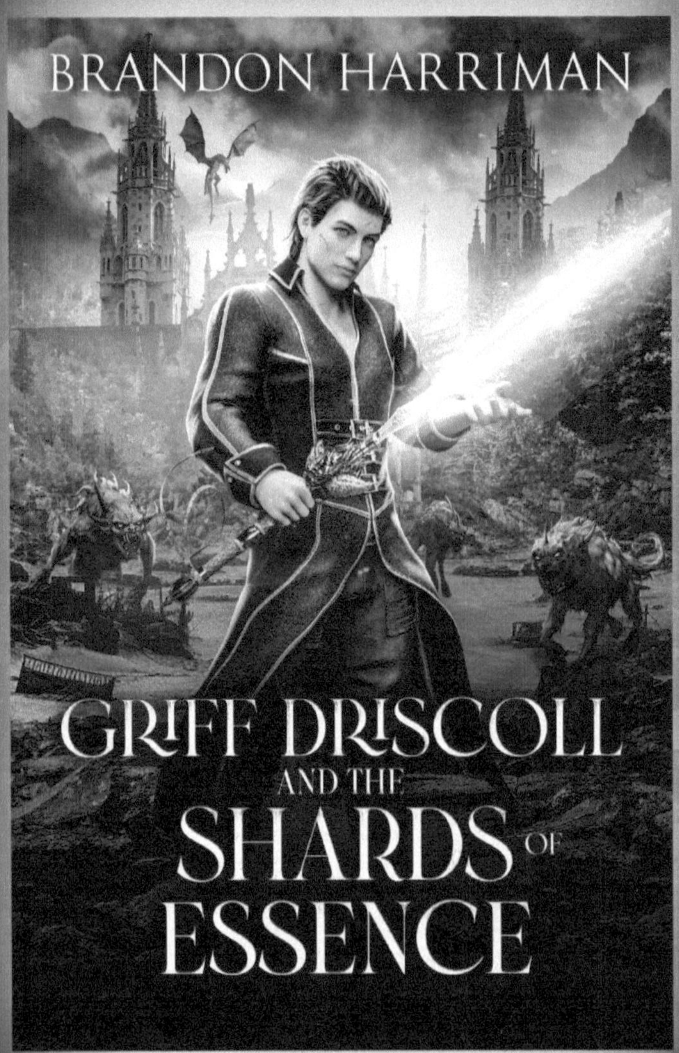
BRANDON HARRIMAN
GRIFF DRISCOLL
AND THE
SHARDS OF
ESSENCE

PROLOGUE

They stalked him from the shadows. The man could hear their careful footsteps in the leaves and twigs, disturbing the otherwise peaceful night. Stars sparkled brilliantly overhead, illuminating the dusty, well-traveled path on which the man walked. A gentle summer breeze playfully kissed the back of his neck, as though Mother Nature was flirting with him. He chuckled quietly to himself as he casually strode through the forest, not minding the shuffling that followed him just out of sight. The moon above was bright enough, and after years of traveling through this same beaten path at night, the man had grown used to walking by its pale light. Even the shadows that stirred in the darkness were like his constant companions. Though they never stepped out onto the path, their constant presence just out of the moonlight's reach was a strange comfort to him. Not that he desired for them to come any closer, but he also knew they never would. They knew who he was, and what he carried.

No one in their right mind would have dared to venture out in the night as he did, which meant that loneliness was part of the burden of responsibility he carried. The man hummed quietly to himself, his pack bouncing lightly against his back as he strolled. Suddenly, the slow, methodical crackling of the forest undergrowth stopped. The man paused his midnight stroll and cocked his head to the side, listening to his companions. In a frenzied rush, the shadows in the woods turned and darted away, their footsteps fading into the dark.

The man raised his eyebrow, curiosity heightening his senses. He shut his eyes and listened to the regular sounds of the nocturnal nightlife just out of sight. Opening his eyes again, he scanned ahead, looking for whatever it was that scared the shadows away. There. Off in the distance were small orbs of light floating as if in formation. They were headed his direction. The man crossed his arms and furrowed his brows, planting his feet firmly in place.

Bobbing in the sea of darkness, the orbs floated closer, growing larger and more vibrant with every passing second.

"Oh, hurry up already, wouldya?" the man called out. "I haven't got all night!"

Within moments, a group of men burst from the forest, their orbs of light illuminating their angry, rugged faces. They surrounded a young woman, whose hands were tied and mouth was gagged. Wet streaks smeared the dirt underneath her pleading eyes that said what she herself couldn't.

"What'cha doin' there, friend? Walkin' 'round here at night like this?" the man standing at the front said. He swayed back and forth, the crazy look in his eye making it clear that his intentions were about as crooked as his teeth.

"I might ask you the same question … friend." He met the man's eyes with total confidence. He knew the type of person that was standing in front of him. Desperate and yet overly confident he would walk away from this "chance" meeting.

Crooked Teeth stepped forward. "We're out here lookin' for someone. Middle aged. 'Bout mid-thirties. Light brown hair. Kinda like you, matter fact. Heard they might have somethin' reeeeal special. Know where I might find someone like that?" He cocked his head to the side, his eyes never blinking.

"Well, ya know … friend. Matter of fact, I think *I'm* lookin' at someone who's got somethin' real special… and my guess is she doesn't belong to you. Is that right?" He gazed over at the woman, her watery eyes meeting his. She nodded furiously before one of the other men shoved her to the ground, silencing her.

The man kept his arms crossed, but clenched his fists as he watched the woman struggle on the ground. Still, he remained motionless. For now.

Crooked Teeth took another step forward, anger flashing across his face. "She ain't none of yer business! Now ... my gut tells me that you're exactly who we're after. All by yourself in the middle of the night. Not a single nightstalker scratch on that pearly white skin of yours. Why is that?"

The man rolled his eyes. "Listen. You want gold? Take some gold." He tossed a couple of coins in the dirt in front of Crooked Teeth.

"Oh, no, friend. We're not here for gold." He spastically shook his head from side to side. "We're here for somethin' so much more than gold. Now, you'll give us what we want, or we'll *take* it from ya."

He took a few more steps forward, stopping just a foot away from the young man. His crooked teeth jutted out from his maniacal smile, but he said not a word. The summer sounds of the crickets chirping were the only noises that could be heard. It was as if everyone had held their breath and were waiting to see who could hold it the longest.

I am protector and defender.

Words passed down from his master echoed in the back of his mind.

I wield my magic; it does not wield me.

I brandish my power with wisdom and resolve.

The young man eyed the group before him. His arms still crossed, his feet still firmly planted, and his eyes never leaving Crooked Teeth's.

I do not strike first, but I strike true.

"GIVE IT TO ME NOW!" Crooked Teeth shrieked, leaping forward toward the man.

"I want it! I want it! Give me!" he screamed.

The man dodged to the left, just in time, as the deranged leader flailed past him. In one swift motion, he kicked the man's knee with his boot, sending him barreling to the dusty floor.

I do not seek battle, but I will end it.

He swirled his hand and hurled a giant wave of fire at the man fumbling on the ground. Crooked Teeth's shrill screams echoed through the night. The man turned toward the rest of the group, who had fanned out and was inching toward him. Their leader may be gone, but their objective was not.

"Last chance," the man said. "Leave the young lady here, unharmed, with me, and turn back towards town, and you won't end up like your ... friend here."

Their eyes narrowed at him, and they inched even closer. The man sighed. It was going to be a long night. Lightning crackled from his fingertips. With a single jab in the air, he arced it across several men, who crashed to the dirt upon impact, their orbs of light diminishing as they fell. One man grabbed at his arm and received a kick to the ribs. Another went for his feet. The man swirled his hands and flung a large boulder that smashed into his attacker's side. Whether by his fists, his feet, or his spells, the assailants all eventually succumbed to the man's abilities. With each person that fell, their orbs of light disappeared, darkened by their own foolishness. When every single body lay motionless on the dark forest floor, the man approached the woman, and gently removed her gag and ties.

"You okay?" he asked quietly.

She rubbed her tender jaw before slowly nodding in response. He sat next to her, not minding the dust that he knew would collect on the back of his otherwise clean linen trousers. She looked to be a couple of years younger than him: late-twenties, maybe early thirties. Even though dirt covered her face, it would be impossible for it to cover her beauty. Her kind brown eyes no longer showed fear but gratitude. It was too dark to tell if she wore a wedding band, but the man tossed that thought aside. No woman would ever want to live the life he lived.

"Thank you," she finally said, her voice cracked with the trauma of the night.

"Here, drink some water, m'lady." He pulled a large stagmoose skin canteen from his pack and handed it to her, which she avidly accepted.

After a rather long and greedy drink, she lowered the waterskin, and heaved gulps of air in satisfaction.

"Ugh," she sighed, and leaned back against a tree trunk. "Thank you. I was ... so thirsty ..." Her eyes started to close.

"Oh, no ma'am. Now's not the time to fall asleep, I'm afraid." The man glanced at the floating white eyes that had come back to stare at him again. He cast an orb of light that hovered around the two of them and shook her awake. He knew the beasts in the shadows would never attack him. In some ways, he could always guarantee his own safety. His new, temporary traveling companion, though, was a different story.

"Don't worry, you'll sleep soon enough, but we've still got a ways to go before you're safe."

He reached down and helped her up. After dusting herself off, and wiping the dirt from her face, she looked up at him.

"What's your name, sir?"

He smiled at her. No wedding band. "The name's Einar Falkenburg." He bowed low. "At your service."

She smiled back and did a slight curtsy. "Fedelma."

They gathered their supplies and continued on the path, doing their best to ignore the snarls and sounds of his traveling companions feasting in the dark behind them.

CHAPTER I

Small pebbles tumbled down the steep incline with each strained step. Sweat poured down Griff's back and it wasn't just from the climb. The intense heat from the summer sun beat at the back of his neck as though it were angry with him. But he hadn't done anything wrong. King's crown, he didn't even know how he'd gotten here. Or where *here* even was. As though the wind thought the sun was being unfair to the poor young mage, she blew gently and steadily across the rippling waters below, rising up to wick the moisture from his body.

He reached the top of the steep, stony slope, brushed the dirt off his trousers, and allowed his eyes to feast on the breathtaking surroundings. The island on which he stood was like a lush, grassy oasis protruding from a never-ending desert of blue. As far as the eye could see, deep waters surrounded him from every direction, save for the tiny sliver of land to the north.

Griff plopped onto the soft, grassy floor and allowed himself to catch his breath and enjoy the moment, knowing that it wouldn't last long. There was a mystery that lay before him, some small thing that was tugging at the edges of his consciousness like a word almost remembered, but still forgotten. Where was he? And why was he here? Considering his previous year, and the dreams in the lava caverns, he assumed that this was another dream. He was at least thankful he wasn't underground with the bats and Korrun's pet again.

Once his ragged breathing had returned to normal, it was time to investigate the rest of the island. It was going to be difficult to find answers to questions he didn't even know to ask. Tall grass playfully swiped at his legs as the salty ocean breeze drifted around him. Happy birds chirped with delight from the trees above, and the steady rippling of the surrounding waters threatened to lull Griff into a deeper sleep, if that was even possible. This would have been a restful, almost even luxurious place to be, had it not been for the unnerving feeling at the edges of his consciousness.

He cautiously approached a wall of shrubs and trees. The bushes almost seemed smashed together, and the trees towered over Griff, standing tall and proud. It was as though they were the guardians of the shadows within the tiny forest atop the island. That small, lingering pull at the edges of his mind egged him forward. There was no sound, no words, nothing. Just this ... knowing feeling that there was something calling to him. This mystery that was begging to be solved. And not just by anybody, but by him, and him alone. Like a personal invitation to a party where he was the only guest.

With every step closer, it was as though the trees bent lower, investigating the tiny ant that dared to tread on the guardians' hallowed ground. Though this was just an illusion brought on by the height of the trees and the shadows they cast, Griff still half-expected them to place their branch-like hands on their hips and say, "And where do you think you're going, boy?"

There was no opening in the shrubbery, just tightly packed leaves with thorns — yet another sign of unwelcome. And yet, that feeling that he was supposed to go beyond these guardians continued to beckon him forward, like the smell of fresh bread from the baker's window. Griff cleared his throat and was about to say, "Excuse me," but realized how dumb it would be talking to inanimate objects like these thorn bushes. Suddenly, there was a rustling sound coming from within. At first, he thought there might have been a rabbit who'd just realized his presence, but the rustling sounds grew louder, and the shrubs trembled. He leaned in closer and noticed the intertwining branches were moving. Sliding across one another, like tangled snakes. They unwound themselves from one another until an opening appeared right in front of him

Though the shrubs had unraveled themselves, Griff's stomach did the opposite. As he took his first steps forward into the shadows of the guardian trees, a knot formed in the pit of his stomach.

It's just a dream. It's just a dream. He thought to himself. *Nothing can hurt you here. You're safe.* The words felt empty and hollow. Leaves and twigs crunched under his feet with every step. Their sounds, the only sounds Griff could hear, echoed in the shadows. It seemed that not even the wind dared to follow him here. An eerie feeling swept over him as he peered into the shadows. Were the trees watching him? No. It must have been another illusion brought on by the shadows. And yet, Griff couldn't help but feel as though he was a foreigner.

Ahead, Griff saw light trying to break through the shadows; a clearing. The still, small voice in the back of his mind, that mysterious presence that lured him into the shadows in the first place, jumped with excitement. The young mage accelerated, his once slow and careful steps replaced with quick, agile strides. As he ran, small plants with large leaves slapped at his torso and legs, as though they were trying to stop him. Leaves swirled around him, blocking his view. Vines snaked across the ground behind him, inches from his feet. It was as though the entire forest was sparing no effort to keep Griff from reaching the clearing.

Griff sprinted faster. His feet pounded against the forest floor. Strange mixtures of opposing emotions flooded his mind: Fear—which was his own—and excitement—which was not. Finally, just as Griff was beginning to think the entire forest would cave in on him, he broke through the darkness and was swallowed whole by the light of the sun. Thankful for its endearing light, Griff laid on the ground and closed his eyes, allowing the golden orb in the sky to welcome him into the clearing.

He heaved huge, desperate gulps of air. It was strange to think that knowing he was in a dream did nothing to still the fear he had felt in the shadows. Finally, his beating heart was starting to slow and that inkling in his mind urged him to continue. He was so close. He could feel it. Well, he could feel *something* telling him he was close.

Griff sat up and reached his hands behind him to steady himself. Just then, the ground rumbled. It was faint at first and came in small, consistent bursts. But with every second that passed, the tremors grew in intensity. Something was coming. Something big. His heart sank and he felt as though he was glued to the ground. The overwhelming fear inside him grew, but the other mysterious presence in him felt excitement.

His hands were shaking, and not because of his fear, but because the tremors had intensified to the point that he could visibly seem them shake. Loud booms and crashes echoed from the woods, as though trees were snapping in two. Whatever it was, it was big, and it was getting closer. Griff tried to scoot away from the edge of the forest, but his hands and feet wouldn't cooperate. They were at the mercy of his own fear and the quaking of the ground.

Suddenly, it was quiet. The tremors had stopped, and the forest was still. Griff's eyes zipped back and forth, scanning the edge of the woods. There was no sign of life. No sign that anything had been there at all. He wiped the sweat from his forehead. Then the wind, which was absent in the shadows, now cast a gentle breeze that teased his messy black hair. He quickly regained control of his limbs and stood. Eyes still scanning for life, he turned and faced the forest. Without warning, the world behind him erupted in a flurry of activity and sound. The ground convulsed and it sounded like lightning had struck at his back.

His heart seized. He twisted and fell to the ground. Pure terror gripped his every thought and emotion when he found the source of the commotion. Beady, red eyes stared into his soul. Long, deadly talons gripped the dirt in hatred. Smoky, gray scales seemed to almost absorb the sunlight instead of reflect it. Large, elegant wings gracefully extended, blocked out the sun. Pitch black smoke billowed from its snout. He sat frozen. His heart beat loudly against his chest, and his pulse thumped in his ears. And yet strangely enough, the presence at the edges of his consciousness leaped for joy. Towering over Griff stood the final guardian of the forest—and the last clue to his location: a Nightflame dragon.

The monster's eyes narrowed at him, and it leaned its head closer. Griff stared at the jagged teeth that looked as though they had been dipped in a bucket of red paint. Teeth that were so close, he could smell the overwhelming metallic odor that came from the blood. It sniffed him, going up one side of his body and down the other. Its shoulders rose as it inhaled deeply, lifted its head to the sky, and erupted in a ferocious roar that chilled Griff to his very core.

Then, the dragon stumbled backward and fell on its side. It lay motionless in an awkward position, not breathing. It was dead.

"Griff!" A dirty pillow thumped against his head before falling to the tent floor.

He sat up and groaned from the pangs of waking from his deep slumber. The cot underneath him creaked from the years of use.

"You were muttering in your sleep again last night," Leena Driscoll said from the other side of the tent.

"Yeah?" Griff said, flinging his feet to the side and sliding on his dirty socks. "Sorry if I kept you up."

Leena shook her head and rolled her eyes. "That's not why I'm telling you that." She stared at him. It was that mother's stare that demanded more information.

"I dunno why I was mutterin' in my sleep."

"You sure about that? No strange dreams or anything? No lava caves or nightstalkers or Korrun Aldamund?"

Griff paused and pretended to look for his shoe, knowing full well he had placed it under his cot the night before.

"No," he finally said, realizing he had been quiet for far too long. "Not that I remember, anyways."

"Remember that the king said if you have any more dreams about Korrun, you're to tell Professor Coen ri—"

"I will, mom! I promise! Now, can I *please* go get some breakfast? I'm starving."

Leena paused as though she was wrestling with how to handle her son's outburst. She sighed and said, "O-okay, honey. Go get you some breakfast." Then she walked out of the tent.

Griff sighed. He knew he hadn't been fair to her. But after telling the king his recent dream about Korrun in the catacombs not long after Cordelia had fallen, he was tired of people treating him differently. Whether it was his parents watching his every moment, especially as he slept, or whether it was other Cordelians staring at him like he was a human nightstalker, he just wished things could go back to normal. Griff promised himself he would make amends with his mom once he got some breakfast in him. He may have lied about his dreams, but he hadn't lied about being hungry.

"Hey Griff!" Sylva said as soon as Griff drew back the tent flap. "Sleep well?"

"Literally, Sylva, I can't even take a single step outside my tent before somebody comes barging at me."

"Oh ... sorry, Griff. I'll just ... I'll go." The look of hurt on Sylva's face was like a dagger to Griff's heart.

"Sylva, wait. I'm sorry. I-I just ... I'm hungry and I'm tired."

They walked through the ruins of Cordelia, down familiar cobblestone streets that were no longer familiar. Ash-covered debris littered the ground, and the smell of the fire still lingered. It was strange to be at the heart of the town and still see all four walls of Cordelia. Only two weeks ago, shops and houses used to block those views, and now there were only plots of land with rubble and maybe a fence at best. Some yards housed humble tents that the king had provided, but they weren't as tall as the buildings they had replaced.

"Yeah, you must be tired and hungry," Sylva finally said after walking beside Griff in silence. "Let's get you some food."

"...That's ... that's what I was about to do."

"Oh. Right." Sylva shifted uncomfortably and continued walking in silence, periodically looking at Griff, then back to the ground. It was like he didn't know how to talk to his childhood friend anymore.

Finally, Griff halted and looked at his friend. "Sylva. I need you to do something for me."

"Yeah? What's that?"

"Treat me normal."

"Normal?"

"Yes." He put a hand on Sylva's shoulder. "Everyone here looks at me all crazy like. Some treat me like I'm carryin' some sort of disease that'll spread to them if they get too close, and others treat me like I'm some sort of celebrity or that I'm famous or something. And I'm neither of those things!"

"Well ... you are apparently a really, really, *really* strong mage or whatever. And you have had those dreams that interest the king..."

"Yeah, but nobody else knows that." Suddenly, a thought occurred to Griff. One he hoped wasn't true. "They *don't* know that ... right, Sylva?"

"…right," he said and continued walking toward the food tent.

Griff raced to catch up to him, grabbed him by the shoulder, and turned him around. "What did you say?"

"I didn't say anything!" he said, holding his hands in the air.

"Then how does everyone know about my dreams?"

"I-I dunno. Maybe your parents told them?"

"My parents know better than to go spoutin' off important information like that. I guarantee you it wasn't them. And you're lookin' awfully guilty."

"Fine!" Sylva said, looking like a terrified mouse. "I … I was just so proud that *my* best friend is important … you know? And – and he's strong! Crazy strong! And that he saved my life! So … yeah, maybe I said a little too much about you, Griff, but nightstalker's fury, I'm thankful you're my best friend, okay?"

Griff sighed deeply. It was one of frustration, but it was also one of contemplation. He calmed himself before he spoke again.

"I'm thankful you're my best friend as well. But … Sylva … this is *important*. We don't know what these dreams mean or why exactly I'm having them. And we're at *war*. That means if any important information gets into the wrong hands, it could be bad. And last but not least … I, as your best friend, am *begging* you not to tell anyone else about this stuff, ya hear? Please."

"Okay, Griff, I promise. No more. My lips are sealed shut."

"Good," Griff said. "Because I got something really important to share with you. And I need your help …"

THE ADVENTURE CONTINUES...

Cordelia is destroyed, Korrun is after the shards of essence, Tyrell's mission is incomplete, and the Driscolls are relocating to Solastran. So much has happened and yet Griff's journey has only begun. The adventure continues in:

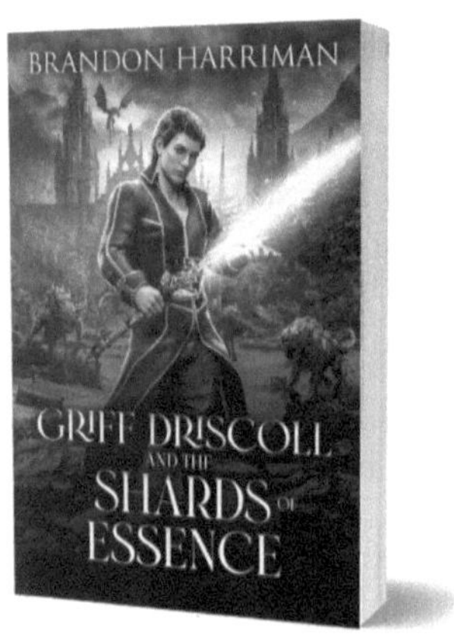

START the next book in the series now! Read **Griff Driscoll and the Shards of Corruption**

SUBSCRIBE to my newsletter to stay up to date on the next installment in the Corruption of Essence series! More info at www.Brandon-Harriman.com

THANK YOU for joining Griff on his journey through the land of Oriel! If you enjoyed the adventure, would you consider leaving a review so more people can experience the magic and mystery Oriel has to offer? I truly hope you had fun alongside Griff and Tyrell, and I hope you are as excited as I am about their stories moving forward!

ABOUT THE AUTHOR

As a baby, Brandon Harriman could barely get the Miami sand out of his diaper before he was whisked away to the Southern charm of North Alabama. Growing up in Decatur alongside his twin brother, Brandon traded salt air for sweet tea, and developed an early love for reading.

That love of reading frequently had him tuning out his teachers (much to their displeasure) to dive headfirst into the magical worlds of books like *Harry Potter*. In hindsight, he probably should have paid more attention in class, but he recognized the pull a good story had on his focus.

Brandon earned a business degree from Harding University before completing a Master of the Arts with a dual focus in Youth Ministry and Pastoral Ministry at Grand Canyon University. After six fulfilling years as a youth pastor in Sarasota, FL, he and his wife, Annette, along with their son, Jayce, made the move to Tulsa, OK. As part of the discussion to leave Florida, Brandon decided to pursue his dream of writing young adult fantasy novels full-time while embracing the role of stay-at-home dad. Since then, the Harriman clan has grown with the addition of their daughter, Haley.

When Brandon isn't exploring the fantastical worlds he creates, he's busy being playful at heart. Whether it's board games, video games, sports, or assembling (and inevitably stepping on) Legos, he's always up for some fun. He's also an unapologetic beach lover, with a passion for tropical weather, deep-sea fishing, and snorkeling.

Thanks to the unwavering support of his family and friends, Brandon has completed his debut novel and, at the time of publishing, is hard at work finishing The Corruption of Essence series.

www.ingramcontent.com/pod-product-compliance
Lightning Source LLC
Chambersburg PA
CBHW051141130726
47988CB00005B/1939